998-A131

D0393721

# OUR
# YEAR
# IN
# LOVE
# AND
# PARTIES

**ALSO BY KAREN HATTRUP**

*Frannie and Tru*

# KAREN HATTRUP

An Imprint of HarperCollinsPublishers

HarperTeen is an imprint of HarperCollins Publishers.

Our Year in Love and Parties
Copyright © 2019 by Karen Hattrup
All rights reserved. Printed in the United States of America.
No part of this book may be used or reproduced in any manner
whatsoever without written permission except in the case of
brief quotations embodied in critical articles and reviews. For
information address HarperCollins Children's Books, a division of
HarperCollins Publishers, 195 Broadway, New York, NY 10007.
www.epicreads.com

ISBN 978-0-06-241023-8

Typography by Ray Shappell
19  20  21  22  23   PC/LSCH   10  9  8  7  6  5  4  3  2  1
❖
First Edition

*For Mom and Dad.*
*Thank you for everything.*

# OUR
# YEAR
# IN
# LOVE
# AND
# PARTIES

# THE PARTY AT THE CAVE AND THE PARTY AT ADAM'S

# 1

## TUCKER

This was their last time together, but Tucker tried not to think about that. He tried instead to focus on the best parts. The speed and rhythm of her breathing, the feeling of their bare chests pressed together. The little joke about whose turn it was to go first. Those awkward moments that made them both laugh, because there were always awkward moments.

His leg cramped. Her arm got stuck. Some ridiculous noise came from their bodies connecting.

And then, of course, the end, the end. That was the point, wasn't it? He hit it now, his cheek against hers, cresting and crashing into that just-after hollow, the place where all the lightness and tingling turned heavy, making Tucker wish he could curl up and close his eyes . . .

Right away, though, Suzanne was moving and the feeling

was gone, replaced by her carefully disengaging from him, whistling some song he knew but couldn't name.

It was a hot, humid day in mid-August, the two of them in his basement like always. And like always, she slipped quickly into the bathroom and then back out, getting dressed in front of him, forcing and wriggling her way back into her damp sports bra, her tennis skirt—a shed skin that no longer had the right shape.

"You can do it," Tucker said. "I believe in you."

She told him he was a dork, and he went quiet, watching her from under the blanket on the floor, replaying in his mind their last six weeks together.

He'd had classes with Suzanne all through high school, and the two of them had been friendly if not exactly friends. Then came that day in July. Tucker had been getting the mail, and she'd driven right by, then backed up her car to say hello. It turned out her tennis club was down the street from Frank's house, which was now Tucker's house too, since his mom had married Frank in June. The two of them had been out that day, and Tucker had invited Suzanne inside to drink Gatorade and watch Wimbledon on the big TV in the basement.

Half a match later, she was kissing him and he was kissing her back. When things had started to get intense, she'd pulled back to say she didn't want anything serious, not on the cusp of senior year, but maybe she'd keep coming by? He'd said yes—of course he'd said yes—and by the beginning of August, Tucker had fumbled his way through losing his virginity without even mentioning that it was his first time.

Now Suzanne was busy looking through her bag, so Tucker grabbed his clothes and hurried to the bathroom. He cleaned up, wrapping the condom in a tissue and hiding it in the deepest recesses of the trash can before taking a moment to stretch out his shoulder.

He'd had three months of physical therapy now and was almost back to normal, he was sure of it.

When Tucker came back, she was collapsed at one end of the couch with her phone. He grabbed his own and sat at the other end. Their feet lightly touching, they both got lost in the glow of their screens. This had become part of their routine, and usually he liked it, the two of them smiling and sighing at their own little worlds.

Today he clicked and clicked and didn't see a thing.

He felt her gaze on him and looked up, found her with an eyebrow raised. Suzanne had very serious eyebrows, stark black lines against white skin.

"You remember I leave for the beach tomorrow?" she asked.

"Of course."

"You going to miss me?"

Tucker tilted his head and scrunched up his mouth like he really had to think about it, and she threw a pillow at his head. He dropped his phone on the floor then, crawling down to her end of the couch and wrapping her in an embrace. He liked looking down at the two of them tangled together, limbs on limbs, almost indistinguishable from one another.

Suzanne turned to look at him, squinting like a cartoon villain.

"What's going on in there, Mr. Deep Thoughts?"

He sighed and gathered himself, looking off into a distant corner of the room.

"This is awkward, but I feel you should shower before you come over here. Is it too late to mention that?"

"Oh my god, Tucker."

He was laughing and she was covering his mouth with her hand, trying to make him stop, forcing him to fight his way free.

"I'm all covered in tennis sweat and secondhand sunscreen," he said. "It's kind of a turnoff."

"Oh, for sure. I can tell how much it's bothered you."

She was shaking her head at him, and Tucker smiled, but really he was feeling a little lost, a little low. He'd been wondering if she might change her mind, insist that this shouldn't be the end. That didn't seem to be happening.

"Are you going to Adam's house tonight?" she asked.

*Adam's house.* Hearing those words, Tucker could practically taste the lukewarm beer and feel the bass from those junky old speakers throbbing under his skin. People still talked about Tucker's little performance on Adam's coffee table last October. They always told the story like he was drunk, but actually he wasn't—Tucker just liked to dance.

He couldn't quite imagine doing that anymore, certainly not in front of Suzanne.

"Yeah, for sure. I'll be there."

"Okay, then. No goodbyes yet."

"Not yet."

Suzanne climbed out of his arms and off the couch, quickly gathering her things and then disappearing with a wave through the sliding glass door.

As soon as she was gone, Tucker got a text from Bobby, asking if it was safe to come over and play Mario Kart. Normally he would have said yes right away, but he was feeling restless.

**Do you want to go to the batting cages instead? The ones next to the Cave?**

The sun beat down, one of those unbearably sticky Maryland summer days. A few practice swings and Tucker was already sweating. He was thinking about how it had been ages since he'd been here.

He looked up to see Bobby heading his way, grinning and shaking his head, a bat slung over his shoulder.

"What?" Tucker asked. "What's so funny?"

"I'm having flashbacks. Eighth grade? It was hot as hell, just like this. You had stolen your mom's Juul and you were trying to share it with those girls, right over there by the snack machine."

"Oh my god," Tucker said, covering his face with his hand.

"Because they were definitely going to want to smoke that thing. Here. Between the four of us. Why did your mom even *have* that?"

"Don't you remember? She still smoked like three cigarettes a day then, and she was trying to quit. And those girls were super into us."

"Um, no. They really, really weren't."

"How would you know? You went to the bathroom and never came back."

"That was the only reasonable thing to do, given the situation."

"Well, sorry. I had to try. I have a thing for softball players."

The boys had known each other for as long as either could remember, born two months apart in adjoining houses, a circumstance that had turned their mothers from neighbors into friends. Bobby was an only child, too, a miracle baby his parents thought would never come. Growing up side by side, Bobby and Tucker had honed a lifetime's worth of jokes about being brothers-who-didn't-exactly-look-like-brothers, since Tucker was white and Bobby was black.

This year Bobby was starting at left field. Tucker was a relief pitcher.

"How's your shoulder?" Bobby asked.

Tucker's hand went to it instinctively, as he rolled it a couple of times.

"It's fine, it's fine. Or it will be by the spring. You ready?"

They both pushed the start button and then got into their stances, falling back into their old routine without discussing it, ready to call out and keep track of their hits. Tucker's swing felt different, everything felt tight, and yes, there was a pull in his shoulder. He told himself that was from being out of practice and kept going. At first he was missing and missing, hitting half-assed little hoppers, but then—finally—he made one big slamming connection.

He paused to enjoy the ring of the aluminum, the arc of the ball through the air, riding the brief high it gave him for as long as he could.

After that, Tucker let a couple of pitches fly by as he stretched and considered the squat, ugly building next door—a windowless brick warehouse full of arcade games and a glow-in-the-dark mini golf course. Fun Cave was the official name on the sign, but everyone just called it the Cave. Tucker had worked there the summer he was fifteen, his first job, and he could still picture it perfectly, the beeping and the shouting and the grime, the counter where kids turned in tickets for candy and crappy plastic toys.

As he was settling back into his stance, someone called his name.

"Dude, is that you? I almost didn't recognize you. You're like a foot taller than you used to be."

Standing on the other side of the chain-link fence was a smiling face that Tucker knew right away—his old coworker Mikey. He'd been a few years older than the rest of the crew, but he'd hung out with them anyway, always coming along when they went to Pizza Hut after the late shift.

Right now he was clinging to a bag of trash, apparently on his way to the dumpster. Tucker smiled as he walked over.

"Mikey! Hey. It's, uh, good to see you. You still working there?"

"Wild, right? I mean, I'm the manager now, or I *was* the manager, since the place is done."

"What?"

"You didn't hear? It's finally out of business! Today was the last day. I'm closing up early, and some company's coming tomorrow, to liquidate everything and do who-knows-what with it. Nobody plays pinball anymore."

"Oh, man," Tucker said, sadness fluttering in his chest as he pictured the place ravaged and gone. "I'm sorry."

Mikey threw the trash bag over his shoulder and waved at the building dismissively. "I'm over this dump, honestly. The kids that worked here this summer were total douches. Nothing like when you were here."

Tucker smiled and kicked at the ground, remembering all those times he'd scrubbed the toilets and vacuumed the carpet that refused to get clean. He thought about singing that weird, terrible version of "Happy Birthday" whenever there was a party, which had basically been every day. The place was ridiculous, but he had loved it. It was like being in another dimension where nothing really mattered, where all anyone wanted was to have fun. Plus all those hours joking around with Erika . . .

Struggling a bit under the weight of the bag, Mikey said he'd better take off. Tucker watched him go, trying to turn his mind back to the party tonight, but thinking instead about the

Cave, how much time he'd spent laughing there, being silly. He wished he could go one more time and say goodbye. That sounded a lot more fun than a night at Adam's, where Tucker would be stuck trying to act cool around Suzanne while wondering if she thought he was terrible in bed.

Tucker tapped his bat on the fence and called Mikey back.

"So I might have an idea . . ."

Bobby took his final swings, slamming the last ball all the way to the distant net.

"Twenty-five," he said, dimples showing as he smiled. "You lost bad. What was that about?"

Tucker wiped the sweat off his brow, grinning.

"The Cave. It went out of business. A bunch of us are going to meet there tonight, after hours. Like a goodbye party."

"Officially? Or unofficially?"

"Unofficially."

Bobby's eyebrows went up.

"Do you want to go?" Tucker asked.

Somehow, Bobby's eyebrows managed to go even higher.

"Me? No. I'm going to pass on the casual breaking and entering. And c'mon. Don't make me go to Adam's without you."

"Isn't Lawrence driving you anyway? It doesn't make sense for us to go together. And I just—I don't feel like dealing with Suzanne right now."

Bobby paused, fiddled with his bat. "So you guys are broken up or whatever?"

"I think it's more like I've been dismissed."

Tucker tried to say it like it was all a joke, but it didn't quite come out that way, and he could see that Bobby was struggling with how to respond. Tucker cleared his throat.

"And get this—my mom just told me that my dad is in town. Living nearby, I guess. And she wants me to have dinner with him once a week."

"Seriously?"

"Seriously."

"Can you say no?"

Tucker avoided Bobby's eyes, frowning and shaking his head.

"She wanted to have some big talk about it this morning, but I kind of blew her off and now I'm trying to avoid her."

"I'm sorry. Maybe he'll bail anyway, and you won't have to deal with it."

Tucker nodded, then took a couple steps away, straining to see out beyond the cages and the field. Across the road was the neighborhood he'd grown up in, with Bobby. Three quick turns and he would be there, to the tiny crackerbox house that had once belonged to his mother's grandparents, and that they'd rented to her all those years for almost nothing, so that she and Tucker could get by. He missed the place fiercely.

"One more round?" he finally asked.

Bobby nodded, and they both got ready to push their start buttons, but first Tucker paused.

"Would it be funny or stupid if I wore my old work polo tonight, the one from the Cave? I still have it."

Bobby leaned on his bat and sighed loudly.

"That thing was ugly as shit. And that would be hilarious."

# 2

## ERIKA

Erika was going for a long, hard run when Marissa texted to say she needed her as soon as humanly possible. Erika stared at the message, gauged where she was, then immediately turned around and sprinted back the way she had come.

The heat was brutal. She had no business running outside right now, but her mind was a jumble at the thought of heading back to school and to dorm life, so she'd taken off on this miserable swamp of a run.

Seven minutes and a mile later, she was knocking at the familiar door. Marissa threw it open, red hair flying, green eyes wide.

Even in her current state—clearly stressed about something—she was a welcome sight. Their vacation and work schedules had conspired against them this summer, and Erika felt like she'd barely seen her best friend.

"Yuck," Marissa said, wrinkling her nose at Erika's sweatiness. She hugged her anyway, then dragged her upstairs to her room. Once they were in with the door closed, Marissa promptly crawled into bed and pulled the sheets over her head.

"Everything all right?" Erika asked, hovering in the middle of the room.

"Nope, nope. Not even a little. I need you to look at the thing on the dresser."

Erika took a single step, but stopped dead when she saw the plastic wand.

"Oh, shit."

"Oh, shit indeed."

"Am I giving a second opinion? Or am I the first one looking?"

"You're the first one."

"Okay, okay. What's the code? How many lines am I looking for?"

"No lines. I bought one that says words."

"Like it talks?"

"No it doesn't fucking talk!" Marissa was almost, but not really, laughing. "The words show up on a digital screen or some shit, I don't know. What am I, a freaking pregnancy test engineer?"

"That's probably more lucrative than— Did you officially declare your major?"

"Yes! Art history."

"Jesus. Definitely more lucrative than that."

A sound came from underneath the bumpy sheets—halfway between a laugh and a scoff. Erika's heart felt very funny, going from the run and the heat to this, and oh god, she wanted some water, a gallon of water, but that would have to wait.

She stepped forward and grabbed the test, then exhaled hard.

"Not pregnant. It says not pregnant."

Marissa burst from under the covers, hands clasped in prayer. "OH MY GOD. THANK MARY AND JESUS."

Erika hadn't moved, her fingers still clinging to the little piece of plastic. It was the first time she'd ever held one, and she was surprised by how light and flimsy it was. Erika's mom was a nurse and far from shy about sex. She'd gotten Erika an IUD when she was sixteen, and that thing was good for five years. Erika had no idea what this kind of scare felt like, and she found that she was imagining her future self, holding this stick and hoping for—what exactly? She didn't really think she was mom material. Although very soon she was going to be somebody's big sister, or half sister, whatever . . .

Erika placed the wand back on the dresser, then climbed into bed next to Marissa. They lay on their backs and stared at the ceiling while Marissa cried.

"I forget to take the stupid pills, all the time. What's wrong with me?"

"It's easy to forget. But you might want to listen to my mom's canned speech about how all college girls should have some kind of long-term birth control. She's very passionate."

"Not necessary. This almost killed me. I'll get that stupid patch or whatever. Maybe that ring you stick up there—that sounds fun."

Marissa was trying to laugh again, and Erika scooted closer to her. The two had met in ninth grade, when Marissa had appeared next to her in the bathroom to ask about her lip gloss, segueing directly into a plan for the two of them to share all their makeup, since they had the same complexion. Erika had been trying to figure out how best to escape from this total weirdo, when Marissa started rambling about how they were probably distantly related, descended from the same Irish peasants. Erika had started laughing and couldn't stop.

"Being home again is so bizarre, isn't it?" Marissa asked. "When do you go back to St. B's?"

"Next Saturday."

"That's right, that's right. I'm headed to Maryland on Tuesday, thank god. Sophomore year, here we come."

"Sophomore year, here we come."

The words sounded so hollow when Erika repeated them, but she wasn't sure if Marissa noticed. And why would she? Erika didn't really complain, since St. B's was basically fine. There were even things about it that she loved, like her lit classes, the quiet room in the library, the green expanse of the quad. The problem was the rest of it. Everybody mad for drinking and staying out late and hooking up—things she had done plenty of by the time she'd arrived. Things she had expected to throw herself back into without a care, a new start after the senior year of high school from hell. But no. Not quite. Freshman year, come and gone. She hadn't kissed a soul.

She'd barely touched another person, come to think of it.

"Can we talk about the fact that you're going to be an RA?" Marissa asked. "That's still blowing my mind."

"How many times have I explained it to you? Free room and board."

And almost as important: her own suite with a bathroom. Sweet, blessed privacy with no one looking at you like you were a sad, pathetic loner because you didn't feel like going out.

Next to her, Marissa sighed. "I need a distraction—like a serious distraction—and there is absolutely nothing going on tonight."

Erika's thumb slipped to her mouth, and she gnawed on the nail.

"I've got something. Maybe."

"Bring it."

"Ugh, I really don't know if I want to."

"C'mon! You owe me."

"I *owe* you? Am I the one who almost knocked you up? Seems like I'd remember that."

"Oh, you'd remember. They always remember. And by *they* I mean Marco. Since he's the only one who's had the pleasure."

They were laughing again, and then Erika sighed, covering her face with her hands.

"The Cave just went out of business. One of my old coworkers texted a bunch of us, inviting us over tonight. For a party or whatever. After hours. Sneak in the back."

"I'm sorry—a secret party at the Cave?"

"I guess."

"Booze and Skee-Ball?"

"Sure?"

"How did you not tell me this? How did you not invite me yet? Please, please take me to the creepy, abandoned arcade party."

Marissa was propped up on her elbow now, batting her eyelashes. Erika gave her a withering look.

"That might work on Marco, but it doesn't work on me. Speaking of—I thought you guys agreed that you were officially done? After he visited his grandmother in Colombia for a month and you finally accepted that you are terrible at doing long distance?"

"I know, I know. Oops? Big-time oops."

Marissa was smiling a little, but her eyes were glassy, like maybe she was going to start crying again. Erika felt the creep of guilt coming on. Maybe she should take her out, let her have her fun. Erika should probably try to have a little fun herself, but she just didn't like parties anymore. The last time she'd really enjoyed a party had been who-knows-how-long-ago.

Since back before the entire world had seen the video.

"Okay, maybe we'll go."

Marissa squealed. "Is that funny kid going to be there? The one who used to flirt with you?"

*Oh my god—why does she have such an elephant memory?*

"I guess. He asked who's bringing the beer. So clearly he's grown into a total tool."

"What's wrong with beer? I like beer. Tell me his name again."

Marissa took out her phone, and Erika rolled her eyes.

"Tucker. Tucker Campanelli."

"That's right, he did look like a nice little Italian boy. Watch me work. This will take no time at— OH MY. Mr. Campanelli has gotten very yummy."

Erika snatched Marissa's phone from her hand and took in his photo, one of those carefully posed profile pictures that wasn't supposed to look posed. She groaned and tossed the phone back.

"No, thanks."

"You've got problems, E. Serious problems. And whoa, hold up. He's a senior at Gaithersburg? He would totally know our precious, perfect Nina."

"Sometimes I think you like Marco's sister more than you like Marco."

"No shit. How about I text her and ask about your little friend?"

"How about not, or I'll murder you."

Marissa pushed Erika toward the edge of the bed, and Erika clung to the sheets, playacting like it was a disaster and then accidentally falling over for real, taking the comforter and Marissa with her. The two of them were laughing in a heap on the floor, and Erika remembered for a moment what it was like to be stupid and have fun with her friends.

Erika made her way home at a jog. Saturday afternoon was slowly turning into Saturday night, and there was so much bustle. The overpriced organic grocery store, the new Chick-Fil-A, the third-best Thai place in town—all of their parking lots were packed. Erika wasn't dying to go back to school, but she supposed she wasn't dying to stay here either, in this congested little corner of suburbia. What was good about this place except for Marissa and her mom?

Toward the end of her run, Erika passed the brick behemoth that was her old high school, keeping eyes firmly on the sidewalk as she did.

She sprinted up the front steps into the townhouse where she grew up, headed into the front hall. Her mom was there wearing her scrubs, her dark hair in a low ponytail, no makeup. Youngish-looking for forty-five, tall and athletic to Erika's short and athletic. It had been all of two hours since they'd seen each other, but her mom hugged her.

"You don't really have to go back to school, do you?"

"Oh my god, you're a freak. Unhand me."

Her mom kept holding her, rocking her back and forth. "You're so full of it. You know you love this."

Erika wormed away from her, hopping onto the couch and turning on the television, which was set to HGTV, the channel from which it hardly ever moved.

"Do you need anything before you go back?"

"Existential fulfillment? Expensive boots?"

"Ha ha. You're very cute. Are you going out tonight?"

"Not sure yet. I'll text you."

Her mom hitched her purse higher on her shoulder, came to stand next to the couch.

"Are you excited to see your St. B's friends?"

Erika had been about to turn the volume up, but now she dropped the remote, fiddling pointlessly with the buttons. Her mom had asked that question casually enough, right? Or was it screaming with subtext that Erika didn't *have* any real friends at St. B's?

No, there was no way her mom knew. Erika dropped plenty of names, acted like everything was fine. This was nothing her mom needed to worry about. Not making friends was not a real problem. Having a sex tape on the internet—*that* was a real problem, and her mom had helped her live through that, so she wasn't going to bother her with silly bullshit.

Her mom was still looking at her, though, with that worried little crease in her forehead.

"I'm super pumped, for sure," Erika said.

She turned the volume up too high, watched a guy sledge-hammer a wall and then frown at what he found inside. Her mom came and stood in front of the screen.

"One more thing, and then I'm gone. Don't you think you should try to see your dad before you go back? You guys had, what, one lunch all summer? You still haven't met Jennifer."

Annoyance flared in Erika's chest, because that was the last thing she wanted to think about now, and the chances of her making an effort to hang out with the two of them were pretty much nil.

"His *fiancée*? Isn't that the most annoying word in the world?" Her mom cocked her head, sighed loudly.

"Do you think she got knocked up on purpose?" Erika asked.

"Well, hon, I'm not sure if it matters, since they seem happy. But she is a high school health teacher, so I'm going to guess she knows how all that stuff works."

Erika raised her eyebrows very high. "But what if she's exceptionally bad at her job?"

Her mom gave her a smile, then finally left. Erika exchanged her remote for her phone and started peeking at the profiles and feeds and pages of everyone who was going tonight, trying to figure out where they were in their lives now, looking for any signs of misery or desperation. Everyone seemed fine, perfectly fine. She searched for Tucker, but his pages were all private. He did have a Facebook account, so she started scrolling through his old profile pictures going back, back, back until he looked like the kid she had known. As she looked at his face, a memory came to her.

A few weeks after the video got posted, those boys had come into the Cave. Kids from her school. Freshmen, maybe? She'd been at the prize counter with Tucker, debating which character's death from Harry Potter was the most emotionally devastating, when one of the boys had appeared in front of her and asked if she wanted to suck his dick.

By then, Erika had gotten very good at not flinching, but words like that had still gotten her every time, shrunk her down to something small and hard. A marble to be flicked around at others' will.

"WHAT?" she'd shouted. "I didn't hear you. Could you repeat yourself and speak up?"

That sometimes worked like a charm. Sometimes it back-fired in the worst way. That day, they'd taken off, and Erika had turned quickly around, almost bumping into Tucker.

"Hey!" he'd said. "Uh, hey. I was definitely on standby to kick those guys' asses, but now that seems almost insulting, since you dispatched them so easily."

He'd tried to do some kind of martial arts move with his hands, then got a little red in the face.

"For the record, I barely know anything about . . . you know, whatever. The thing. Tim tried to tell me, but I told him to fuck off."

Erika had nodded, staring at the ground. Then she'd reminded him that the candy bins were a mess, and the two of them had set to work organizing them. They'd never spoken about the video again.

She'd never thought much about that moment, buried as it was by the endless sidelong glances from her classmates, all those jibes from people she thought were her friends, her own dad barely able to look at her. Then there'd been those awful ladies on the PTA taking the issue up like their own personal mantle, organizing that assembly that was supposed to be about the bigger issue, but felt like it was all about her, a whole hour of absolutely absurd advice wrapped in a thick layer of slut-shaming . . .

As Erika was preparing to drown out those thoughts with an

episode of *Fixer Upper*, a text came in from Marissa.

**Marco's being ridiculous.**

In Erika's experience, Marco wasn't usually the ridiculous one, but her approach to friendship was unconditional and one-sided, so she certainly wasn't going to point that out.

**Sorry M. You know my offer to be your platonic life partner always stands.**

Marissa responded:

**I love you for that, but what I really want is to go out and have fun tonight.**

Then she sent an avalanche of the *please* hands.

Erika sighed. She needed to loosen up, she knew that she did, and could there be any better test run than this? An abandoned-arcade party with her best friend, and possibly being fawned over again by some harmless kid?

**All right, bitch, all right. Put your Skee-Ball pants on.**

# 3

## TUCKER

"I'm sorry—explain this to me again?"

"It's a joke. Because we all hated them."

Suzanne appeared almost-but-not-quite amused as she considered the monstrosity of this tie-dyed polo shirt that had "Fun Cave" written on the back in peeling hot-pink letters. It was also ridiculously small now, but that was half the point, half the reason it was so funny, right?

Tucker still couldn't believe she'd asked to come, when he'd texted her to explain why he wouldn't be at Adam's. He still had no idea what it meant. Was there a chance this whole thing wasn't over? Part of him hoped that might be true. Another part of him wished she wasn't here at all, because the whole point of tonight was that he wanted to goof off without having to look over his shoulder and worry what she was thinking.

They'd just arrived at the employee entrance in the back, and Tucker sent a text to announce their arrival. A minute later the door opened and Mikey was there, a flashlight in one hand and a beer in the other, gesturing wildly for them to hurry inside.

"Tucker," he said. "You're a genius. This is so dope."

Tucker was in fact worried that this was not going to be dope at all; he'd become increasingly convinced on the drive over there that he and Suzanne would be stuck in a dirty cavern of unplugged machines, in the company of whoever happened to show up . . .

But then they walked into the main room, and Suzanne said, "Ooooh."

The place was inky dark, lit eerily by the security lights on the floor and the exit signs in every corner, plus the six holes of mini golf whose windmills and archways were neon with phosphorescent paint. Tucker's eyes adjusted, and everything came into sharper view. The Whac-a-Mole and the tiny four-horse carousel. The air hockey table and that zombie game that never worked. A few people were already there, drinking and watching that kid Noah shoot at the basketball hoop without the benefit of the flashing lights and tickets. He was missing every shot, and the air was filled with laughter and boos.

Tucker was disappointed not to see Erika, but not really surprised since she'd never responded to the text chain. Who knew if she was even around? He didn't have any online connection to her; back when they knew each other, she'd erased all her profiles and stories and timelines because of what happened with that video. He'd looked for her before he came here tonight, but if she had pages now, they weren't easy to find.

Mikey's phone was buzzing, and he took off for the back door again, pointing Tucker and Suzanne to where the beer was, over by the ball pit.

"I'm going to go grab one—you don't want anything, right?" Tucker asked.

"Nope."

Suzanne had officially given up drinking because she was in hard-core training mode this year, trying to get picked up by a college program. She'd offered to drive tonight, which worked out for Tucker. Guided by the light of his phone, he headed for the corner and rooted around in the cooler for the least shitty of all the shitty beers. As he came up and cracked it open, he expected to see Suzanne waiting for him, so that he could introduce her to everyone, but no.

She had already taken over at the hoop and was making basket after basket.

*Swish, swish, swish.*

The small crowd went wild, and some of them looked in his direction, waving and calling his name. Noah was jumping up and down, demanding that he get his ass over there. Tucker smiled and waved back, but stayed rooted to the spot as he watched Suzanne, feeling both impressed and annoyed.

And then, over his shoulder, he heard someone clapping, loud and slow.

"That is some A-plus vintage fashion."

He turned to see two girls, and it took him a second to realize that one of them was Erika.

She'd had a pink bob before, so he'd been looking for that, but her hair was brown now, chopped very short in a way that showed off her blue eyes, her smooth skin. Freckles. He'd forgotten the freckles, but there they were. He could just barely see them in the dimness of the room.

She was with her friend, the redhead who used to show up at Pizza Hut sometimes. Melissa, Marissa? She was the one who had clapped and made the joke, and now she was taking in Tucker with a big smile, while Erika kept her lips pressed together, eyes shifting away.

Tucker started to sweat. They were both looking at him, waiting, and he couldn't read Erika's expression at all, but he had to say something. In a panic, all he could come up with was the truth.

"I'm starting to have a lot of regrets. I didn't realize how weird it was, having people look at your belly button."

He saw it happen, right in front of his eyes—the exact moment when Erika gave in and started laughing.

Whether it was at him or with him, he wasn't entirely sure.

In the end, more than a dozen people came, and as the minutes ticked by and the beer disappeared, the evening started to turn into a debauched version of the kids' birthday parties that had once filled the place. The girls were crowding onto the mini-carousel, taking selfies while Mikey freaked out and begged them not to post pictures anywhere public. A game of putt-putt was dissolving into laughter and shrieks, no one able to make a shot. An epic quest to find the missing air hockey puck was finally fulfilled, and people cheered like they'd found the Ark of the Covenant.

Tucker, meanwhile, had been hovering on the edge of things. He'd introduced Suzanne to Erika and Marissa, and now the three of them were cackling together in the corner about who-knew-what, while Tucker was standing there alone in his not-quite-crop-top, telling himself to forget about them and just have fun.

"Remember that kid who wet his pants and you saved his life? None of his friends saw. NONE OF THEM."

Noah had appeared at Tucker's side, slapping him on the back. He recounted Tucker's small-time heroics before asking him about school and work, then rambling on about his new band. He suddenly broke into a rendition of the Cave's bastardized version of "Happy Birthday," which—like some kind of rallying cry—brought everybody to the center of the room. As he finished, Tucker elbowed him.

"You should have brought your guitar. You could have done 'Shake It Off.'"

That set off a chorus of groans. The song had been on a mix that played for six months straight, and the system was always glitching and starting over, meaning they'd heard it five times a shift until they'd all loathed it beyond words. Tucker could remember singing it in a falsetto one morning before they opened while Erika threw bouncy balls from the prize bin at his head . . .

And now here they were again, those opening beats, playing thinly but surely. When he looked around to find the source, there was Erika, holding her phone straight up in the air.

The two of them locked eyes, and then Marissa was tugging on Erika's arm, trying to get her to dance, but she wouldn't budge. Marissa took the phone from her, wielding it like a baton as she approached Suzanne, who joined her somewhat reluctantly, followed by Noah and some other girls. Mikey got in the middle, pretending to mosh.

This was Tucker's moment, what he'd been waiting for, but he couldn't quite get there, not yet. Instead, he grabbed a beer and sat on the prize counter, scrolling through his phone like he had something important to check.

And then suddenly Erika was there, boosting herself up and sliding in beside him.

Tucker put his phone in his pocket and sat up a little straighter.

"We spent a truly disturbing amount of time talking about Harry Potter, right in this very spot," she said. "Remember how you were always putting spells on the customers with those toy wands?"

Tucker was glad for the dark, because he couldn't think of what to say, too busy remembering what he was like back when he knew her. A loud, silly kid with such an obvious and hopeless crush.

"I like your girlfriend, by the way," Erika said.

*Say thanks. You should probably just say thanks.*

"She's not my girlfriend."

Erika glanced at him, looking skeptical. "So it's complicated?"

"No, no," he said, louder than he'd meant to. "It's nothing like that. It's nothing at all."

As soon as the words were out, his mind raced to justify them. Technically it was true, right? It had always been true, and now it was more than ever.

"Okay, okay. Didn't mean to assume." She shifted a bit to sit on her hands. "So where did you work this summer? Some place better than here?"

"I was at my stepdad's office. He's an orthodontist. So, you know. Dumb stuff like making the retainers."

"Hey, retainers are very important. Don't sell yourself short."

She had a little smile on her face now, and Tucker started to loosen up.

"Oh, for sure. I would never undersell the importance of retainers. But to be honest, I wasn't very good at it. If I ever end up murdered, go to the police and tell them it was Steph, the tech who had to fix all my screw-ups."

Erika looked down at her shoes and laughed. He loved that sound.

"Well, I was at Applebee's. Very glamorous. Hey, you know who worked with me? Nina Martinez. She's your year, at Gaithersburg. Her older brother is Marissa's ex."

Tucker whipped his head in her direction and then started rubbing his temples.

"Un-fucking-believable."

"What?" Erika asked.

"You know Nina Martinez?"

"*Yes?*"

"It's just . . . nothing. I . . . nothing."

Her eyes were on him with an angry glitter. "What's your problem?"

"No, no, no. It's nothing bad. I shouldn't tell you this. If you know her."

She was looking more pissed by the second, and it undid him.

"My friend Bobby. He's liked her forever, and he never tells me things like that, so I'm pretty sure he's massively in love."

The tension in her face broke, and she bit her lip, considering him.

"Bobby . . . Did he used to come in here sometimes? To visit you?"

"Yeah. Black kid? Baby face? Probably never spoke to you because he's terrified of women?"

She laughed and looked at the ceiling. "I remember Bobby."

"I definitely shouldn't have told you that. Please don't say anything."

"I won't, I won't. I helped Nina get a job this summer, as a hostess." Erika was smiling now, swinging her feet. "She's pretty awesome, so I get it."

"Bobby did one project with her sophomore year, and now he can barely say hi to her."

Erika was laughing again. "Aw, Bobby. C'mon."

"Last spring—she was in our lunch period. I'm pretty sure he was timing his trips to the trash can, to bump into her. But then he'd just run away."

"Oh my god, stop it. You're killing me."

And he was, he could see it in her face, a gentleness that had come into her eyes. He started swinging his feet, too.

"Maybe you can subtly drop a hint to Nina that you know him, while you guys are delivering mozzarella sticks. Tell her that he's really nice and good at math. Say he's amazing in bed."

"Hold up. Now *I'm* kind of interested," she said, glancing over with a different kind of smile.

He adjusted his position on the counter and had to look away.

"Erika Green," he said, shaking his head.

"Tucker Campanelli."

Hearing his whole name on her lips gave him a little rush.

"So, are you heading back to school soon? Where do you go?"

"Next week. I'm at St. B's?"

"That's the place on the Chesapeake Bay, right? The little artsy one?"

"You got it."

"That's right where my dad grew up. My grandmother still lives there, practically around the corner."

"So you spent a lot of time there?"

Tucker paused, looking out into the gloom. "Not really."

The music shifted then. The dance party hit a new gear,

people moving closer, hips swinging lower. A smile crept onto his face.

"I feel like you pulled that first song up pretty quickly. Do you have Taylor Swift ready to go on your phone?"

She turned to him, scowling.

"There are two kinds of people in the world, Tucker— people who say they like Taylor Swift songs and liars."

He nodded very seriously, like he was really taking that in.

"Have you heard this one? There are two kinds of people in the world—people who *think* there are two kinds of people in the world and people who are smart enough to know better."

She tried not to laugh and ended up snorting instead.

"Got you," Tucker said, and as soon as the words were out, he regretted them.

*Got you* was a little game they had played when they worked at the Cave. He'd say it any time he made her laugh, and she would say it any time she managed to embarrass him. Usually he got her a couple times a shift. She only got him about once a month, despite her near-constant efforts.

But that was all so long ago, ancient history. He got embarrassed a hell of a lot easier these days. Right now, for instance. He was sure that he'd come on way too strong . . . but then he saw that she was smiling.

"Okay, you got me, after all these years," she said. "What can I say? Irony will get you everywhere."

"Not flattery?"

"No, not flattery."

"All right, then. I won't tell you I like your hair."

The music shut off suddenly, and Erika mumbled that her phone must have died and she should probably go retrieve it.

She hopped off the counter, and as Tucker watched her go, he realized with a sad pang that the party was almost over. Mikey was kicking them out right at eleven, a good half hour before he knew the security company patrolled the parking lots all along this strip. This rendezvous with the Cave was coming to an end, and even though it had been fun, Tucker felt a little hollow. He'd barely hung out with Suzanne at all, and had officially given up on the idea that she might be here because she wanted something more with him.

Talking to Erika just now—that had been something, that had felt special. But wasn't she about to disappear from his life again?

Looking out into the dark room, he wished he could keep that from happening. He wanted a little more from this night, some reason to keep it going, a way to hold on to the spell that had been cast by nostalgia and circumstance and glow-in-the-dark mini golf.

Tucker took out his phone and typed a message to Bobby.

**Are you at Adam's yet? Is Nina there?**

# 4

## ERIKA

Erika had brought a charger cord in her purse, and she found a quiet corner where she could plug in her phone and wait for it to come back to life. She also wanted a chance to breathe, to re-center herself after that conversation, which had made her feel a little giggly, a little nervous.

As soon as the screen was glowing again, Erika saw a message from her mom.

**Out late for once??? I am both happy and worried, because being a mother is terrible that way.**

Erika looked around the room, taking stock of everyone and everything around her. She liked how the darkness turned all the people into shadows, how it made everything seem secret and special.

**I'm with Marissa. We're doing some light trespassing and**

**checking out younger men.**

**And I wasn't invited?**

**EW. Go join an old lady book club or something.**

**I'm already in an old lady book club, remember? We can't find anything we hate-love as much as 50 Shades.**

**Ew, ew, ew. Goodbye**

**Okay—I love you. Have fun, but be safe, but have fun?**

Erika fiddled with her phone and sighed. When your mom had to tell you to have fun, that was pretty sad, wasn't it?

Her mom and Marissa: they were the only ones who were really there for her during that darkest period. No one else had any idea of what it had been like, when she'd had the apocalypse inside her head, all this noise, noise, noise that was part anguish and part defense, her mind churning up horrible thoughts and then screaming at itself to drown them out. She'd spent weeks talking out loud when no one was there and screeching into pillows at night and driving the heels of her hands into her eyes whenever she remembered the very worst part, the part when she'd started going faster, her head bobbing. All of it had been too much for her to stand, and eventually she'd started pinching herself with her nails, leaving little crescent moons in her skin.

It was Marissa who'd seen those and told Erika's mom, and because her mom had wept, Erika had finally agreed to go to therapy. She'd talked a bunch of shit out and learned all these coping techniques, and she was better now, so much better. There were hurdles still, but they were stupid things, right?

Kissing someone, that would be a start.

Erika looked out again at the dim room. She raised her phone and took a picture, thinking there was a chance that this would be a night she'd want to remember.

Marissa had taken up residence in the ball pit, was lying there like it was a nice, warm bath, the most comfortable place in the world. Erika climbed the ladder that led up the side, but she hovered at the edge.

"Plenty of room," Marissa said.

"Not happening."

"It's a ball pit, Erika. If you don't want to come in, I'm going to develop serious concerns about your well-being."

Erika thought again of the text conversation she'd just had with her mom, then lowered herself down into the rainbow of plastic as nonchalantly as humanly possible. Marissa made her way over to Erika with a butterfly stroke, speaking in a dramatic whisper when she'd gotten close enough.

"So how's our little Italian friend in the crop top?"

Erika sank slowly into the balls until she was entirely covered, muttering to Marissa that she was absurd.

"Can you believe he's as yummy in person as he was online?"

Marissa asked. "That never happens. I mean, too bad about the girlfriend, who—I have to say—is delightful, if slightly terrifying. I kind of want her to follow me around and straighten out my life? She could pluck unhealthy foods out of my hand. Make me do my homework."

From her safe space at the bottom of the pit, Erika laughed. After a pause, she said, "Actually . . . she's not his girlfriend."

Marissa went very still, then poked the top of Erika's head. "So he randomly volunteered that information?"

"It came up naturally."

"Oh, I'm sure that it did."

Balls flew everywhere as Erika resurfaced, and she and Marissa were laughing and flailing as they tried to get resettled. Wanting to derail this Tucker conversation, Erika asked about Marco, which set Marissa off on a tirade about the current state of their relationship, how he'd freaked out when she told him about the test, saying he would have been there with her. Erika half listened, making all the appropriate murmurs, while her mind was busy replaying the conversation she'd had at the prize counter, lingering on certain moments . . .

Marissa had trailed off, and Erika realized she'd completely stopped listening. Right as she was about to apologize, Marissa broke into a grin.

"Incoming," she said.

Erika turned in time to see Tucker crashing down beside them. The girls both screamed and then pelted him with balls while he begged them to stop. He had his hands up to guard his face, and because of that stupid shirt, Erika could practically see his whole damn chest.

It was pretty cute, a little fuzzy.

"Stop, please stop!" he yelled. "I need your help. Desperately."

Erika looked at Marissa, and by silent agreement, they ceased attacking him. Slowly, he lowered his hands.

"I texted Bobby. He's at a party and you-know-who is there, and if you two come with me, we can finally get them to have a conversation. PLEASE."

Erika turned to Marissa, who was wide-eyed and waiting for an explanation.

"Tucker's best friend is apparently madly in love with Nina, but he's too shy to talk to her."

Marissa sucked in her breath. Then she used both arms to scoop up a bushel of balls and toss them joyously into the air.

"This is incredible. We have to go. That's what nights like this are all about—stars aligning! Didn't Romeo and Juliet meet at a party?"

"Indeed," Erika said. "And then they died."

"Killjoy," Marissa whispered.

"I'm stating a fact. And can I also state for the record that I'm not going to some party to serve Nina up like a piece of meat?"

Marissa scoffed, gestured at Tucker. "Did he ask for that? It sounds like he just needs us to facilitate some pleasant conversation that could lead to a meaningful, well-paced relationship."

Tucker was nodding, an earnest look on his face. "Exactly.

Yes. That thing that she said."

Erika ran a hand through her hair like she was thinking, but what was there to debate? The whole point of tonight was to loosen up, and wasn't it working? She was in a ball pit. She was laughing. She was maybe, kind of checking out a boy.

"Fine," she said, with the biggest eye roll she could manage. "Bring on the star-crossed bullshit."

Tucker and Marissa cheered and high-fived, then started pelting Erika with balls. She batted them away, screeching, doing her best to act like it was the most annoying thing in the world.

# 5

## TUCKER

Tucker sat in the passenger seat of Suzanne's mom's SUV, fiddling with a Magic 8 Ball that he'd swiped from the prize counter right before they left. He felt a little embarrassed looking down at it because he remembered playing with one at work, quietly taking some small reassurance every time it gave the answer he'd hoped for, when he'd obviously been way too old for that.

"No one ever got one of these, not in the entire summer I worked there. You needed like nine million tickets. It was impossible. A total scam."

Suzanne stared at the road ahead and didn't answer. He knew things had gotten a little awkward when he'd asked to go to Adam's and explained that Erika and Marissa were coming, too, but now the atmosphere in the car shifted another degree.

"Should I ask it if you'll end up playing tennis at Northwestern next year?" he asked. "We know you will, so it's a perfect test case, for whether this thing works."

He shook the ball, still trying to elicit a smile from her.

"Did you guys work together for a long time?" she asked.

"You mean all of us?"

Before she answered, there was a pause, great and yawning.

"Yeah, sure. All of you."

"I was there for the summer. People were in and out."

She nodded, then leaned over to spin the volume up on the radio. Beyoncé came on, raucous and joyful. A few seconds later, Suzanne turned it off with a slap.

"You didn't have to take me, if you didn't want to."

Tucker stopped shaking the ball. His pulse kicked up a notch, and he fired back instinctively.

"What? No. What are you talking about?"

He waited for her to say never mind, to tell him they could drop this, but she kept silent.

"Honestly, I was kind of surprised," Tucker finally said. "You've never wanted to hang out with me before."

She started blinking too much, and her jaw went tense.

"I've been really busy with training, you know that. I . . . Jesus, Tucker. I'm sorry for thinking that you'd want to say goodbye. To this summer."

Tucker wanted to ask her why they were saying goodbye at all, why it was so easy for her to walk away, but of course he didn't—saying any of that would have been humiliating.

Instead, he decided to get angry.

"I didn't think you cared. At all. I mean, this whole thing happened because you drove by me one day, right? You were bored, and I was there, so you backed up your car."

The harshness of his own words made Tucker's heart thump harder. He waited for her to blow up at him, ready even, for the release it would bring.

Instead, she gripped the wheel hard and kept her voice steady.

"I wasn't *bored*. I don't hook up with people because I'm *bored*, all right?"

She gave him a look that clearly demanded an answer, so Tucker finally mumbled "all right, all right," and then she went on.

"I was stressed that day, yeah. And then I saw you, and you made that goofy surprised face, and it made me smile."

Tucker knew there was nothing wrong with what she'd said, but it needled him, set him on edge. He wanted her to stop talking, but she wouldn't.

"I backed up *my fucking car*, because you've always seemed like a nice guy. I remember you took Christa to homecoming sophomore year, and she said you asked before you kissed her."

Face red, Tucker squirmed, trying to figure out why in the world she was telling that story right now, what it could possibly have to do with anything.

"I didn't know what else to do," he said. "She looked nervous, but I couldn't tell if it was normal nervous, and I didn't want to do the wrong thing."

Suzanne stopped too hard at a red light, and both of them jerked against their seat belts. She turned to him with a look that was now more incredulous than angry.

"I'm trying to explain what I like about you. Why do you sound so defensive?"

He stared down at the cheap toy in his hands, the plastic oracle floating aimlessly inside. He didn't know what was wrong with him—*I thought you were nice* should be better than *I was bored*, but right now, for Tucker, it wasn't.

He mumbled a half-assed apology, then stared silently out the car window for the rest of the drive.

"You *told them about Nina*? Tucker, what the hell."

"They won't say anything to her, I swear. They're just here to hang out."

"They're just here to hang out?"

"Yes."

Bobby pursed his lips and nodded his head, like he believed absolutely none of that. He and Tucker were standing alone in a corner, trying their best to take refuge from the chaos that had taken over the great open swath of space that was Adam's living room and kitchen.

The keg was busted and foaming by the fridge, a couch upended. Empty cans and crushed Solo cups littered the tables and the counter, and the kitchen floor was a mess; a hiccupping girl tried to sweep up broken glass and spilled Cheetos while her friends cheered her on. All of it was set to a Drake song screaming from a speaker, and to a couple of kids in the corner who were just plain screaming.

Bobby turned back to Tucker. "And Suzanne. She's also here, just to *hang out*? Or did she go home?"

The conversation from the car was rattling around in Tucker's brain. Had he been a jerk at the Cave? He guessed that he had. After she'd walked away from him initially, he'd stayed away, hoping she'd be the one to come to him. When she didn't, he sort of dug in on not going to her either. He felt embarrassed about it now, like he'd been childish. But at this point, wasn't it best to let it go? She probably didn't even feel like talking to him.

"Uh, I think she went down to the basement. She's kind of pissed at me."

"Does that have anything to do with the fact that one of those girls who knows Nina is that girl you were totally into? The one who was always laughing at your dumbass Harry Potter jokes?"

Tucker paused and looked at Bobby, surprised he remembered that. He nervously looked over at Erika and Marissa, who were scouring the fridge for something acceptable to drink.

"But what does that really mean?" Tucker asked. "Does it mean she thinks I'm funny or does it mean that she thinks I'm a dumbass?"

"Get up on the coffee table and do your little dance again. I'll watch her reaction, and then we'll know for sure."

Tucker could almost imagine trying exactly that, but then

Suzanne might emerge. She'd stand there watching him with a knowing little smile on her face, wondering why she wasted so much of her summer in his basement . . .

"This night got really weird, really fast," Tucker said. "I might have screwed everything up."

"Nah," Bobby said. "You'll find some way to fix it. That's kind of your thing. Hit the mound in the seventh inning and save the day."

"Uh, maybe half the time. The other half I run the whole game into the ground."

There was no time to say more, because Erika and Marissa were coming their way, each holding a beer. Once they'd squeezed their way through the crowd, Tucker introduced everybody, Marissa looking at Bobby with an absolutely ridiculous smile, while Erika did her best to play it cool.

Bobby rolled his eyes. "So how was the Cave?"

"MAGIC," Marissa said. "Pure magic."

"Sorry I missed it, then," Bobby said.

"Oh, the night is still young," Marissa said. "There is so much magic yet to come, so much."

Bobby officially looked mortified, which made both girls laugh, and then Tucker was laughing, too. Bobby announced that he hated all of them, which set everyone off even harder.

*This night can be saved. This night is worth saving.*

As Tucker started to seriously consider the coffee table, he heard a yelp.

"OH MY GOD. Marissa? Erika? What are you guys *doing* here?"

Nina had popped up behind them. She stood there with her cute glasses and her curly hair up in a bun, a big, bright smile making her whole face glow.

Tucker felt a light splash on his shoes, and looked down.

Bobby had dropped his beer.

# 6

## ERIKA

In the far corner of the yard, there was a big, beautiful tree house that Adam's parents didn't have the heart to get rid of, even though Adam was seventeen and his brothers were off in college. That's where they'd convened, seven of them sitting in a circle—Erika, Marissa, Tucker, and Bobby, plus Nina and her two friends. Kara was teeny and pale with a blunt bob, and Yrma was tall and brown-skinned with a shiny ponytail. It took Erika a minute to pick up on it, but the two girls were clearly together.

After they'd had a go-round introducing themselves, Yrma pointed at Marissa, grinning.

"I totally remember seeing you at Nina's house, hanging out with Marco. And her mom still has your prom picture on the fridge. I *knew* I knew that hair!"

Marissa ran her hands through her mane, shaking it out

even bigger than it already was. "My enormous, flaming-red hair? I had no idea it caught people's attention!"

"Where did you meet him, if you didn't go to Gaithersburg?" Yrma asked.

"Where else? At church."

Marissa looked up at the ceiling and did the sign of the cross, Kara and Yrma cracking up while Nina groaned and covered her face.

Erika gave a distracted smile. Tucker had ended up across the circle from her, after he'd done some subtle maneuvering to make sure Nina and Bobby were sitting next to each other. Now Erika was stuck trying and failing not to look at Tucker's stupid, cute belly button.

"What about you two?" Marissa asked, motioning to Kara and Yrma with her beer bottle. "I love a good meet-cute. Lay it on me."

Nina put a hand up in protest.

"Oh, hell no. I can't listen to this again."

Kara ignored her and sat up straighter.

"It was freshman year. First day of JV soccer. I accidentally got Yrma with my cleats—just barely, mind you—and she called me a very, very, *very* offensive name."

Yrma scoffed. "I did *not*. I wouldn't have even *known* that word when I was fourteen! And I have never, ever *said* it."

"END OF STORY!" Nina said.

People were laughing, a new energy filling the air as Marissa peered around the circle.

"All right, all right," she said. "Let's keep going. Platonic meetings can be cute, too. Kara, how do you know Nina?"

"Kindergarten," Kara said. "Nina was crying for her mom, and I held her hand. Besties ever since."

That set off a round of *awwww*s while Nina begged for this to stop, but Marissa's eyes were alight now. She was really getting going, and that made Erika nervous.

"Okay, okay," Marissa said. "Let's switch this up. You. Tucker. What do you remember about meeting Erika?"

Erika went completely still and silently cursed her best friend, the freaking queen of subtlety. She tried not to look at Tucker again, but couldn't help it. Tucker seemed a little anxious as he toggled the tab on his beer can.

Then he put it down and started to smile.

"How much time do you have?" he asked Marissa.

That led to snickers and chatter, and Erika did her best to look annoyed, but her pulse was racing now.

"I'm fifteen, right? First job, at the Cave. I come one day for training or whatever. I hear this girl giving an elaborate explanation of why she hated a *very* specific plotline on *Game of Thrones*. And you know what? It's a really good point, something I'd never thought of. I'm about to say that, but she's down behind the prize counter with some other kid, unpacking more plastic spiders or whatever, and I can't really see her. But then the manager walks over, and the girl pops up. She's got pink hair and she's beautiful, but she's giving me this look that clearly says, *Holy shit, who hired this fetus, he's not old enough to work here.*"

"You looked straight-up eight years old when you got that job," Bobby said.

It was the first thing Bobby had said the whole time they were in the tree house, and people were laughing, were loving this—the ridiculous story, of course, but also what was happening between Erika and Tucker.

They'd all noticed, right? How could you not notice, the way he'd dropped *beautiful* in there, so nonchalant?

The word had hit Erika's chest like a firework.

"So I stand there, speechless, and she goes, 'I hope you know we get paid in Laffy Taffy and bouncy balls.' Then she walked away and I spent days thinking of all the funny things I could have said."

Marissa announced that this was "the most Erika story" she'd ever heard, and Nina agreed. People were laughing and watching her, waiting to see what came next.

Erika kept her cool, but she was feeling overwhelmed, thinking back on all that. She'd been in so much pain that summer, and that silliness with Tucker, those hours together . . .

They'd been a sliver of light when she'd had so little.

"My turn?" she asked, looking over at Marissa.

"Of course."

Erika made a point of casually examining her nails.

"So I'm seventeen, working at the Cave, and this fetus shows up."

Everyone laughed hard at that, and she waited for them to calm down. In that pause, she found Tucker's eyes, big and brown and shining.

She held them just long enough for it to mean something.

"So I meet him or whatever, but before he leaves, the manager tells me to put him on for three shifts the next week. So I pull the calendar up on the computer, and it's weird—he's only available on the days where he can see my name."

Marissa was dying. Bobby was shaking his head. Nina and her friends were having silent exchanges with their eyes about what exactly was happening here.

Tucker, though—he couldn't manage to look at her right now. He was staring very earnestly at his shoes.

"Every time I try to schedule him on a day when I'm not there, he tells me he's busy. Sports stuff, or when that doesn't make sense, he says he has to meet with his English tutor."

Bobby leaned over to see Tucker better. *"English tutor?"*

"So he's leaving, shoving paperwork in his backpack, and *Slaughterhouse-Five* falls out. I ask if it's summer reading, and he says no, just for fun. So I point out how very *interesting* that is. That he needs an English tutor, but reads Vonnegut for fun. And do you know what he says?"

She waited for a second. Two. Three.

"He says: 'I'm much better at extracurriculars.'"

Everyone was cracking up now. They had gotten much too loud, but nobody cared—even Nina had given up on hushing them. She was too busy chugging her beer, after which she leaned over to talk to Bobby, her hand on his knee.

In the middle of it all, Tucker had his face hidden away in his elbow, but Erika was pretty sure that he was blushing. He'd never expected her to remember all that, not in a million years.

When he finally looked up, she mouthed two words to him, careful and slow.

*Got you.*

Marissa was halfway through a story about her and Marco sneaking off into the woods during a CYO retreat, Nina howling for her to stop, when Adam's angry face appeared in the doorway of the tree house.

"You are way too loud. Your tree house privileges are officially revoked."

Everyone started filing out, but Erika pinched Marissa on the arm, and the two of them hung back in a corner, pretending to look at something on their phones, while everyone else took turns climbing down the ladder.

Tucker went last, and seemed on the verge of saying something, but then he too disappeared over the edge.

As soon as they were alone, Erika sat down cross-legged and Marissa settled right in front of her in the same position, their knees almost touching.

"You okay?" Marissa asked.

"What? Yes. I thought you'd be doing a victory dance or something right now."

"I am, in my head. But you look kind of nervous and sweaty, so I'm also a little worried." Marissa pulled a ponytail holder from her pocket. "Do you want to braid my hair? It's disgustingly hot out here."

Erika told Marissa to swing around, then quietly went to

work. It helped having something to focus on, and it also helped not having to look her in the eye.

"Sometimes I kind of miss Truth or Dare. Seven Minutes in Heaven," Erika said. "Wasn't it nice, having a dumb excuse to say the things you wanted to say, do the things you wanted to do?"

"Oh, people still have those kind of excuses. Only now they're called beer and vodka."

"Because that's so healthy."

Marissa laughed. "Fair enough. But you're a mature, empowered woman. If you want to do something, shouldn't you just do it?"

Erika stared at the thick woven strands in front of her, then pulled them loose again, told Marissa she was going to try a fancier braid. They were both quiet as she did.

As Erika tied off her handiwork, she took a breath.

"I think I need a reset button."

"A reset button?"

"It's . . . I suck at college. Seriously. I never have fun. You realize I haven't even kissed someone, since everything happened?"

Marissa turned around and gave her a questioning look.

"And tonight could be the night?"

"Maybe. He's a puppy dog, right? I can't imagine anything feeling safer. If I can't get through this, then I might as well join a convent."

Marissa had been holding out the braid, admiring Erika's

work, but now she dropped it and raised her eyebrows.

"If you're just trying to *get through it*, I'm not sure I endorse this decision."

"That's not what I meant."

"Are you sure?"

Erika scoffed and mumbled a nonresponse, then stood and pulled Marissa up after her.

*Sophomore year, here I come.*

# 1

## TUCKER

Tucker stood at the bottom of the old, sprawling oak. With a distressed sort of wonder, he considered the perfect acoustics of this spot, how clearly they had sent the girls' conversation right to him.

His plan had been to wait here until Erika came down, make a play for her in the grass and the moonlight, but instead he turned and went inside.

Tucker did not want to be anyone's puppy dog, but he did want to get very, very drunk.

A few guys from the baseball team were standing in the corner of the basement, so Tucker went and joined them, and they started laughing about his shirt, or at his shirt—whatever, who cared, right? He rummaged around in the cooler and pulled out a Bud Light, tried to drink it quickly.

When Tucker was about eight years old, his dad had given him a sip of beer, and Tucker had told him it tasted "ugly." His dad had cracked up, had repeated the story to everyone they saw that day, laughing every single time he did.

It was one of the only times Tucker could remember him laughing at all.

Tucker still thought beer tasted ugly, but right now that didn't matter. Right now he started drinking faster, pounding the whole thing down, feeling a little dizzy, a little woozy, listening-but-not-listening as the guys talked about Fortnite, about summer hookups, about how they couldn't believe it was finally senior year.

Bobby appeared, eyeing him suspiciously, asking Tucker if he was okay, but Tucker shrugged and said he was fine.

"Does anybody have a key?" Tucker asked.

Pete, the starting pitcher, pulled one triumphantly from his pocket.

The only other time Tucker had tried shotgunning a beer had been a year ago—and he'd choked on it, practically thrown up. Now he was convinced he could do better. He took a breath and steeled himself as Pete jammed a hole in the side of a new can with a loud pop.

Tapping into some inner will, Tucker pressed the stream to his lips and took it all, feeling the buzz hit him hard while a couple guys chanted his name.

He made it to the end, and by those last drops, he welcomed

the bitter taste of something gone purposely bad. It had felt awful going down and filling his stomach, but that's how he knew that he was on his way. When the swallowing made him wince. When the sour taste was stuck there on the back of his tongue. When he thought the word *bubbles* and that suddenly seemed hilarious, parties were hilarious, everything was hilarious.

Peter slapped him on the back. "Way to take it like a man, Campanelli. I'm impressed."

Tucker swayed, noticing that a space had opened at the flip-cup table.

Each round started with two people squaring off, their arms crossed and their fists meeting across the table, answering a this-or-that question before they drank. Every time it came to Tucker, he'd ask about two of their teachers—Mrs. Smith or Miss Mendoza? Mr. Chen or Mr. Robinson? People were laughing so hard, and Adam was filling everyone's cups way too high. Tucker was spilling almost as much as he was drinking.

He suddenly wanted pizza, and he knew he needed water. Gripping the edge of the table, he waited for his vision to steady, trying to decide if he had it in him to make it up to the kitchen.

And then he saw Suzanne, standing across from him, keys in her hand.

"I'm leaving," she called, and oh wow, she looked pissed. Now would probably be a good time to excuse himself and go talk to her. He was pretty sure he could pull himself together enough to hold a conversation. He should apologize and tell her that this summer had meant a lot to him, that he hoped they could still be friends.

Instead Tucker said, "Cool," and went back to his game.

He meant not to watch as she left, but his eyes followed her as she went up the basement stairs, brushing past Erika, who was coming the other way. Erika gave her a friendly wave, which Suzanne did not return, and he saw a flicker of hurt on Erika's face.

Tucker thought about yelling *not your fault*, but he didn't have time—he was up again.

Pete and Dre put out their fists, waiting for Tucker's question. For a few seconds, he was too far gone to think of anything, but then it came to him.

"Hermione or Ginny Weasley?"

"Which one's Ginny Weasley?" Pete asked, and he was already behind, because Dre had screamed "Hermione forever!" and chugged his beer faster than Tucker thought possible.

As he clung to his cup, Tucker realized Erika was standing there and smiling at him, teasing and sweet and all alone. Like she was waiting for him.

Couldn't she tell he was busy? Couldn't she see he was locked in an epic competition that would soon make it almost impossible to think?

A space opened up on Tucker's team, right next to him. Tucker hiccuped and offered to play both parts, but as he did, a familiar face appeared by his side.

Christa—Miss Kiss-and-Tell herself.

"Hi, friend," she said, bumping her shoulder against his. "How's it going?"

A giggle bubbled up inside him, and he thought about explaining that she had been responsible, in a very roundabout way, for getting him laid. He was trying to form the words, and only barely stopped himself when he saw her concerned expression.

"Are you okay?" she asked.

"Yeah, yeah. I just—I need a shot of something."

He'd heard Adam was keeping the hard booze out of sight in the laundry room, so he went looking for it. The first door he opened was the bathroom and the second was a hot water heater and the third was a home office, windowless and cluttered. He paused on the threshold, taking in the messy desk and packed shelves, remembering that Adam's mom was an English professor.

"BOOKS!" Tucker yelled to the empty room. "I like books."

He wandered in and grabbed the closest one and then sank down onto the floor, squinting his eyes at the tiny text. After repeated tries, Tucker finally made it through a few lines of "The Love Song of J. Alfred Prufrock," mumbling *what the fuck is this shit* as he did.

His phone beeped. It was a message from Bobby, asking where he was.

Tucker typed **unfortunate tree house situation**, or tried to, and then lay back down on the floor, resting the book on his chest, wondering in a vague, detached way if he was some kind of masochist. He could have walked away before he'd heard everything Erika said, but this seemed to be a chronic problem he had—eavesdropping on conversations that he didn't want to hear.

Tucker let his mind flow back to when he was a kid, to those intermittent days when he actually spent time with his dad. Ray's appearances in Tucker's life were mostly unpredictable, but Tucker could always depend on seeing him in May. Every year without fail, Ray would take Tucker to the place where he grew up—those acres near St. B's, the place that everyone called the farm, even though it hadn't been one in years. The family always had a party to celebrate Tucker's grandfather's birthday, which seemed like a strange tradition, considering the man was long dead and everyone clearly had hated him. Still, there were fireworks, barbecue, and music, all that beautiful green. Tucker had a pack of cousins who made him nervous— loud, fearless kids from big families. They all knew one another so well.

Tucker would come home dirty and sunburned and tired, and always he'd run to his room, while his dad stood on the front porch talking to his mom, and how stupid could the two of them be, not to realize that he could hear?

He remembered exactly how it felt, inching open his window only to be hit by words that would cling to him like burrs. His dad had said a lot of things that Tucker could never forget, but the absolute worst was when Tucker had been struggling with a speech impediment, and his dad could not let it go.

*If you don't get that fixed, nobody is ever going to fuck him.*

"Nine," Tucker said out loud. "I was nine."

His phone beeped again, but this time it was his mother, asking how late he'd be home, reminding him that they still needed to talk about his dad.

This night was officially a disaster, and it was his own fault— because he'd had some pathetic urge to relive the summer that he was fifteen. He felt newly ashamed as he realized there was zero chance of slipping by his mom without her noticing how drunk he was. No, not just his mom. His mom and Frank.

*Frank, Frank, Frank.* Only a total asshole would complain about Frank. He was a great guy, the opposite of Tucker's real dad, and Tucker was happy for his mom, really he was. Still, there was something so hard about this new life, in a new house, the proximity of it all, suddenly having a stepfather who was an unavoidable witness to Tucker's lowest moments. It was an intimacy Tucker hadn't asked for, one he hadn't figured out how to navigate, one that made him feel that he was hopeless at bonding with any kind of man—a fact that didn't seem to bode well for him ever trying to be one . . .

As Tucker was on the verge of falling asleep, he heard someone open the door.

# 8

## ERIKA

Erika froze, her hand still on the doorknob. Tucker appeared to be wasted out of his mind, and seeing him lying there made it painfully clear that her whole plan had gone to hell. Or maybe it had been stupid from the start.

She turned around to leave but couldn't quite do it, because she had a vision of Tucker puking all over the rug with no one to help him . . .

Slowly, Erika tiptoed around him, settling into the desk chair and considering the T. S. Eliot collection that lay open on his chest.

"A little light reading?"

Tucker picked it up like he'd forgotten it was there, then tried to focus on the open page. *"In the room the women come and go, talking of Michelangelo.* I'm usually pretty good at this shit, but what the hell does that mean?"

Erika spun herself around a couple times before stopping again to face him.

"I think that part doesn't mean much at all, on purpose. People are just wandering around a party, trying to sound important or something."

"Well, that's depressing."

Erika didn't respond, but she kind of agreed. She'd let her hopes for tonight get so high, and now they'd come crashing down.

She sighed, looking down at Tucker, who was rubbing his shoulder, wincing a bit.

"Hope that didn't happen in the ball pit."

He looked up at her, confused.

"Your shoulder?" she said.

"Oh, *that*. No, no. It's from the spring. It's almost better."

"I'm sorry, I didn't mean to joke if it's something serious. Sports?"

Tucker closed his eyes, and for a second Erika thought he'd passed out, that she was going to have to go and find Bobby so he could drag Tucker out of there . . .

"I crashed the fuck out of an ATV," he said.

Erika let out a loud laugh, spinning herself in a circle again. This time when she came to a stop, she looked at his face and realized he wasn't joking.

"Wait, *what*?"

He was the one laughing now, an arm draped over his eyes.

"I crashed the fuck out of my dad's brother's ATV. At the farm that's not a farm. I haven't seen my dad since that day, and now my mom wants me to have dinner with him. Like a lot of dinners. So many dinners. What the fuck, right?"

Erika was chewing on her lip, staring at his prone form and feeling bad for him.

"Tucker, I'm not really sure what all that means, but it sounds like it sucks."

Right then, Erika wished that he was sober enough to make sense, and she also started to feel ridiculous, for this whole silly mission she'd put herself on. She'd been having fun tonight when she was just talking to him, and wasn't that what she really missed? How nice he was to talk to?

Tucker mumbled to himself, then laughed again. He shifted around, then very carefully sat up, his eyes focused on the wall in front of him.

"That was nice of you to notice my shoulder. Suzanne never asked about my shoulder."

She took in those words slowly, and as she did, a tingling started on the back of her neck, subtle but sure. At first she wanted to deny it, to think that she had it wrong, but no.

He was saying exactly what she thought he was.

"All this summer, we were down in my basement, and I don't think she ever noticed. She was always leaning on it wrong."

*On purpose. He's telling you on purpose.*

Why he was doing that, Erika had no idea. Maybe he was too drunk to do anything, so he didn't care anymore. Maybe this whole thing had been some weird joke at her expense, who knew?

The air in the basement office was stifling, and Erika hated herself in that moment, more than she had in a long time. She could not believe that she was still so stupid.

*So. Fucking. Stupid.*

She left the room without another word.

Erika went first to the backyard, to have a minute to herself, a minute to look at the stars and breathe and be glad that she hadn't made a horrible mistake.

When she felt calm enough not to cry, she went inside, in search of Marissa. She eventually found her huddled in the living room with Nina, Kara, and Yrma. Marissa appeared to be regaling the girls with more stories that Nina didn't want to hear.

When Marissa spotted Erika hovering on the edge of the room, she hopped up and headed her way, a smile on her face that Erika could tell was masking her concern.

"Everything okay?" Marissa asked when she reached her. "I hope this isn't you after being reset, because you don't look reset at all, if I'm being perfectly honest."

Erika kept her lips tight and shook her head. "He's an asshole. I'll fill you in later—I really don't feel like explaining right now."

"That's fine, that's fine. Come over here. Have fun with us."

The music was too loud, the room was too hot, and all Erika

wanted was to go home, but Marissa was dragging her by the hand, calling to Yrma that Erika would braid her hair next, so Erika gave in. She settled on the couch, taking Yrma's shiny locks and dividing them into careful sections.

Five more minutes. She'd give this five more minutes, and then she'd drive her and Marissa home.

"We were asking Marissa for all of her senior year advice," Kara said. "So if you want to add anything . . ."

It was such an innocent question, but Erika's cheeks went pink, and she had no words to offer. What could she possibly say, after all?

*I kept my head down, worked my ass off, and somehow managed to survive nine months of jokes and stares.*

Quiet seconds ticked by, and then Marissa jumped in.

"The news may not have traveled beyond the walls of our high school, but Erika had a bad senior year. Some dickhead shared a thing that should have stayed private on his phone."

Erika's hands went still, her eyes flashing up to her best friend, silently asking her *what the hell?* Marissa wasn't looking at her, though; she was just sitting there on the floor, casually picking at the carpet.

"Oh no," Nina said. "I'm sorry, that's terrible."

Yrma whipped her head around, undoing all of Erika's hard work, staring at her with wide eyes.

"Do you want me to murder him?"

"Ooooh," Kara said. "I like that idea. You and Erika have no connection. It would be completely untraceable."

Nina clucked her tongue and raised her beer. "Not to put a damper on this plan, which I would love to support, but what about the fact that literally *dozens of people* can see the two of them talking right now?"

"We'll kill them, too," Yrma said. "Collateral damage."

The conversation continued that way for some time, slowly and steadily gaining in silliness. Eventually, Erika took Yrma's hair in her hands again.

Resuming her careful work, she did her very best to smile and laugh along.

"Maybe check with me next time, before you spill that to *a bunch of strangers?*"

"They weren't a bunch of strangers. It was Nina and her two friends. And I knew they'd be cool."

"That's not your call to make."

Erika had said she needed a breather, so she and Marissa were outside, standing shoulder to shoulder against Erika's car and avoiding each other's eyes. They looked instead at the clear night sky, the white moon.

Marissa sighed and crossed her arms. When she spoke again, her tone was gentler.

"Okay. You're right. And I'm sorry. But also—I think you need to give people more of a chance."

Erika struggled to respond. It was almost midnight, and all around them, the cicadas swelled like an orchestra, louder now than the muffled clamor of the house behind them.

"Do you not remember how many of our friends totally sucked after everything happened?" she finally asked.

"Yes, one hundred percent I remember. But, E . . . I think you might be happier at school if you tried a little harder. You've always kind of been like this, to be honest. Even before. You are really slow to open up."

Tears pricked the corners of Erika's eyes, because nothing hurt like the truth. At the same time, Marissa knew exactly what she'd done back there—she'd told just enough of the story. She certainly hadn't mentioned that the guy in the video was some other girl's boyfriend—one of their friends, no less . . .

Erika swiped at her face with the back of her hand, a defensiveness growing in her chest.

"Well, I gave Tucker a chance tonight. Or tried to. And that was a total disaster."

Marissa closed the gap between them, put her head on Erika's shoulder.

"Do you want to talk about it now?"

"Absolutely not."

"We could see if Yrma would murder him, too, since she's got such a long list going anyway?"

"No, no. I don't want to talk about it. I want to go home."

Swallowing hard, Erika kept her gaze on the stars and took a deep breath before pulling her keys from her purse. She noticed that the heat of the day was finally dying, and that came as a small relief.

Summer was ending; a new season was on the way.

# THE CHRISTMAS PARTY

# 9

## ERIKA

Erika's closet was empty and her mini-fridge cleared out. All the girls on her floor were gone—those freshman souls she thought of in some small way as hers. Cleaning the bulletin board in the hallway was the last task she had to do, and she kept putting it off because she was sorry to see it go. She'd worked so hard, putting up something new every month. She'd even bought a Polaroid camera and was always taking photos of everyone, posting fresh ones. She had an eye for it, and she knew the girls liked to pause and see themselves there, looking pretty.

The midday sun was shining from the big window as she opened the trash bag and picked up her staple remover.

"Need some help?"

She turned with a start to find it was Salma, the RA from a couple floors above.

"Sure, okay," Erika said. "I mean—if you don't mind."

Erika moved over to make room for her, and Salma slid in, started taking things down gently.

"I need to up my bulletin board game," Salma said.

Erika was about to shrug it off, say it was nothing, but Salma was smiling at her, and Erika started smiling, too.

"I'm not going to lie, this was a masterpiece," Erika said.

She watched Salma out of the corner of her eye, her dark brown hair wrapped in a neat bun, that perfect beauty mark above her lip. As Erika was trying to figure out what she was doing down here on her floor, Salma started talking.

"It was you, right? Who found her? You don't have to say yes or no, because I shouldn't really be asking, but . . . I heard you did everything right. Or as right as anyone can, with something like that."

Their eyes met, and Erika managed to give Salma a tight little smile.

"I don't know," she said. "It wasn't much."

They went back to ripping down the board, and Erika started to take some pleasure in it. She leaned into the noise and destruction, the clearing away.

Erika had tried to come back this semester with a good attitude, with hopes for this year being better than the last. But then came that night near Thanksgiving.

The campus had been mostly deserted, and Erika had been the last RA left on duty before the dorm officially shut down. It had been so late and dark and quiet, and then she'd stumbled on Makenzie in the stairwell.

Everything had gone to hell so fast.

Erika had spent hours talking to the police, to the Title Nine office. The story had appeared in the local news, then circulated further online—hard, sparse sentences about a student sexually assaulted on campus. A vague collection of words that said nothing about how Erika had found her in a heap on the landing, thinking at first it was just a pile of clothes until she spotted the tangle of her hair.

For the past couple weeks, Erika had been anxious and struggling to sleep—but still, she was here. She was standing.

"So, um, where's home?" Erika asked.

"Outside Philly."

"You leaving soon?"

"Tomorrow. I'm going to the Daily Grind tonight, with Grace and Hailey?"

"Oh yeah. I write papers there sometimes. Or try to."

"They stay open late on Fridays, for an open mic. There are some super-cute townies with guitars who make it worth it, if you want to come."

That actually sounded fun, and Erika felt a swell in her chest. Her tongue loosened up a little.

"I'm leaving in a few minutes," she said. "Otherwise I would totally go. I'd like to expand my options, to be honest. Last week I made out with a kid in a trucker hat, at that stupid SGA-sponsored luau."

Salma laughed hard at that, and it echoed down the hallway,

making both girls look around at the emptiness that surrounded them.

"Who was it?" Salma asked. "That's the best and worst thing about this place. It's so small, I probably know him."

"Jacob Jones? Senior? Swim team? Horrible fashion choices?"

Salma was laughing again. "Yes, yes. I had a class with him. He's really cute."

Erika was blushing as she unhooked the last sheet of paper from the board, let it drift into the trash.

"Oh, he's totally cute. And nice. Probably not my soulmate, but you know. Fine for ten minutes of kissing outside the dining hall."

At the time, Erika had walked home from the luau swinging her heels in her hand, not quite sure how she felt about everything. There was no one whose door she could knock on to gossip about what she'd done, so she'd pushed it to the back of her mind. Now suddenly the whole incident seemed kind of adorable. Charming, even. Not a reset button or anything, but not the worst thing in the world.

"So, big plans when you get home tonight?" Salma asked. "Or just eat normal food and sleep in an actually comfortable bed?"

Now Erika couldn't contain herself—she turned to Salma, a smile taking over her face.

"This is so crazy. I'm going to this house that's famous where I live, in the DC suburbs? The decorations are beyond ridiculous, like Christmas threw up all over it and then some. The cops have to direct traffic because so many people drive by to see it. I've never been inside, but my best friend got us an invite."

"That sounds amazing."

The garbage bag was shut tight now, and Erika was swinging it back and forth.

"Do you want to hear my deepest, darkest secret?"

"Oh god, yes," Salma said.

"Are you sure you're ready?"

"So ready."

"I fucking love Christmas. Every tacky thing about it."

Salma was laughing again, really laughing, and Erika loved that feeling, of cracking somebody up.

Salma cleared her throat. "Well, anyway. Sorry if it was weird, what I said before—I just wanted to say it. I guess I'll see you around."

"It wasn't weird. It was . . . thanks. For saying it. And yeah, I'll see you around."

As Erika watched her retreat down the hallway, her heart was beating fast. How many people were there in the world who were meant to be your friends, your real friends? It was the kind of math problem that she did during those darkest hours when she couldn't sleep. Marissa, divided by four hundred people in her high school class . . .

Maybe it would be better if she stayed at St. B's tonight. Erika imagined calling down the hall to Salma, and started to think she might actually do it.

But no. She was too exhausted and too desperate to be free of this place. Besides, she'd finally stopped stressing about not having much fun here. Instead, she'd made a comfortable little nest out of the idea that bulletin boards and lit classes were going to be the extent of her college experience.

Hanging out with Salma would mean flying out of that sad but safe space—right now that wasn't an option.

# 10

## TUCKER

Frank held up a shoulder wrap made of soft, real fur, the tail still intact, the kind of thing that women wore in black-and-white movies. He looked at Tucker expectantly.

"Is this hideous enough? It's pretty hideous, but I'm not sure it's the best I can do."

"Is that *real*?" Tucker asked. "How much does it cost?"

Frank poked around until he found the price tag and cursed softly, quickly hanging the wrap back up. For as long as he'd been with Janet, the two of them had a strict gag-gifts-only policy, which explained why the house was full of things like a director's cut DVD of *Sharknado*, a kitchen tool that only cut bananas, and a now-wildly-out-of-control Bernie Sanders Chia pet.

But right now, Frank stood there—trim and bald and wearing

his wire-rimmed glasses—looking absolutely hopeless.

"Okay, that's way too expensive for a joke. I'm striking out here."

Tonight, Frank, Janet, and Tucker were all going out for sushi, but they'd decided to make a quick stop at the mall, so that Frank and Janet could get their "shopping" out of the way. Frank had wanted Tucker to come with him, had been sort of insistent, so here they were. As Tucker was wondering how long this was going to take, a familiar-looking woman appeared next to them and gave a little yelp.

"Dr. Blume! Hi! Oh my goodness, it's so nice to see you. I just hung Sarah's senior portrait over the mantel, and I was totally thinking of you, when I was looking at her pretty, perfect teeth!"

As Frank was saying thank you, telling her how lovely that was to hear, the woman's eyes flicked over to Tucker. She had a moment of confusion before she started laughing.

"Oh my god," she said, reaching out to squeeze Tucker's arm. "He worked at your office this summer, right? For a second, I couldn't figure out why he was shopping with you. I had no idea he was your son!"

"Oh, um—yeah. Yes. That's right."

The woman was shifting her bags around on her shoulder now, talking about how Tucker must take after his mom. When she started asking about when to bring in her younger daughter, Tucker took the opportunity to walk quietly away. He texted Bobby to make sure he was coming tonight, asked if he was going to bring his girlfriend, Skylar. Tucker kind of hoped that he wouldn't, because he and Bobby hadn't been to a party together in a while, and he wanted to have fun with him without feeling like a third wheel.

Tucker wandered aimlessly among the hats and gloves and scarves, and a minute later Frank caught up to him. The two of them hovered in front of a rack of NFL ski caps, and Frank gave it a spin but didn't seem to be actually looking at them.

"Do you need to shop for anybody?" Frank asked. "Do you, uh, need anything for Ray?"

Tucker went still at the mention of his father's name, because that was the last thing he'd expected Frank to say. Frank tried to give him his space, to stay out of his business when he could.

"Ray's not really the gift-giving type," Tucker finally said.

Frank moved on to a rack of gloves, continuing to pick up and examine things he had absolutely no interest in.

"Listen. I don't agree with your mom, that you should have to see Ray every week. She knows that, and I know it's not really my call, but . . . If it's not working, you should talk to her, and maybe I can talk to her, too, if you need me to."

Was that what this whole trip was about? Frank checking up on him? Tucker had been lying to his mom for months now, telling her their weekly dinners were fine. Apparently those lies were pretty transparent, but whatever. The less he thought about his dad, the better. One hour, once a week. People endured worse.

Tucker was trying to be an adult about it. This is what adults did, right? Ate shit and kept quiet?

"It's really no big deal," Tucker said.

Now Frank was the one wandering aimlessly with Tucker following, and they found themselves in the fragrances. Right at Tucker's eye level were two different kinds of Taylor Swift perfume, and he gave an irritated poke at the shiny boxes. Taylor Swift always made him think of Erika, and because Taylor Swift was everywhere, he was constantly being reminded of that horrible night at Adam's.

Infinitely worse, of course, was the story he'd seen online about the sexual assault at St. B's. He'd known the chances of it being Erika were slim, that there were over a thousand girls there. Still, he'd been worried, so he'd asked Nina, who'd asked Marissa, and that was how he knew what he wasn't supposed to know—that Erika was the one who'd found the girl and called for help.

And now he might run into her tonight.

Earlier today, Nina had mentioned that she'd invited her brother to Ryan's Christmas party, adding that Erika and Marissa might come, too. And somehow, as mortified as he was about what had happened this summer, part of him wanted to see her again, was dreaming that somehow he could erase what had happened . . .

Just then, the John Lennon Christmas song came blasting out of the store's speakers, the most irritating thing he could possibly hear right now. Tucker actually loved Christmas music, but not this. It was his mom's favorite, but he'd never understood the appeal. Christmas was supposed to be about pure happiness—cookies and presents and no school—not some complicated swell of emotion.

Frank cleared his throat awkwardly.

"Listen, I'm sorry that I said yes when she asked if you were my son, and didn't clarify. I . . . well. I'm sorry. If it bothered you."

Tucker's chest felt strange and tight.

"It's fine. It's totally fine."

The words had come out a little blunt, and the two of them were looking anxiously around at the bright lights and the decorations, staring pointlessly at all these things they didn't need.

One time, right in front of Tucker, someone had asked Janet if she and Frank were going to try to have a baby. Janet had blushed and shaken her head, said that they'd talked about it, but decided no—she was getting a little old for that, and they were happy the way things were.

Had Frank wanted kids with his first wife? Probably he had, but Tucker knew she'd gotten sick and died so young . . .

Those thoughts were entirely too much for Tucker to sort through right now. It was all too big and too sad and too messy. He and Frank were friendly. Neither of them seemed to know how to make this relationship into something more, but that was okay—they were both doing their best, weren't they? Nine months from now, Tucker would be living in a dorm room anyway.

"Do you have something to wear tonight?" Frank asked. "If

you wanted to get something new . . ."

"No, no. I'm going to wear the suit you got me for the wedding."

Tucker loved that suit—he knew he looked good in it, and it made him feel grown-up. Besides seeing Erika, the main reason that he wanted to go to the party tonight was because he wanted an excuse to wear it. He tried to think of a way to say that out loud, but it seemed so silly.

Instead, he told Frank he was going to go look around on his own.

# 11

## ERIKA

"The Mariah Carey song. It has to be the Mariah Carey song. This isn't even a discussion."

"That's the best *pop* Christmas song. Your heathen ways make it impossible for you to know the actual answer, which is 'O Holy Night.'"

"Oh my god, it's not like I haven't heard that song. Everyone's heard that song. But the Mariah Carey song makes you feel infinitely hopeful and happy—you know, for three whole minutes. *That* is the pinnacle of a Christmas song."

"Again, your heathen ways fail you. 'O Holy Night' briefly convinces you that you're going to be pious for the rest of your life. That's real power."

"I like 'Blue Christmas.'"

Erika had stopped at an intersection, and she and Marissa

turned around at the same time, staring into the back seat at Marco.

He sipped on his coffee and didn't look up from his phone.

"*The Elvis song?*" Erika asked.

"Yeah. That's my favorite."

The girls looked at each other and then turned their disgusted gazes to Marco again.

"You are epically weird," Marissa said. "So, so weird. How have I slept with you? How are we even a thing?"

Marco shrugged and started humming "Blue Christmas" under his breath while the girls kept arguing.

"Okay, let's please forget Elvis for a second and focus on the real problem," Marissa said. "That Mariah Carey song is contorting Christmas so that it's all about falling in love."

"So what?" Erika asked. "Lots of Christmas songs do that."

"BUT THAT'S NOT COOL. This is a Jesus-centric holiday, or it's supposed to be. Christmas songs about your baby coming home are just a capitalist ploy to make people get googly-eyed and buy diamonds or whatever. Our songs have nothing in common. Nothing!"

Erika was laughing now, trying not to spill her gingerbread latte.

"I don't really think it's that different," Marco said. He finally put his phone away, and leaned forward, his head between the two front seats. "Believing in God, believing in love. Or wanting to. Either way, you're putting your faith in the idea that life is ultimately beautiful. That it makes sense."

He kissed Marissa on her cheek, and she rolled her eyes, but couldn't keep from smiling.

"Georgetown has made you hopelessly pretentious, but okay, I'll buy that," she said. "Actually, I like it because it means E and I aren't that different. I'm fighting to believe in God, and she's fighting to believe in love, and we just need our own personal anthems to get us there."

Marissa was about to turn the music back on, but Erika reached out to stop her.

"Whoa, whoa. You've got it all wrong. I love those songs, but I know that they're a trick. They make us buy into the magic for three minutes or whatever. And that's fine, I'll take the rush, but I'm not trying to believe."

Marissa sucked in her breath and frowned at her friend.

"So Christmas is your version of drugs?"

"Yes, exactly."

"So young and yet so cynical," Marissa said with an annoyed huff.

Erika rolled her eyes and turned up the music.

Every inch of the mansion, every branch of every tree in the yard, was twinkling. An army of inflatable nutcrackers was coming in from the left side, while a ten-foot-tall Santa and a snow globe the size of a small car loomed over on the right. Up on the roof, a pack of reindeer pulled an enormous sleigh full of toys while the Grinch hung from the chimney. At the end of the impossibly long driveway, there was a pack of carolers dressed like they were from a Dickens novel. Next to them, children were acting out the nativity with live animals.

Marissa shook her head in wonder. "Holy fucking Christmas, Batman."

Erika elbowed her, indicating the children that were a few feet away. "Shhh. You're corrupting the young people."

"Oh, please. They spend half their days on YouTube. They've heard much worse."

"You were totally Mary in one of these things, right?"

"Me? No. I have Mary Magdalene hair, not Virgin Mary hair! I was always the donkey."

Erika patted her arm. "You're my special donkey."

For a couple minutes, they walked around the yard and gawked, and then they shed their coats and took photos of one another in their party clothes. As Erika and Marissa posed together, they congratulated themselves on how their outfits were perfect. Erika was in a red velvet shift with candy cane tights and black boots, Marissa in a green sweater dress covered with Christmas pins that belonged to her Catholic schoolteacher mother. Erika had been a little embarrassed, going out like this—she hadn't worn anything this flashy in ages—but now she was glad that she'd let Marissa talk her into it.

"This has to be the biggest house I've ever been to. Explain to me again how we were invited?" Erika asked.

Marissa's eyes drifted a bit. "So, here's the thing . . ."

"Oh my god. Are we not actually invited?"

"Oh, we are *very* invited. Nina is on the debate team with

Ryan, who lives inside this glorious monstrosity, and the two of them are total besties. He knows we're coming."

"Okay . . ."

"Just the smallest of side notes: Tucker seems to have joined the debate team this year, and he's maybe, probably, definitely going to be here."

Erika groaned. There was a name that she had absolutely no interest in hearing again. But so what? That whole thing this summer had been stupid from the start—she'd been in the wrong state of mind, thinking that one night was going to change anything.

"Whatever," she said with a wave of her hand. "I'm here for Santa and champagne and cookies. And did you not see the size of this place? We could be here all night and not even see him."

Marissa gave her a smile that turned into gritted teeth, as she focused on something over Erika's shoulder.

"Love that attitude. The second part might have been a tad optimistic."

# 12

## TUCKER

"I'm sorry—I know I'm cramping your style, and I swear we will leave in five seconds, but we must, must, *must* get a photo here."

"Oh my god, Mom, it's fine. I'm happy to take your picture."

"Do you think we're allowed to climb into that sleigh? No wait, let's stand in front of the giant snow globe, the lighting will be better."

Tucker was starting to think that letting his mom and Frank drop him off here after dinner had been a massive mistake. He rubbed his temples, half-annoyed, half-amused, while Frank was trying very hard not to laugh.

"OH MY GOD," Janet said. "Is that *a giant mistletoe made of smaller mistletoes*? Okay, that's it. C'mon, c'mon."

Janet was now scurrying down the driveway, Frank and

Tucker following behind, with Frank mumbling apologies. By now Tucker was laughing, though, starting to get caught up in it all, ready to have fun and . . .

There was Erika.

Tucker's stomach dropped to the ground and his eyes quickly followed. He turned and looked back at the car, like maybe he'd forgotten something. He'd thought he was prepared for this, but he wasn't expecting to see her so soon, right here in the driveway with his mom and Frank.

He should hurry by as quickly as possible, right? Maybe nod without looking at her? Just as he'd committed to that plan, he realized that *of course, of course, of course.*

His mom was talking to her.

Still stuck to his spot, Tucker cursed under his breath, and Frank backed up a few paces to stand next to him.

"Everything cool?"

"I . . . it's nothing. I just need a second."

Frank's eyes slid up the very long driveway and then back again. "Should I pretend like something important happened on my phone and we need to talk about it? Look, here I go. I'm actually really good at this. Sometimes I do it when people try to start long conversations about their kid's teeth when I'm trying to shop."

Tucker was barely listening, his mind too busy running through and discarding his options for how to handle this. His shoulder was acting up tonight and it was distracting him, making it particularly hard to think.

"Is she still talking to them?" Tucker asked.

"Yes, and they're definitely looking over here. Sorry?"

Mumbling that it was fine, Tucker gave himself a few more beats before he accepted that it was time to stop stalling and start walking, though he was still completely unsure of how he should arrange his face.

Janet was beaming as he and Frank came up the driveway.

"I stopped to compliment their outfits; I had no idea they knew you!"

Tucker opened and closed his mouth a couple times, coming up with absolutely nothing in response—partly because there seemed to be no proper words for this situation, and partly because his brain had been hijacked by the sight of Erika in red lipstick and candy cane tights.

Luckily, his mom barely seemed to notice, turning right back to the conversation.

"St. B's is *so pretty*. What are you studying?"

"English."

"Janet was an English major," Frank chimed in.

"Oh my god, don't tell her that. She'll ask what I'm doing now, and then she'll think it's her fate to be a real estate agent, selling overpriced suburban condos with her face on a stupid magnet."

"Hey, hey," Frank said. "I love that last magnet. You look so trustworthy."

The girls were smiling now, even if Erika's lips were a little tight, even if Marissa seemed to be side-eyeing him. There was a guy with them, too, but Tucker was pretty sure it was Nina's brother—Marissa's boyfriend or not-boyfriend or whatever.

"Okay," Janet said. "We're leaving, I swear, right after this picture. This place is like a dream come true. Is 'dream come true' too strong?"

"Ummm," Frank said, handing Tucker his phone with a *help-how-do-I-answer-that* face before turning to follow her.

The girls laughed as they headed for the door, Marissa yelling over her shoulder to Frank and Janet that they had to do "the prom pose."

Right then, Tucker couldn't help imagining some alternate universe where this was a perfect moment—the beginning of some amazing night where he got to see Erika again. But that would mean he'd have to get over what she said in the tree house, and she'd have to get over the fact that he not only lied, but acted like a total and complete dick, and there was no way that was going to happen.

"Okay," Janet said, once she'd arranged herself and Frank exactly as Marissa had suggested. "We're ready."

Bobby was running late, so Tucker hung out with Nina, Kara, and Yrma in the big, grand foyer—a two-story space with twin, curving staircases leading up to the second floor. The four of them ate a disturbing number of tiny appetizers and the girls pounded hot chocolates and punch, after which they watched with slow-growing horror as the lines for the bathrooms got worse and worse.

After a while, they realized they were mostly surrounded by adults and little kids, so they escaped to the heated tent in the backyard to look for their other friends, debating whether or not the bartender would serve them alcohol, while admiring the beautifully decorated trees and the pond ringed by giant inflatable penguins. Someone was handing out glow-in-the-dark reindeer antlers, and they all put them on.

"OH. MY. GOD," Kara said. "Is that glass box thing *an indoor pool?*"

"More importantly, can we piss in it?" Yrma asked. "I literally care about nothing but a place to piss. Help me find the biggest tree. No, wait, the least lit-up tree. That's the one we want."

"Tucker can create a distraction," Kara added. "Do his little dance again, the one from Adam's coffee table."

Tucker ripped the antlers off his head. "Oh my god. That was a year ago. When are people going to let that go?"

"Probably never," Yrma said. "It was a very memorable dance."

Nina started laughing, and then they all started laughing, Kara screeching that she was officially going to pee her pants if they didn't do something soon. Right then, Ryan wandered outside and Tucker jumped in the air, waving him over, shouting that if he didn't find them an open bathroom, there was going to be a situation out here with one of his Christmas trees.

Ryan made a faux-panicked face and hurried over.

"There's one in the mudroom. The outside door is locked,

but you can get in through the kitchen. It's also a good spot to hide and drink, since my dad's being a total asshat about it. I'll take you guys, okay?"

The girls cheered and followed Ryan inside, leaving Tucker alone in their wake, in the glimmering backyard. Smiling, he put his light-up antlers back on, trying to decide where to go, what to eat, what to drink.

How best to avoid Erika.

Tucker was so close to losing himself and just having fun. This fall had been strange and unsettling because of his dad, but joining the debate team had been a bright spot. He'd found something he was really good at and he'd made new friends and he was excited about tonight. Now that moment in the driveway was weighing on him, bringing back memories of Adam's party. The fact that he'd cared so much, about what Erika had said in the tree house, that he'd acted like such a jerk in response . . . What had it done but prove her point, about what a baby he was?

There was no way for Tucker to hang out in the same house as Erika tonight without thinking back on his behavior and cringing the whole time, so he figured he had three options.

He could leave. He could stay and have no fun. He could apologize.

Tucker took out his phone and started typing.

# 13

## ERIKA

Marissa and Erika lounged together on a chaise in the corner of the dimly lit basement, where most of the people their age seemed to have congregated. A strobe light was flashing on the crowd that was swaying and shimmying to the DJ, but Erika said she wasn't quite ready to dance. Instead, they laughed and sipped champagne that Marissa had sweet-talked the bartender into giving them. Now they were dishing about Marissa and Marco being officially back together, Marissa describing their elaborate attempts to find some alone time over winter break.

Erika was laughing and begging her to stop with the details, and finally Marissa conceded, her face growing serious.

"Are you okay? That was a hell of a semester."

"I'm okay, honestly. I mean, I'm not okay, but I'm dealing with it."

"Are you still seeing that campus therapist lady?"

"Yeah, yeah. She's cool. I like her."

"Sorry," Marissa said. "I shouldn't have brought this up. I'm totally ruining our Christmas high."

Erika forced a smile, then swept an arm around the room. "Nothing could ruin this high, right? Nothing."

"We haven't taken nearly enough selfies. Get your phone out."

Erika obeyed, and as she did, she saw two messages that stopped her short.

> I'm really sorry that I was such an asshole this summer. And I'm sorry I didn't say that sooner. I swear it was true that Suzanne wasn't my girlfriend—it was a summer thing, and it was supposed to be officially over that day. I know that doesn't make it okay, just trying to explain.

> Okay, me again. My mom always says the only way to apologize is with no excuses and no caveats, so I'm rereading that text and realizing that I failed miserably. Here I'll try again: I'm really sorry that I was such an asshole this summer.

She stared at the screen, then showed it to Marissa, who scrutinized the words like they were the Dead Sea Scrolls before handing back the phone.

"Is he forgiven?" Marissa asked.

Erika read the message again, thinking. "Well, high school parties are kind of a petri dish for terrible behavior, are they not? No one knows that better than me."

Marissa kept quiet at that, of course knowing exactly what she meant: Erika and that complete douchebag, Grayson, holed up in his room while unsuspecting Dana had been downstairs with the rest of their friends . . .

"Whatever," Erika said, shoving the phone away. "I'm over it. I'm just not sure I owe him a response."

"Totally, totally."

Erika scowled. "Why does he have a suit that nice? Teenage boys never have suits that nice."

"Look, if you need me to pretend he doesn't look extra yummy, I will, but that will take a superhuman act of will."

"Am I dressed like a Christmas elf? I need you to be honest with me."

"No! Oh my god. You look smoking hot, you know you do."

Erika rolled her eyes, then looked over at the dance floor, all those close-knit bodies churning, churning. She could easily stay down here all night, making smart little comments from the edge of everything, but that wasn't fair to Marissa. Announcing that their girl time was over, Erika hauled her friend upstairs, where they found Marco listening to a ten-piece soul band in the library, watching grown-ups dance and drink cocktails with sugared rims.

Marissa went off to the bar to try to procure them another drink, but came back empty-handed.

"This bartender was not as accommodating," she said, then held up her phone with a smile. "But Nina has intel on the location of a secret bathroom that's also convenient for swiping champagne. Pit stop?"

"For me," Erika said. "Not for you."

She got directions for the secret bathroom, then shoved Marissa and Marco together, demanding they slow-dance while she set off to find Nina.

Erika cut through the restaurant-sized kitchen, ducking and dodging her way to the back corner, feeling like a trespasser. Slowly, she opened the door a crack. Then she heard Nina's voice.

"It's not happening. Not tonight. I'm going to college next year without ever having my boobs touched. Do you realize how tragic that is?"

Erika bit her lip and covered her mouth with her hand. Then she peeked her head through the door, calling into the room.

"If you just want them touched, I can't imagine that would be difficult. I could find a waiter back in the kitchen, I'm sure . . ."

Nina swung around and then squealed Erika's name, Kara and Yrma dissolving in a fit of laughter. They were all double-fisting pilfered drinks. Erika slipped into the mudroom and took in Nina without the benefit of her winter coat. She had on a pencil skirt and boots, a V-neck sweater.

"Actually—that *is* tragic. Look at those things."

Kara and Yrma were cracking up, but Nina seemed nervous.

"It's not as weird as you think, for the record," Erika said.

"Asking a waiter to touch my boobs?"

"Not being experienced. High schools are full of virgins. Regular virgins and boob virgins and kissing virgins. All the virgins!"

"So you say, and yet I don't see any boob virgins in here except for ME."

Erika told her to hold that thought, then squeezed her way into the tiny bathroom, feeling happy as she did, her mind hard at work on how to help Nina. This was the task she hadn't known she needed tonight.

Erika burst back into the mudroom.

"Okay," she said. "So who do you have in mind? For touching your boobs?"

Nina still had that tentative look. Kara and Yrma were exchanging glances.

"We have the full power of Christmas magic all around us, right? If you're trying to make something happen, tonight is the night."

"If you're suggesting mistletoe," Nina said, "the answer is hell no."

"Who is it?" Erika said with a grin. "Show me a picture."

A strange silence descended, and the back of Erika's neck started to tingle. Was she being too pushy? Why did it matter who Nina liked, unless it was someone she knew . . .

*Oh shit.* For a second, she held out hope that it was Bobby, but Nina wouldn't be looking at her like that if it was.

Erika started to blush. "I'm sorry. I shouldn't have asked. Ignore me."

Kara mumbled that she needed something to eat, and she and Yrma slipped out of the room, though Erika felt one of them squeeze her arm gently as she went by.

As soon as they were gone, Nina hid behind her hands.

"Oh my god, this is so embarrassing. And don't be sorry, *I'm* sorry. I thought there was something with you and Tucker that night in the tree house, but then you were back at school, and I didn't really know him before, but he joined the debate team this year, and I . . ."

Erika was waving her hands, telling her to stop. "Is he good at debate? I feel like he'd be good at debate."

Nina sighed. "You have no idea."

Erika nodded and laughed a little, smoothing out her dress. She could see that Nina was still nervous. Erika was nervous, too. She couldn't decide if she should tell Nina about this summer, that Tucker had been such a jerk. Because if she did tell her, Erika wasn't sure if she could honestly pinpoint her motivation. Would it be an innocent warning? Or did some part of her still like him and want to drive them apart?

Marissa would probably want her to say all of that out loud, but there was no way, right? Nina liked Erika, and Erika wanted to keep it that way.

Honesty was way too fraught. She would just keep her mouth shut.

"Erika, if you . . . if he . . ."

"No. Absolutely not. We're not even friends. I haven't said one word to him since that night."

Nina sighed. "I haven't kissed someone since eighth grade. Eighth grade! That doesn't even count. It never works out for me."

That got Erika, right in her gut. She had to swallow before she could talk.

"Not kissing anyone doesn't mean shit, okay? You're beautiful and you're smart and you're funny. I *guarantee* there are boys living for when they see you at school."

Nina was still looking at her doubtfully. Erika fidgeted.

"I thought . . . I guess I thought you were flirting with Bobby that night, in the tree house?"

"Oh god, I know, I know. I had a thing for him last year, but nothing ever happened. Besides, he has a girlfriend now."

Erika took that in, chewing nervously on her nail. The air in the mudroom seemed to be growing warmer, and she needed to get out.

"Just go party. Get close to him. Smile. Use mistletoe as backup. You need to do this, for the sake of your boobs."

Nina groaned, and Erika gave her the gentlest of pushes, leading her back out into the kitchen.

Kara and Yrma were waiting right by the door to collect their friend. Erika managed to give them a smile.

"Did you want to head to the library with us?" Nina asked.

"No, no," Erika said. "I, uh, I heard the dining room is set up like the Great Hall from Harry Potter, and I kind of have to see that. And listen, if I see him, I'll make sure we come find you, okay?"

Were they going to fight harder, tell her that she had to come with them?

Erika was too afraid to find out, so she turned as quickly as she could and left.

# 14

## TUCKER

Tucker had lost all his friends, and Bobby still wasn't there, but at the moment he didn't care about any of that, because a guy dressed as Dumbledore had handed him a goblet of pumpkin juice, and Tucker knew that tonight was totally worth it, that he had clearly found the very best room.

Besides, he'd apologized. Even if Erika hadn't texted him back, even if she didn't care in the slightest, he felt better.

Tucker walked around slowly, taking in the elaborately laid-out tables, the flags from each house hanging on the walls. There was even an owl in the corner of the room, a *real* owl. It looked kind of pissed off, hooting loudly at everyone who came in through the far door. Tucker watched it happen again and again, people jumping with fright and then smiling and laughing.

A waiter walked by with a tray that had exactly one chocolate frog left on it. Tucker grabbed it and held it in his hand, examining its tiny perfection. Wishing he had someone to show it to, he turned around to scan the room . . .

Erika was right behind him, scowling. Tucker jumped and almost dropped the frog right on the ground.

They stood there, facing each other, neither of them saying a thing, until finally he extended his hand, making her a silent offer. For a second, he thought she was going to turn around and leave. Instead she plucked the frog from his palm and ate it in a single bite, without a thank-you, without looking at him, letting the silent seconds continue to stretch out.

At least she wasn't walking away. Or punching him in the face.

"Was it good?" he asked.

She didn't answer at first, too busy standing on her tiptoes and looking this way and that, taking in the room. "Delicious. This is a pretty nice setup."

"I was going to say dream come true," he said. "Is *dream come true* too strong?"

She turned away from him, acting like she was trying to see the owl, but he was pretty sure she was laughing.

"Big night for you and your mom. So many dreams coming true."

"Yeah, yeah. She was a little excited about this place."

"Well, I hope you got a good picture."

"Oh, it was perfect, don't worry. A framer for sure."

Erika glanced at him, her expression curious, but still a little suspicious, too.

"He seems nice. Your stepdad. I feel like they'd just started dating, that summer you worked at the Cave?"

Hearing that, it came back to Tucker—how much he had joked about it, because joking about it had made it seem less overwhelming. He fiddled with his goblet.

"Yeah. She hadn't had a boyfriend in years, and was totally freaked out about telling me. I already knew, though."

"How?"

Tucker rolled his eyes. "She came home one day and said that some guy had stopped to help her change a flat tire. All of a sudden, she was going to all these dinners with 'her friends' and getting a million texts."

A smile flickered across Erika's face. Then she took a deep breath and turned to him, starting to say something about going to find Nina. Before she could finish, Dumbledore appeared at their side.

"Are you two a team? Because it's time! Everybody who's playing needs to be at that table over there."

"No, no," Erika said, at the same time Tucker asked, "Playing what?"

"Harry Potter Trivia! We have excellent prizes. I wouldn't miss it."

Dumbledore gave them a wink and then swept off, robes trailing behind him. Erika and Tucker turned to look at each other, officially making eye contact for the first time that night.

She wanted to do this—he was sure she wanted to do this. He did, too, but more than that, he wanted to do whatever he could to make her happy. And the best way to do that was to forget entirely about trying to be cool.

"So I'm going to take off, like I was saying before . . . ," she said.

Her foot was nervously tapping. Tucker didn't even try to keep the goofy smile off his face.

"Like hell you are."


"These scarves are really nice. It's not like some crappy prize we gave out at the Cave. This is a high-quality piece of clothing."

"To be fair, we earned these. We know a truly unsettling amount about Harry Potter."

"The fact that they let us pick our houses really takes it to the next level. Yours looks weirdly nice with your suit."

"Yours looks weirdly nice with your candy cane tights."

Erika's eyes narrowed when Tucker said that, and *oops, oops, oops*—he was forgetting himself. He'd been trying so hard to be reserved and polite around her, but the last half hour had undone all that. Sometime in the lightning round, when they'd started high-fiving at all their right answers, he'd given up trying to be mature . . .

"Are you making fun of my tights?"

*No, I like your tights entirely too much* was definitely not the right thing to say, so Tucker stammered for a few seconds, then blurted out the first question he could think of.

"So what's the best thing about college?"

She cocked her head, smirking at him. "What are you, my aunt?"

"It's just . . . I can't really imagine it yet. Living in a dorm. Frat parties, whatever. It might as well be Hogwarts—that's how real it seems. I know that sounds dumb."

Erika fiddled with her scarf.

"It's not dumb. Honestly, I think my favorite thing is being an RA. I like looking after the little freshmen on my floor."

They had wandered to the edge of the library. Erika had said again that she wanted to find Nina, but so far they hadn't seen her.

"Do you want me to text her?" Tucker asked. "I can ask where she is."

Erika glanced over, blushing a little. "Sure. Yeah. Or I can do it. I'll text her."

She took her phone out of her dress pocket, but then she paused, looking out over the beautiful room and sighing.

"Oh my god, they even have a ladder. How is this place real? You're friends with the kid who lives here?"

"I am. He's pretty nice, actually. I've come over to hang out in his video game room."

Erika's eyes went wide as she turned to look at him.

*"His video game room?"*

Tucker was laughing so she flipped him off, but smiled as she did. He was almost starting to feel like this summer had been erased, like they could pretend it never happened.

"I guess it's not officially a video game room—it's just one of the guest rooms, but Ryan's kind of taken it over for that."

She was fiddling with her phone, but still not texting Nina.

"You can ask," he said. "Go ahead."

Erika paused, licked her lips. He thought for sure she was going to say no, and his heart sank a little, but then she whipped her head toward him.

"Does he have Super Smash Brothers?"

"Of course."

"Well, I'm Pikachu. You can't be Pikachu."

"I think I can live with that."

# 15

## ERIKA

The bed was a queen, and they were each perched on a different corner, so not particularly close to each other. Still—there was something about his tie and his jacket lying on the bed behind him, and his sleeves rolled up over his forearms, that felt distracting.

She shouldn't be here. She knew she shouldn't be here. She had stood right in front of Nina, swearing she didn't like him, promising to help her out tonight.

But Erika was tired—very tired—of feeling alone. Right now she was having so much fun, playing games and joking around for the first time in weeks. She needed this, if only for a few more minutes. She'd even insisted to Tucker that they play just one round.

The problem was, one round seemed very short, so they'd

agreed to a couple more. Now he took off his shoes, scooting back a little so that he was leaning into the absolutely absurd pile of decorative pillows that adorned the bed. After hesitating, Erika kicked off her boots and did the same.

They kept playing, Erika looking occasionally at the time, convincing herself they hadn't really been up here that long. She noticed that Tucker was humming "Jingle Bell Rock" without seeming to notice that he was doing it, and she found that irritatingly cute.

"You are freakishly good at this," he said after she'd beaten him three times in a row.

"It's my game of choice when I can't sleep. Playing it by myself is very soothing."

"You play this *alone*? That's sad. Very sad, Erika."

That stung a little, but she knew he hadn't meant anything by it, so she tried to brush it off.

"Whatever. Insomnia sucks, and Pikachu is the only cure."

There were a few seconds of silence, and then he seemed to get squirmy, shifting around and coughing. She looked over and he was staring away from her at the wall, red-faced and trying desperately not to laugh.

"Oh my god, what? What is wrong with you?"

"Nothing, nothing."

"*Nothing?* You look like you're choking."

He was shaking his head. He was still bright red. She was feeling simultaneously annoyed and amused.

"What is so funny about . . ."

But *oh, oh, oh.* Suddenly she knew.

Back in high school, Erika had honed a whole bit about having one surefire way to put herself to sleep—and it definitely wasn't Pikachu. There had been a time when she loved saying things like that, things that shocked people, things that proved she didn't give a shit. She'd grown far away from that, of course, after the video. But sometimes at the Cave, with Tucker, she'd felt like she could still act that way.

Now she clucked her tongue, but couldn't quite look at him.

"I cannot *believe* that you remember that," she said.

"Um, I was fifteen and I had a big crush on you. It kind of blew my mind."

She pulled one of the pillows from behind her and whacked him in the chest.

"I'm sorry, I'm sorry," he said. "I have a lot of questions about why Pikachu is better than that now, but I'll keep them to myself."

This time she hit him squarely on the head.

"You know what, Tucker? It's a little tough to do that with a roommate five feet away. You see how it goes for you freshman year and get back to me."

"I'm not sure I feel comfortable getting back to you about that, but thanks for the warning."

She tried not to laugh, which made her snort as usual, and then she was yelling at him that she wanted another round. He got everything ready, was about to push start, but then he paused.

"One more question. If you're an RA, don't you have your own room? I'm just wondering why you still need Pikachu, if you have some privacy."

She grabbed the pillow again and started hitting him repeatedly. After half a dozen blows, he picked up a pillow of his own, and was trying his best to fight her off. She got on her knees so that she'd have a better shot, but he whacked her first and she fell over, grabbing the hem of her dress as she did, to keep it from riding up.

"Oh my god—are those candy canes *fuzzy?*"

"Stop making fun of my tights!"

She hit him a final time, with the smallest pillow, and the end of it popped right open, sending up a big burst of feathers.

As the fluffy white down drifted all around them, she realized they were way too close to each other. She made a show of gathering herself and moving back to the edge of the bed, reclaiming her controller. She kept her voice low-key and steady when she asked him to please start the game. As she did, her phone beeped from the nightstand.

> **Hey, it's Salma. I found your number on the RA spreadsheet. Just wanted to say that if you want to talk about anything over break, I'm here.**

"Is everything all right?" Tucker asked.

Erika glanced quickly at where he hovered on his corner, his brow furrowed. She realized her eyes had gotten watery.

"What? Yeah. Sorry. Some weird stuff happened at school this semester, and it's . . . It's nothing. Seriously."

She picked up the remote and stared at the television, silently willing him to start the game and stop looking at her, but he didn't. Instead, he was nervously shifting and clearing his throat, and then he was talking in a rush.

"I feel like I should tell you this . . . I, uh, I saw the story online. And then I asked Nina, because I was worried about you, and she asked Marissa, so I know what happened. That you were the one who found her. I'm so sorry. I mean—I'm really sorry that it happened, and I'm also sorry if it seems like I was prying in your business or something."

Long seconds stretched out, and then she mumbled that it was fine, that she wasn't mad. It was hard for Erika to think right now, though, because in her head she was hearing Makenzie's voice.

*My wrists hurt, he hurt my wrists.*

She heard the echo of her own voice too, how she'd somehow kept it from shaking.

*I believe you, I believe you. Can I please call for help?*

"Do they know who it was?" Tucker asked.

Erika swallowed hard. "He was a friend of a student. I guess he hung around the dorms all the time. She knew him. They just filed charges, but nobody really knows yet what's going to happen."

Maybe there would be a trial. Maybe Erika would have to testify. And who knew what they might ask her about if that happened. Did they really dig up dirt on people, or did that only happen on TV?

*Chill out. Breathe. Don't worry about this right now.*

"I'm sorry," Tucker said quietly.

She didn't look at him. She took a few deep breaths.

"One more round?" she said. "For real, this is the last one. Winner take all."

"Yeah, yeah. For sure."

The game started. She was destroying him within seconds. He cursed softly, then cleared his throat.

"I hate to tell you this when you already picked your scarf out and everything," he said. "But I don't think you're a Ravenclaw. I think you're a Gryffindor."

Erika's cheeks went pink. Stupid Pikachu was not behaving, and she started banging harder on the buttons.

Was she brave? She'd like to think so, but she certainly didn't feel that way right now, hiding out with Tucker when she should be helping Nina. If she thought about that too hard, this lump in her throat was going to get the best of her.

"Well, I'm sorry to tell *you* this, when you've already picked out your scarf, but I'm pretty sure you're not a Slytherin, Tucker. You're a Hufflepuff."

Something in the room shifted then. Tucker seemed to go still, and when she looked over, he was wearing a complicated smirk.

"Um, that's not an insult," she said. "Cedric Diggory was a Hufflepuff."

"Fair enough. And I know I'm a Hufflepuff. I know I'm a puppy dog. It's cool."

116

*A puppy dog?* That set off a distant bell in the back of Erika's mind, but she couldn't quite place it or figure out what he was talking about, why he seemed suddenly more distant. But it didn't matter, did it? She needed to get out of here as soon as possible.

But as she was putting down the controller, *whoosh*. The door was flung open.

Ryan was holding it wide, gesturing for his friends to walk in. Four people crowded through the doorway, and the last one was Nina.

Erika couldn't look at her. She couldn't look at anyone. Her eyes swung sharply to the right, to the opposite wall, but unfortunately, there was a giant mirror there.

The bed was a mess, and Erika's hair was full of soft, white feathers.

# 16

## TUCKER

Tucker was still in the guest room, watching a round of Fort-nite, when he got a text that Bobby had finally arrived.

Erika had left, having practically sprinted from the room when everybody else showed up. Meanwhile, Tucker was back to feeling terrible. First he'd let himself get annoyed by that Hufflepuff comment, which shouldn't have been a big deal, and then she'd gotten so embarrassed when Ryan and everyone walked in. He hadn't realized it would upset her so much—if he'd known, maybe he could have said something, made it clear that nothing was going on. By the time he'd thought of that, though, she was long gone.

Tucker found Bobby standing in the foyer alone, devouring a plate of crackers and fancy cheese, looking around like he couldn't decide if this place was amazing or ridiculous.

"Finally," Tucker said, settling in next to him. "Did you see the pictures I posted, of the Great Hall?"

"All fifty million of them? Yes."

"It's even better in person. I'll show you. Where's Skylar?"

Bobby shook his head, then refilled his plate with fancy nuts and crackers.

"She's not coming?" Tucker asked.

"It's a long story."

Tucker nodded, secretly glad that just the two of them could hang out. He looked around at this enormous space, which was as big as the entire first floor of the house he'd grown up in.

In the far corner, there was a mountainous man dressed up very convincingly as Santa, posed perfectly in a red velvet chair. A professional photographer was kneeling on the floor in front of him, while a snaking line of children waited for their turn to say their wishes out loud, to have their pictures taken.

"I think we missed a few years," Tucker said. "Are you ready or what?"

Bobby shook his head and gave Tucker a *don't even think about it* kind of look. Their moms used to drag them to the mall together every year. Tucker was sure that there were half a dozen photos of the two of them on Santa's lap still haunting Facebook or Instagram.

"Can you imagine if we did that, and sent it to them?" Bobby asked.

"They would die. We might have to do it."

"I'm not waiting in that line—no way," Bobby said. "And

you know your mom would post it everywhere, even if you asked her not to."

"She can't help herself," Tucker said.

Bobby laughed, then started running his hand back and forth across his hair, a nervous habit he had. His face grew serious.

"Is everything okay, with your dad?"

Tucker purposely hadn't been drinking tonight, but that suddenly seemed like a mistake. He could really use a beer right now. A very light buzz would be nice.

"It's fine," Tucker said. "I mean, he's still an asshole, like always. But that's to be expected."

He'd asked his mom not to talk to Bobby's mom yet, not to tell her why his dad was here, and why they were suddenly spending all this time together. He wanted to tell Bobby himself, he'd said.

Except days went by, then weeks. Months.

He should have told Bobby the truth right then; he knew he should. But there was no way he wanted to talk about it with these happy, screaming kids all around them. This was a Christmas party, and they were supposed to be having fun.

Tucker pointed at the line.

"Bobby, I'm sorry, but we have to do this. For our moms. Because not long from now, we'll be off at college, ignoring all of their calls except when we need money."

Bobby sighed very loudly and put down his plate.

\* \* \*

"Don't worry," Bobby told Santa. "We're just going to stand next to you."

"No, no," Tucker said. "It will be much funnier if we sit on his knees."

Santa rubbed his temples and sighed loudly, wearily.

"Look, I get paid either way. Do whatever you want."

"Fake Dumbledore was much nicer than Fake Santa," Tucker whispered to Bobby.

"I'm concerned about the way you're using the word *fake*," Bobby whispered back. "You do know there's no real version of *either* of those people, right?"

Tucker pretended to look hurt, and then as soon as they sat, he started laughing and couldn't stop. That made Bobby laugh, too, even though he kept acting like he was pissed, yelling at Tucker to shut up and get this over with. As soon as they were done, they gave their email addresses to an elf, who promised they'd receive their photos momentarily.

They both took out their phones and waited. The message pinged through seconds later, and Bobby immediately insisted that the file be destroyed.

"Too late," Tucker said. "I sent it to my mom."

Bobby rolled his eyes, then looked out at the room, asking what it was like to be Ryan, to live here. Tucker mumbled that he was actually really nice, and that was true, but he felt funny saying it. He was uncomfortably aware that he'd been here half a dozen times since school started in the fall, more times than he'd been over to Bobby's house. It was just hard to go over there, to see some other car in his old driveway . . .

Tucker was struck by a sudden thought that he and Bobby might be drifting apart, but no—he was being paranoid, right? They were a little out of sync maybe, because of the move, this stuff with Tucker's dad, Bobby being busy with Skylar. All of that would pass; none of it could change them. He and Bobby were too good a team, had always balanced each other perfectly. Tucker was outgoing where Bobby was quiet; Tucker's sense of humor was goofy where Bobby's was dry.

Bobby's phone beeped, and he looked at it, his face growing serious.

"Who is it?" Tucker asked.

Bobby frowned down at a text. "It's Skylar. She's just . . . checking in."

Tucker almost let it go at that, but Bobby seemed upset.

"Is everything okay?"

Bobby put away his phone, crossed his arms. "I didn't want to get into all this before, but we had a long talk tonight, and . . . it's not working. She broke up with me."

"Oh!" Tucker said, genuinely surprised. "I'm sorry. That sucks. I thought . . . the way she was talking outside of History the other day, I can't imagine her breaking up with you."

Bobby crossed his arms and looked away, and Tucker could instantly see that he was pissed off.

"You were annoyed that day, when she was talking," Bobby said. "I know you were. You rolled your eyes."

Tucker's stomach dropped. He stuttered for a second, and

wanted to bat this conversation away, but that Santa picture had brought up all these feelings in him, about their friendship, how much he cared about Bobby. He felt like he needed to be honest.

"I'm sorry. You're right. But she kept going on and on about how cute it was that she was your first girlfriend and you were her first boyfriend. It's not even true! She was totally seeing Tyler Reed at the beginning of the year."

For a second, Tucker thought Bobby was going to walk away, but then he took a step toward him instead and spoke more softly.

"Do you know Tyler?"

"No, not really."

"Me neither, but apparently he's a creep. She wants to pretend that never happened. And she decided she doesn't really want to date anybody for a while, which is why we're not together anymore."

Tucker tried and failed to come up with something to say. His skin tingled all over, and he wanted to crawl under the table, to curl up and hide there.

*Skylar can say whatever she wants, one million percent. The world would be a better place if everybody's first boyfriend was somebody like you.*

Tucker wanted to say all that, but the words got caught in his throat.

"I'm sorry," he finally mumbled. "I'm really sorry. I . . . I didn't know."

"It's fine."

"Okay, okay."

As they stood there, Tucker started to remember things from the past couple weeks, times when Bobby had clearly been trying to talk to him about this and Tucker hadn't picked up on it, or worse, hadn't wanted to deal with it. He'd been too distracted by his own stress or too annoyed by his friend being wrapped up with a girlfriend when he didn't have one.

Tucker couldn't believe how pathetic he felt.

"I'll go look at the Harry Potter stuff with you, but can we go to the video game room first?" Bobby asked. "I really want to see this video game room."

Tucker told him where it was, adding that Ryan and Nina and everybody were probably still up there. Then he said Bobby should go ahead without him.

Tucker needed a few minutes alone, a few minutes to walk around and clear his head.

# 17

## ERIKA

Erika made her way back to the library, pulled by the sound of the horn section happily blaring, the singer's voice coming through bright and clear on the chorus of "Sleigh Ride." When she arrived, though, she could barely squeeze her way in, the room was so packed. She scanned the crowd and finally spotted Marissa, who was hopping up and down and waving to her, looking like she was about to burst.

The girls inched their way toward each other, and as they did, Erika heard the first notes of her song—"All I Want for Christmas Is You."

The band was playing it perfectly, starting quiet with all the promise of a big, grand finish, and Marissa dragged her onto the last square of dance floor available.

"Can you believe we found each other, *right as they are*

*starting this song?* This is total magic. Also, you look even sexier than I remember, and definitely not like an elf. And one more thing, Marco gave me my Christmas present. He gave me a ring."

The song was still in its slow build, as Erika did her best to absorb everything that Marissa had told her.

"Well, that's nice," she finally said. "Though it's awfully romantic, considering you just got back together. I hope it's not an engagement ring."

Erika laughed, a little too loud, but she was feeling jumpy and off, still thinking about Nina, about those stupid feathers. She didn't really want to tell Marissa what had happened, but Marissa might find out anyway, so Erika was anxious to get through this silly talk about Marco and get her confession over with.

Marissa had gone strangely quiet, though.

"It's not a real engagement ring. Like, it's not some big-ass diamond. But it's, I don't know. A symbol of something serious. We're committing to each other. For the long haul."

Silence descended while Erika's brain caught up.

"I don't understand. Are you *engaged* right now?"

"In a way. Yeah."

Was she supposed to say congratulations? She should definitely say congratulations. Or say how sweet it was or something. Her stomach was jittery, though. She had questions, so many questions, and she was pretty sure they were all going to sound judgmental.

"What about this fall? Spain?" Erika finally asked.

"I'm still going to Spain."

There was defensiveness in Marissa's voice, and it brought out the edge in Erika's own.

"Is that why he's doing this? So you don't hook up with people over there?"

She was trying to not talk too loud, and it made it seem like she was hissing at her friend, which was ridiculous. But everything about this was ridiculous, was it not? Her pulse was racing, and Marissa was taking way too long to answer again.

"He's doing this because he loves me. Sorry if that seems pathetic to you, but I'm actually pretty happy about it."

*We're twenty*, Erika wanted to scream, *twenty!* What could she be thinking? And how were she and Marissa supposed to get a crappy apartment in DC together after college like they'd always planned, if Marissa was on the verge of getting married?

*You need to calm down. You're being overly emotional, because this night has been so weird. Chill, chill, chill.*

"What is up with you, by the way?" Marissa asked. "You look totally freaked out right now."

Erika started chewing on her thumbnail.

"This is kind of hard to explain, but Nina told me that she likes Tucker, and she was worried that I liked him, too. So I told her that I definitely didn't, and that I'd try to help get the two of them together. Only then she walked in on us in Ryan's guest room."

Marissa stared at her, blinking slowly. "You were making out with him?"

"No! We were playing video games. And I guess having a

pillow fight. But it's not what it sounds like."

"So you told Nina you didn't like him, then you two went up to a bedroom and had a pillow fight?"

The song was at its peak now, Mariah hitting that pitch-perfect, neverending *you*, and every second of it was grating to Erika's ears.

"Don't look at me like that," she snapped at Marissa. "Jesus, you're the one who's always been so desperate for me to jump his freaking bones."

Marissa was running her hands through her hair, and Erika saw the little ring on her finger, gold and glinting. It was probably really pretty. She should have asked to see it, but it was too late for that, much too late.

Erika's throat was dry. She had to swallow before she could talk again.

"This always happens, you know this always happens. Girls hate me!"

"And that's *girls'* fault?"

Erika's cheeks flared. She had no good response. A waiter went by, and she snagged a champagne when he wasn't looking, chugged it right there.

"Fine. It's my fault. I suck, all right? I'm the same old ho I've always been."

"Don't do that. What are you even talking about?"

"You know, don't pretend you don't know. You always wanted to live vicariously through my hookups, but you think I'm trash, like everybody else does. Whatever, okay? I'm over it.

Go do your thing and be a child bride."

Marissa's eyes went wide. "*What?*"

Erika turned and started pushing through the crowd, desperately needing some space, needing to get away. She'd only made it a few feet, though, when she started to crumble. She turned around, ready to apologize and ask for forgiveness . . .

Marissa was already gone.

# 18

## TUCKER

Tucker barely squeezed his way into the library; he couldn't believe how crowded the place had gotten. He'd been wandering around for twenty minutes now, looking for Erika, not wanting to leave things on a bad note.

He spotted her standing stiffly by the wall, and he made his way over, reaching her as the band launched into that stupid, sad John Lennon song.

*Great. Just fantastic.*

He said hello, but she didn't even look his way, staring instead at the dance floor where everyone was wrapping up in pairs. She was scowling and chewing on her lip.

"Hey, uh . . . I'm sorry if it looked weird before, up in Ryan's room."

Now she looked like she might cry.

"I feel terrible," he said. "You have no idea. I should have told everybody that it wasn't anything . . ."

"I'm not upset about that. It's fine. Forget it."

Tears were officially running down her cheeks. Tucker panicked.

"Do you want to dance?"

Slowly, she turned to look at him. She seemed to be considering if he was the stupidest person in the entire world.

"I'm not trying to hit on you, I swear. When I'm trying not to cry, the only thing that helps is having something to do."

A part of him couldn't believe he'd said that out loud, but it was true. He'd cried way too much as a kid—when he said something dumb in class or screwed up at T-ball. When his dad was being his dad. Eventually, he'd learned to control it by moving around, distracting himself. In his mind, he called it staying busy, and it also helped to say it again and again in his head, while he was sharpening his pencil or tightening his shoestring or whatever.

*Staying-busy-staying-busy-staying-busy.*

Erika was still giving him a disgusted look, but her tears were gone.

"See!" he said. "It's already working. You're so blown away by what an idiot I am, you forgot to be upset."

Erika crossed her arms, and just as he was about to apologize and leave her alone, she turned toward him, her face suddenly blank.

"Why the hell not, at this point? Let's dance."

Erika elbowed her way through the crowd until she found a small opening on the floor, then stood there waiting. Tucker, operating on a delay, finally tripped his way over and planted himself across from her.

After a few seconds, she reached up and put her hands very lightly on his shoulders. He did the same to her waist. Her dress was soft, and she felt nice in his arms, but he stopped that train of thought as quickly as he could.

More people were crowding in around them, and the song was reaching a crescendo now, talking about hope for the year to come, that it would be free from fear . . .

"This song is the worst," Erika said. "It's so depressing. I was trying to explain this to Marissa, on the way over here. Christmas songs are supposed to be *happy*. A three-minute sham that helps you forget how much the world sucks. Give me pure, fake joy or give me nothing."

Tucker started nodding in agreement. "Yeah, this song's awful. Who wants war in their Christmas song? Even if it *is* over."

Was she laughing or was she back to crying? He wasn't sure.

"I drove tonight, and I feel like I drank too much champagne," she said. "I'm going to have to abandon my car. My mom is going to be so pissed."

Tucker kept swaying to the music while his mind worked. He couldn't undo his mistakes from tonight, but maybe he could do something nice for her now. As the last notes of the song were bleeding out, he decided to take a chance.

"I didn't drink at all. I can drive your car home."

He was about to add more, to explain that he was happy to help, that he could drop off Marissa and Marco, too, and then call an Uber for himself . . .

"Okay," she said. "If you don't mind. Do you want to go now?"

# 19

## ERIKA

She texted Marissa and apologized for leaving, promising to pay for her Uber. Then, afraid to see how Marissa might respond, she busied herself controlling the music, pumping out dreamy-sounding women who seemed to be moving the car with their breath and their words, pushing them past strip malls, drug stores, the hospital that never slept.

She'd made this decision in a moment of recklessness, and she'd been hoping to chase that feeling, only now here he was in her car, being very particular and careful about everything—-the lights and the wipers and the side-view mirrors. It was sweet, and that was taking her from all the anger and embarrassment that had sent her down this road in the first place.

She gave him directions, and they merged onto the highway.

Now they had a five-mile stretch of straight driving, and she needed to start talking.

"Where are you going to school next year? I just realized I have no idea."

He hesitated before he answered.

"University of Michigan, I think. I mean, I hope. It's where my mom went—we've got family out there. I always liked the idea of going somewhere big and far away that still kind of seemed like home."

"That sounds nice."

The car grew quiet again, and she could sense Tucker fumbling for something else to talk about.

"So, uh, what are your Christmas plans?" he finally asked.

"Nothing much. Going to see my mom's family in Virginia."

"What about your dad?"

Erika noticed a hole starting in her tights. She covered it with her finger so she wouldn't have to look at it.

"They've been divorced since I was ten, but lately I see him less and less. He's in sales and he travels a lot."

She almost let it go at that, but she felt like Tucker was waiting for more.

"He's getting married soon, and they're having a kid in the spring. They're in Mexico right now on a 'babymoon.' In case you needed any proof that he's a total douche."

"What about her—do you like her?"

The Beach House song faded out, and there were a few long beats before Florence and the Machine crept up out of the silence. As she sat listening to the music, contemplating his question, she realized that she wasn't drunk in the slightest, those couple glasses of champagne just a memory now.

"I've never met her," Erika said.

She was surprised that she was saying all this, but it always felt easy, talking to Tucker. She wondered if he felt the same.

"You don't see your dad much either?" she asked.

His fingers were nervously drumming on the wheel now.

"He's hardly been around. Just here and there, my whole life. He and my mom were never married, they . . . They worked at a restaurant together, right after my mom got out of college. I don't even have his last name."

He fiddled unnecessarily with the windshield wipers, then kept talking.

"Actually, I see him every week now, because he moved up this way. He's been staying with a friend. Not far from your house. We've been having dinner at the Athena Diner on Thursdays. You know that place?"

"I love that place," Erika said quietly. "They have the best pancakes."

She shifted in her seat, looking out the window to search for a few stars that managed to glow brighter than the lights of the suburban sprawl. She watched the landscape pass, much of it familiar, though it was always changing, here and there.

Senior year, she'd convinced herself that she hated it here, complaining to Marissa all the time that she couldn't believe they had to live somewhere so dull and yet so crowded. But had she really meant that? She'd been so ready to run at that point, it had helped to act like the whole place was tainted. Really, it wasn't so bad. It was close enough to DC to have some of its worldliness, a touch of its polish and shine, but still—there were all those sublimely ordinary joys of suburbia. Birthday parties at the Cave. Mozzarella sticks at Applebee's. A Christmas house so tacky it had the power to start a traffic jam.

Watching the lights of the strip malls blur as they drove, Erika was reaching for a certain feeling, wanting to be nostalgic for her hometown. She was close, but couldn't quite get there. Then a familiar sign crested into view.

It was the Athena, etched against the sky in blazing neon.

"We could stop now," Erika said. "For pancakes."

Tucker didn't respond at first, and just when she was about to take it back, he looked at her with that bullshitty smile on his face.

"Because there was nothing to eat at that party, nothing at all."

She flipped him off—very slowly this time, very deliberately.

"Twice in one night? I'm starting to feel kind of special over here."

"Well, whatever. We don't have to. It's late, and you're about to miss the turn."

"Oh, it's happening. It's so happening."

Tucker zipped over to the right lane, and Erika gave a little squeal.

# 20

## TUCKER

The hostess greeted him by name, and then she sat the two of them in Bonnie's section, of course. Bonnie arrived at their table all smiles. *Two times in a week, to what do I owe the pleasure?* They both ordered coffee, even though Tucker knew the coffee there was terrible.

Bonnie left, and they were alone. Tucker kept staring at the menu that he basically knew by heart, because he always needed something to stare at when he was there. Something that wasn't his dad.

"Are you okay?" Erika asked.

"Yeah, yeah. It's just . . . my dad is staying literally around the corner. He can walk over, so he's here all the time. I was actually kind of worried we might see him, but so far so good."

"Jesus, Tucker. We didn't have to do this."

He shrugged, mumbling that it was no big deal. The truth was, as soon as she'd suggested this, he'd imagined sitting with her in some back booth, how that memory could keep him company on nights when he really didn't want to be here.

"Let's talk about pancakes instead," Tucker said.

Erika shifted in her seat, then nodded. "Okay. Sure. I have lots of thoughts about the pancakes here. Deciding between the cinnamon roll pancakes and the chocolate caramel pancakes is almost impossible."

"Okay, wow. You like this place more than I realized."

"I stopped coming for a while because it was always crawling with people from high school, and I hate people from high school, so I've been very deprived. Of the pancakes."

He wondered if he should ask her more about that, but he didn't want to bring all the messiness of their lives into the warmth of the booth. Besides, Bonnie was back, setting down their coffee. She turned expectantly to Erika, who looked physically pained as she stared at the menu.

"All right, all right. Cinnamon roll pancakes. Sorry, that decision was brutal."

Bonnie turned to Tucker. "Reuben and sweet potato fries?"

Tucker handed her the menu. "Can I have chocolate caramel pancakes?"

Bonnie disappeared, and the two of them looked at each other. Erika's face had gone pink, and it made all her freckles pop.

"If you're nice to me, maybe I'll share," he said.

She kicked him in the leg, and he gave an exaggerated flinch, pretending to be hurt.

"Not cool," he said.

She kicked him again, a little harder this time, and now he actually flinched. He told her to leave him alone, and then he felt her foot, hooking around his under the table. She held on for a moment, just a moment, and then she let go.

When he finally looked up, she had ripped her empty sugar packet to shreds. His eyes swung to the window next to them, at the snowflake decorations that were starting to peel off. He could not believe how tense things suddenly felt.

"So, uh, what do you like to do when you're home?" Tucker asked.

*You sound like you're trying to ask her out. Abort, abort.*

Erika was hard at work cleaning up her massacred sugar packet. "Oh, I don't know. This and that."

Her freckles were popping again. He suddenly felt like there was not enough air back there, in that corner of the room.

"I still can't believe you knew the ingredients to Polyjuice Potion," he said.

"I can't believe you knew Hagrid's *mother's* name."

For five solid minutes, they relived the glory of their win, and then a runner from the kitchen appeared with two plates of pancakes, sliding them down, hers and then his.

They were bordering on pornographic. Big and fluffy, whipped cream everywhere. Buried in toppings.

"How the hell," he said, "did these get here so fast?"

"It's always like that. I think they're continually making pancakes all day, every day. I can't believe you come here every week and never get them!"

Erika set about meticulously cutting hers into slivers, and he followed her lead. When she started talking again, she kept her eyes on her plate.

"That was a hell of a party, but honestly, I can't wait to get home to my nice, quiet house." She carefully added more syrup. "My mom's working a night shift."

Tucker's heart started thumping a beat faster, as he started to wonder what exactly was happening right now. He was feeling way too keyed up to eat, and was stuck staring at this giant pile of pancakes, wondering if he could even manage to take a bite . . .

And then there was a cough, a presence.

His dad was hovering close at the edge of their table.

Ray had that stupid bandanna on, the one Tucker absolutely hated and wanted to rip right off his head every time he saw it. He looked like hell, of course. He always looked like hell these days, his skin gray and sagging, his eyes bloodshot.

He had an awful smile on his face, absolutely awful.

"Hello, hello," he finally said. "Who's this?"

Tucker had felt sick as soon as he saw him, but now the sensation went deeper because, of course, the stupid smile was about Erika.

*Don't fidget. Don't let him make you squirm.*

"This is my dad, Ray. This is my friend Erika."

"Your friend?"

His dad put his hands in his pockets, his eyebrows up.

"My friend," Tucker repeated, and he leaned back in the booth, as if he could put some distance between himself and her, like that might help.

"Okay, okay."

Ray was still smiling like he didn't believe him, like it was all a joke, and oh god—this was a fantasy Tucker had had for so long and in so many different ways. That he'd finally find some way to surprise his dad, impress him. He used to picture him showing up to his baseball games, but as he'd gotten older, he'd imagined exactly this. That Ray would see him with a pretty girl, and then . . . what? He'd know that someone *did* want to fuck him? It was stupid, he knew it was stupid, but he'd never been able to kill those little make-believe scenarios. When he was younger, these ridiculous scenes of being with some hot girl with his dad wandering by had been a way to imagine a path toward forgiveness, reconciliation. But as time went on, it became an excuse to picture exactly how he'd tell his dad to fuck off.

Now here they were, it was actually happening, and Tucker didn't want it at all. He didn't even want Ray to look at her. The seconds were ticking by, his dad rocking back on his heels, staring now at the pancakes idling on the table. The whipped cream was starting to sink.

Tucker realized he was still wearing his Harry Potter scarf, and as subtly as he could, he took it off and shoved it under his leg. He began pulling some words together, some *nice to see you now get away from us* kind of words, but it was taking forever to form them.

And then it was too late. Very slowly, Ray was sliding into the booth, uncomfortably close to Tucker.

Tucker moved as far as he could into the corner. It was sticky there, and cramped.

"You two look awfully fancy, for this place," Ray said, his eyes all over Tucker's suit.

"We were at a party," Tucker said.

Ray's eyebrows went up. He picked up the fork and poked at the pancakes with a smirk on his face. Erika still hadn't said a word, and Tucker wanted to rescue her from this, but he didn't know how, and that made him feel weak, pathetic. An ache started in his head at the same time that he got a twinge in his shoulder, and before he could stop himself, he was touching it with his hand, rolling it back.

Ray saw, of course he saw.

"I thought that was finally better?"

Tucker didn't answer, so Ray pushed the pancakes out of the way, leaning his elbows onto the table, taking up more space than seemed logically possible. And now he was looking at Erika.

"Injuries like that, they always come back. Did he tell you what happened?"

Back in the kitchen, there was the crash of a dropped glass.

143

"Maybe?" Erika finally said. "I can't really remember."

She'd spoken in a neutral tone, and now she valiantly took up her fork and knife again, acting as if all of this was perfectly normal.

Tucker had tried that method with his dad plenty of times, though—acting nonchalant, not rising to the occasion.

He knew that it wouldn't stop him.

"We were over at my mom's place, last May. Tucker's cousin Bill asked if he wanted to drive the ATV. Didn't go too well."

Tucker had spiraled down to a place where he couldn't speak, could barely seem to move. He stared at the speckled Formica table, while in his mind, that day he'd tried so hard to forget was coming back in a rush.

He could still picture the thing perfectly. Big black tires and a neon yellow body, all skeleton, like some monstrous insect.

"Tucker got it bad, but Riley got it worse. He's Tucker's little cousin? He was sitting right on Tucker's lap."

Tucker had been staring at Erika's plate, and so he saw her pause, briefly but undeniably, before she resumed her façade of casually eating.

Meanwhile, Tucker's mind became a storm as he thought of Riley, little Riley who belonged to no one. Or rather, he'd belonged to Ray's youngest sister, Jean, but she'd disappeared more than two years ago, leaving Riley to live on the farm with sad, quiet Grandma Ruth.

Tucker had made a point to play with Riley always. He was so much younger than all the other cousins—only six. That day, as Tucker had put his hands on the wheel, Riley had scrambled into his lap, all warmth and flailing, skinny limbs.

"Not your best moment, Tucker, if I'm being honest."

Tucker leaned his head against the back of the booth. He closed his eyes.

"No," he said quietly. "It wasn't."

Aunt Maggie had screamed *no, no, no* and run toward them, arms outstretched to snatch Riley back. But Bill had been laughing, begging him to go, and when Tucker had looked up, he'd seen his dad, watching and waiting to see what he would do.

Tucker had hit the gas.

"Whew, that was one hell of a wreck," Ray said. "Never seen anything like that."

*Blue-green, blue-green, blue-green.* That's what Tucker remembered, from when he first came to. His consciousness had returned slowly, the world coming into focus in such incremental degrees that at first he could not comprehend that he was lying on the ground, his face in the grass, sky blazing above him. He could only think *blue-green, blue-green, blue-green.*

Then he'd seen the toppled ATV. He'd seen Bill sitting up, dazed but in one piece. And finally he'd seen Riley, a limp rag to his left, one of his knees bent wrong. Tucker had wept and tried to go to him, but he'd fallen as soon as he stood, still too dizzy, his shoulder full of pain that was like its own private sun. Tucker had lain there, crying, while Ray took Riley in his arms and ran him to the car to drive him to the hospital.

Tucker had been right behind them in Maggie's car, completely unable to look at her.

All around them, the diner was full of loud talking and clinking silverware, but silence had descended over their party of three. Tucker finally managed to turn and look at his dad.

"Are you done? Have you had enough fun for one night?"

His dad looked at him in mock surprise.

"Well, she should hear the end, right? That Riley's mostly fine? He was in a cast all summer, but he's okay now. I've got scars worse than the one he's got, much worse."

Ray took his elbows off the table, examining his arms, looking at both of them like maybe they would ask to hear his stories, to see the evidence of his wounds. Tucker felt nothing but rage.

"I don't care. She doesn't care. Can you leave now?"

For a few long seconds, his dad just sat. Then he moved to slide out of the booth, pausing first to poke an elbow into Tucker's ribs.

"You remember what Riley always used to say? *I wish Tucker was my brother.*"

And then finally, finally, his father stood to leave.

"Not sure he really says that anymore."

# 21

## ERIKA

They sat in the car in the parking lot, Styrofoam containers full of uneaten pancakes on their laps. Erika had let him know she was sober and could drive, but they hadn't yet clarified where exactly she'd be taking him. Her house? His house? Back to the party?

She hadn't started the engine yet, and was still trying to decide whether or not to say something about what had just happened. Then Tucker cleared his throat.

"My dad's never liked me, even when I was a kid. He's been calling me, you know . . . *a pussy* for pretty much as long as I can remember. Which, yeah, that's a messed-up thing to say, but I guess I know what he means. Because I'm soft, I've always been soft, ever since I was little."

That word had sounded so unnatural coming from

Tucker—it was like it had disrupted the air, rearranged its atoms. Erika was squirming now, trying to figure out how to respond.

"Tucker, you're not a pussy. And a little kid can't be a pussy."

Now he was looking at her, but this stupid car was too small for that much eye contact, and they both turned away.

"There have been times in my life when I should have thrown a punch. I could never do it. You know how people always ask what you want to be when you grow up? I knew I was supposed to say a fireman or a race car driver or something, but I could never picture doing any of that stuff. The only thing I could imagine was, you know, having kids or whatever. Being a dad."

Erika took in a sharp breath, pressed her lips together.

"Those aren't bad things. At all."

"No, but they make me a Hufflepuff."

They were back to that again, which was reminding her of Ryan's guest room, and then she was remembering Tucker's puppy dog comment and *oh*.

Now it finally clicked.

"You heard what I said that night. In the tree house?"

He ran a hand through his hair, then started rubbing his shoulder again.

"I shouldn't have been listening, I know. I'm really sorry. And it was stupid to bring it up again. I just want to forget about it."

Erika didn't know how she felt about that—angry or guilty, just embarrassed maybe. She didn't want to think about that night right now. Also, she was tired of holding these stupid pancakes. Sighing, she took a second to put the Styrofoam container on the back seat, then took his from him and stacked it on top.

Now they were both stuck staring at their empty hands.

Whatever she'd been planning for tonight, it wasn't for the right reasons. She knew that now. She knew, too, that she cared about this boy. She cared about him a lot.

As for what she should do about it—she had absolutely no idea.

"Listen, I'm really sorry you had to sit through that, with my dad," Tucker said. "And I know you had an intense night, remembering everything from school and then you got the text . . . Anyway, I hope you're feeling okay now."

She was too ashamed to admit that she hadn't even been crying about any of that on the dance floor. She'd been crying because of her fight with Marissa. But in this cramped car, with all these words being spilled, she could feel everything weighing on her, and she wanted to talk.

"I keep wondering what will happen if there's a trial, if I have to testify. What if everything that happened senior year comes back to ruin my life? Sometimes I think that's the thing that's stressing me out, more than anything else. So in case you were wondering how shitty of a person I am, the answer is pretty shitty."

Erika was afraid maybe she'd said too much, that she'd made a mistake. But when Tucker spoke again, his voice was gentle.

"You're not a shitty person. At all. Anybody would feel like that."

Erika closed her eyes. *You're not a shitty person* was a phrase that, right then, she really needed to hear. The words kept flowing out of her.

"It was a video. You know that, right?"

"Yeah, yeah. I mean, I guess. I heard stuff at the Cave, but I tried not to listen."

Erika nodded, then steadied her voice.

"It was thirty seconds. Of me going down on him. You can barely tell it's me, except for my stupid pink hair. So the asshole that took it sent it to a second asshole, because it was some bullshit dare that was running through these jerks on the hockey team. The second asshole posted it on this Facebook page that was run by the booster club, this place for sharing stats from meets, clips from games. Tons of people followed it."

A half hour. That was all it had taken to find one of the moms who administered the page, so that she could take it down. A half hour that had become Erika's life.

She could still remember staring at her phone, seeing it there. She'd barely kept herself from smashing the screen.

"You couldn't download it—my saving grace. But people took screenshots and whatever. Made hilarious memes with them. They're probably still floating around."

"What did the school do?"

*Be cool. It's just old shit. No big deal, no big deal, no big deal.*

"It was the beginning of June. The guys were a year older, so they'd already graduated, and it wasn't an official school page anyway. Legally I could have gone after them, but . . . I don't know. At the time I just wanted the whole thing to be over."

She fought back tears now, as she sat there thinking about living her senior year in the aftermath of it all, getting called a slut again and again. By strangers. By people that used to be her friends.

By Dana.

Of course Erika had known that it was wrong, back when Grayson first started flirting with her, but she'd always had a thing for him, so she'd gone along. At some point, their semi-innocent compliments evolved into completely inappropriate conversations, like their joke about how he watched too much porn on his phone.

The tension between them built for weeks, until she'd finally gone off with him that night. He'd begged her to let him take the video. He went on and on about how he wouldn't need anything else to look at, how sexy she was, how he was totally falling for her . . .

It hadn't even been that hard to convince her. He'd played right into that want she had, to be everything to someone. Their whole world, their only desire. That's how you knew you were worth something, right? When their need for you was that extreme, an absolute.

That was the part that was so hard, even now, to come to terms with. How desperate she was for someone to make her feel special. Afterward, she'd been so bitter, telling herself that everyone's relationship was some version of that, that people sought each other only for some flimsy validation. It became another reason to distance herself from other girls, to look down on their silly crushes.

She didn't want to be that way anymore. She wanted silly crushes—boys in trucker hats at luaus. But more important, she wanted friends to talk about it with afterward.

Erika was starting to realize that getting there would take a lot more effort than she'd been giving.

Finally, she put on her seat belt and readied herself to ask if she was taking him to his house. Before she could, his phone started beeping incessantly, and he fumbled with it, trying to turn down the volume.

"Everything okay?" Erika asked.

"Yeah, yeah," Tucker said. "Ryan's trying to get all the debate people together, in half an hour. He wants to get a picture of us jumping into his indoor pool, in our clothes."

"Oh, ha ha. I can't believe there are still rooms of that house that I haven't seen."

"I know, right?"

Erika fiddled with the hem of her dress. "I can drop you back off at the party. It's not that far."

"No, no. I'll call an Uber, have it pick me up here. That makes more sense."

"Okay. I mean . . . if you're sure. But listen, don't mess up that suit, okay? It's a really nice suit."

"I won't, I won't."

Erika was still feeling restless, like she hadn't said all she could, like she could have done a better job convincing him that he was special the way he was. She was still rattled, though, from everything that had happened tonight, and she couldn't seem to find the words.

"Tucker . . ."

He looked over at her, cautiously, expectantly. After a second, she turned away.

"I guess I better head home."

# 22

## TUCKER

Bobby had agreed to trade outfits with Tucker so that Tucker could be part of the debate-jump photo, and now the boys were standing in the changing room located off the pool, considering themselves and each other in the mirror.

"Damn," Bobby said. "I look good in this."

That made Tucker laugh, and he was thankful for that, because he still felt bad about what had happened with Bobby earlier. He was also reeling from the diner and the conversation he'd had with Erika in the car. He couldn't believe he'd said so many deep, secret things out loud.

Now Tucker just had to hold himself together for a little longer. He could do that, he was sure of it.

"Hey," Tucker said to Bobby. "Don't get attached to that. I want it back."

"We'll see, we'll see. If you end up ruining that shirt, I might keep this as punishment."

"Isn't it kind of adorable that we're the same size?"

"So adorable," Bobby said.

Tucker looked at Bobby's jeans and nice button-down reflecting back at him in the mirror. That got him thinking of the Santa picture, so Tucker pulled out his phone, and, of course, his mom had posted it online, where it had already gotten a truly frightening number of likes. Then he saw that Bobby had responded with a line of mortified emojis, and Janet had replied that she missed him. Bobby had responded that he missed her, too.

In that moment, Tucker realized that Bobby was a Hufflepuff just like him. And maybe that was what pulled the two of them together, more than anything else. Maybe it's why they'd been friends for so long. Maybe it would keep them together, even when everything changed next year.

That was something to be grateful for.

"Hey, listen . . . I've been a total jerk. About Skylar. I'm sorry. I . . . she's actually really cool . . ."

"Seriously, it's fine. I mean, we can talk about it later if you want, but I don't want to talk about it now."

Tucker nodded, then walked over to the door, opening it a crack to peer at the pool, which sat inside a glass cavern. Stars and a big fat moon glowed overhead, reflecting down into the water. Ryan was getting everybody ready for the jump, talking about how important the timing was because they'd only get one chance and then everyone would be soaked.

Tucker's emotions were pinballing all over the place, but he was still managing to control them. He was okay. For now he was *staying-busy-staying-busy-staying-busy*.

"Just to be clear," Bobby said. "You did drive off with Erika, and now you're here again?"

"Yeah, yeah. Things got really weird. I took her to the diner, and we ran into my dad."

"*What?*"

"It was bad. Like really bad."

"Is that why you came back?"

Was it? Tucker didn't think it was that simple. He'd left because the circumstances were wrong, both of them off-kilter. If something had happened, it might have been because they were hurting, and that didn't feel right.

But there was another reason, too.

"I had fun here tonight," Tucker said. "I didn't want to miss the end of the party."

Tucker and Bobby walked out into the glass pyramid, where it was steamy, chemical-smelling. Tucker joined the rest of the debate team, all of them lined up, barefoot, at the edge of the pool, their shoes, socks, and tights piled behind them. Ryan was pulling up a Christmas mix, then linking his phone to the speaker in the corner. Tucker was glad when it was a happy song that came blasting out, or at least happy-ish. It was that soul song where the woman was begging her baby to come home.

Standing there with his new friends, while Bobby hovered

in the corner in his borrowed suit—Tucker was overwhelmed. The night suddenly felt strange and beautiful and sad all at once, the way the end of a year always did.

A lump formed in his throat, and Tucker was relieved when Ryan said that it was time to jump.

Across the pool, the professional photographer was waiting, along with a bunch of friends holding their phones. The water, impossibly clean and blue, was gently lapping against the bright white tile. Ryan was trying to get everyone to be quiet, but it was hopeless—there was too much laughter, too much chatter. He gave up and did his best to yell over it.

"All right! Don't mess this up. ONE. TWO. THREE!"

Up they went, and down they fell.

Splash.

Tucker kicked his way up, shocked at how heavy he felt, weighed down by the jeans, the shirt. He burst to the surface, then watched as everyone else did the same. The girls' makeup was running down their faces, and everyone's hair was a disaster, but it seemed like nobody cared.

They were all a mess, so what did it matter?

Dodging bodies left and right, he awkwardly made his way over to the side of the pool, clinging to the rough lip, smiling at everyone . . . and then somebody crashed down next to him.

It was Bobby, who leaned back to casually float there in his boxers.

Tucker splashed water all over Bobby's face, but Bobby barely flinched.

"Don't worry, I laid your suit out very nicely in the corner."

"This is a pathetically obvious way to show off your muscles, just so you know."

"*What?* Whatever. I'm just checking on you. In case you needed to be saved."

"Sure, sure."

As Tucker and Bobby kept bickering, Ryan and Nina were paddling up behind them, situating themselves to hang off the edge of the pool. Nina was looking at Tucker a little funny, and he thought maybe she was going to ask what happened to Erika, but then she started smiling, pointing back and forth between Tucker and Bobby.

"You two sound exactly like my little twin sisters when you fight."

"Tucker's totally like my twin sister," Bobby said.

"Oh yeah," Tucker said. "We're twinsies for life."

Nina and Ryan were both laughing at that, and Tucker was so happy. The wet clothes felt awful, but the water was so warm, and that soul song was ending, the word *Christmas, Christmas, Christmas, Christmas* echoing over and over. Ryan yelled at someone on the sidelines to turn up the volume as a new song began.

And of course. What else would it be? John-Fucking-Lennon.

Tucker sighed, letting the first bars of the song wash over him. And . . . maybe his mom was right. Maybe this was a good song. Right now, it was completely overwhelming him, filling him with entirely too many emotions. Bobby was across from him, still churning, still afloat, his eyes going wide with concern, because he saw exactly what was happening.

Tucker was crying.

Bobby splashed him in the face, asked if he wanted to race to the other end of the pool, and Tucker knew that Bobby was fulfilling his promise from a moment ago—he was trying to save him. But Tucker didn't feel like he needed saving, not this time. He wiped his face, swallowed hard.

"It's okay, it's okay."

"Are you all right?" Nina asked quietly.

"Dude, what's wrong?" Ryan asked.

"Nothing, nothing," Tucker said. "Or lots of things, I guess. My dad has pancreatic cancer and he'll probably be dead in a year."

Beyond them, the pool was still full of laughter and splashing. The camera was still flashing, phones still clicking. In their little circle, though, it was quiet. Ryan and Nina murmured how sorry they were, while Bobby kept treading water, his face crumpled in concern.

Tucker felt very bare, very raw just then. He was sad and he was scared, but he felt freer than he had in a while.

That part was almost exhilarating.

They were asking him questions, and he was answering, giving details in a mindless sort of way, letting the words flow out of him, explaining how his dad was staying with a friend, to be near the clinic where he was getting treatment. And then he told them that his dad was an asshole. That Tucker felt like he barely knew him. It seemed suddenly easy to say all these big, monstrous things, surrounded as he was by people who were looking at him with so much kindness.

When the three of them ran out of things to say, Tucker swore that he was fine, and then he pushed off the edge, floating on his back toward the middle of the pool.

Staring up at the stars, Tucker was glad for this complicated, bittersweet moment, for everything that had led to it.

That night in the tree house, Erika had talked about people wanting an excuse to say and do all those things they secretly wanted to say and do. But maybe parties were more than just an excuse. Maybe they were something a little more special.

Maybe some kinds of magic were real.

Tucker sat in Bobby's soaking clothes, in the corner of the glass cavern. Before he could think too hard, he called Erika.

She said hello very skeptically.

"I took my suit off. Wait, wait. That sounded creepy. Let me start over. Bobby and I traded clothes, so that I didn't ruin my suit. But then he took it off, too, and swam in his underwear. I don't know why that matters. This is getting off on the wrong track."

"Can't wait to hear what the right track is, if there is one."

"There is, there is. I had to call you because I heard the John Lennon Christmas song for the third time today, and it's really grown on me. It helped me come up with a new theory about Christmas songs."

He could hear her shifting around. He wondered if she was in bed, and he wondered what she wore to bed, and then he screamed inwardly at himself to focus.

"Okay, Campanelli. There's nothing I like better at one in the morning than elaborate theories. Lay it on me."

"Oh god, it's that late? Sorry, sorry. Okay. So I think you're right, but only partly. Yeah, those songs are written to heighten our emotions. But I don't think that's a sham or fake, I think . . . okay, this will sound stupid, but I mean it. The sensation you get, at the climax of a song—that's how beautiful life is. But there's no way to always feel like that, right? So we need things like Christmas songs to remind us. A touchstone or something. And when they make you kind of sad? That's because even as they help you understand how much it all matters, they remind you of the times you didn't understand at all."

Now the other end of the line was very quiet. No more shifting. Was she thinking? Had she hung up? Had the chlorine warped Tucker's brain, and this was the dumbest thing he'd ever done?

"Okay, okay," she finally said. "I buy it. I think memories are like that, too. You know how there are big moments in your life that you think about all the time, stories that you tell in your mind?"

"Like a song played over and over."

"Exactly. I think that's how we explain ourselves to ourselves. Or something."

Tucker was smiling, even though he was starting to get very cold and shivery. "That's pretty good. Were you on debate, too?"

"Ha ha, no. But listen, I'm actually glad that you called, because I've been thinking, too. When we were in the parking lot . . . I shouldn't have said you weren't a pussy. I should have said that the word is, you know, invalid. Inherently flawed."

"Yeah, yeah. Okay."

"Don't blow me off! I'm serious." She paused, sighing loudly, mumbling that she needed a second to figure out how to say this.

"So I had the first boobs of anybody in my class—I know they aren't much now, but everything that's here I've had since fifth grade, and that was a lot for fifth grade. I showed up with them at the beginning of the year, and right away boys started calling me a slut. When I was ten. *Ten.* Later I was a slut because of something I wore, because I hooked up with too many people. By then I knew that word was bullshit, but it got harder to believe after the whole world saw what they saw."

All of his friends were out of the pool by now. Ryan was handing out giant fluffy towels, and everybody was laughing about how miserable it was going to be to drive home in wet clothes. Tucker hunched down lower with his phone, trying to block it all out.

"I'm sorry. That's . . . I don't know what to say."

"You don't have to say anything. What I'm trying to explain is . . . I know I shouldn't care, if people think I'm a slut. I know that it's bullshit, the whole idea. But really believing that, deep down, all the time? That's a different story. I'm not there yet. And maybe it's the same for you."

Tucker ran a hand through his hair.

"Yeah, yeah. For sure."

For a few long seconds, neither of them said anything, but it was the nice kind of lull, the kind where you felt connected to the other person.

"So if Bobby put on your suit and is now in his underwear, what do *you* have on?"

"Did you just ask what I'm wearing right now?"

There was a weird noise on the other end of the line, and Tucker was fairly certain it was a snort.

"Got you? Did I get you?"

"Yes, fine. You got me. And now I'm going to bed."

"Cool, cool. Thanks, uh, for talking to me."

"No problem. Get home safe, Tucker. Have a good night's sleep or whatever."

"You too. Are you going to go play Pikachu?"

"TUCKER!"

*Oh no.* His face was on fire. Even though she couldn't see him, Tucker hid behind his hand.

"I didn't mean that—seriously! I honestly just meant Pikachu, not . . . you know. Anything else."

"Well, this is great. Have we ruined Pikachu? I think we've ruined Pikachu."

"No, no. Don't say that. He's not ruined, he's . . . full of new superpowers. Or something."

Now she was really laughing. "Okay, I'm definitely hanging up."

Was this goodbye? Tucker hated the idea of saying goodbye to her, so he searched for something else.

"Merry Christmas, Erika."

She paused, and in that gap, he felt sure that she was smiling.

"Did you know Christmas is my favorite holiday?" she asked.

"I didn't. But that makes me weirdly happy. I hope it's a good one. You know, like John Lennon says."

"Thanks," she said quietly. "I hope so, too."

# THE
# COLLEGE
# PARTY

# 23

## TUCKER

Tucker was watching Bobby furiously write a message, his thumbs flying, his eyebrows scrunched together as he leaned on his locker. He was going through a complicated cycle—writing, waiting, sighing. Writing again.

"Who are you texting?"

Bobby's eyes flashed up and then back down.

"Skylar."

Tucker nodded and kept pulling things out of his locker, while still looking sideways at Bobby.

"So Destiny seriously doesn't care that you still text Skylar that much? I'm not being a dick, I'm just curious."

"She doesn't care. She knows we're only friends."

"Do you ever wake up in the morning and get blown away by the fact that you're dating *Destiny Lewis?*"

Bobby dropped his phone to his side and looked at Tucker. "You realize how insulting that sounded, right?"

Tucker laughed, hitching up his backpack. "I didn't mean it like that! But seriously, aren't you glad you almost ran her over in the parking lot that day?"

"That was completely your fault. You wouldn't stop talking. It's impossible to drive with you."

"But look how well it worked out. Because of me. I'm a key part of your love story."

"Don't remind me. Listening to the two of you together is exhausting."

"Destiny and I have a special bond!" Tucker said. "She gives me good advice, I ignore it, and then she gets to point out how she was right."

Bobby got sucked into another endless text message exchange before he could respond. As Tucker waited, he took in how Bobby's hair was longer than usual, how he was wearing new sneakers. Bobby looked cool in a way that he never had before.

When Bobby was done, he pointed at Tucker. "For the record? If anyone has a texting problem, it's definitely you."

"Am I even looking at my phone right now? Clearly, I'm not."

Technically that was true, but the only reason Tucker wasn't checking for messages was because he happened to know that Friday afternoons were when Erika saw the school therapist, so there was no chance of her writing to him right now anyway. He'd promised to check in once he was on the road, on the way to St. B's.

This weekend, Destiny was visiting her sister at Spelman, and Tucker had convinced Bobby to go with him to visit Erika.

Bobby made a big show of putting his phone away too, and then he was smirking.

"Destiny made me promise I'd say this: girls don't like big, dramatic gestures on the quad. Those are creepy. You should just tell her how you feel."

Tucker scowled at him. "No offense, but I'm definitely not eating lunch with you two anymore. I've explained a million times that Erika and I are friends."

. . . at least for now.

Somehow, a couple texts the day after the Christmas party had turned into a winter break ritual of ice cream and video games at his house or HGTV and pizza at hers. All of it had been very chaste, no pillow fights. But they'd talked a lot; he'd told her what was going on with his dad. Then she'd left, and they'd spent the last couple months texting constantly—about stupid, little things all day, and big, important things during sleepless nights.

In the middle of it all, Tucker's dad had taken a turn.

There was no reason for him to be at the clinic anymore, so he'd moved back to the farm, to Grandma Ruth's house, to wait things out with the help of a hospice worker. They'd sold some of the land to pay for that, because the doctors were saying he had about nine more months, maybe more, maybe less.

Tucker hadn't seen his dad in weeks, so he'd hatched this plan to visit Erika and his dad in one trip, and then had never followed up on the second part. Tucker was so relieved to be away from his dad—he didn't have the will to reach out. So now this weekend was all about Tucker and Erika.

"*Just friends*," Bobby said. "Got it. Whatever you say. Let's talk again at the end of this weekend. See what your story is then."

Tucker ignored that, and said that they should hit the road. He and Bobby were about to head to the parking lot when somebody called to them.

"You guys going to Adam's tonight?"

It was Yrma, and she was with Nina and Kara. Tucker and Bobby walked over to stand with them, kids streaming around their little cluster, headed for the bus, their cars, the practice fields.

"Actually, no," Tucker said. "We're going to St. B's, to visit Erika."

The girls nodded and smiled, telling them to have fun. Nina was only half listening, too busy laughing while she texted. Probably she was talking to her boyfriend—that new kid, Theo.

"Too bad you guys won't be there," Yrma said. "I was thinking we could drink in the tree house again, tell more stories to embarrass Nina."

Nina kicked her without looking up from her phone, while Tucker laughed and said they'd have to do it some other time. As everybody was starting to drift away, Bobby put up his hand. He was fighting a smile.

"Wait, wait. I'll give you one for the road. About the first time I saw Nina."

None of the girls moved. Then Nina smiled cautiously.

"Freshman year, you were showing this really sad girl around—giving her a tour of the school, in Spanish. She was crying really hard, and you were being so nice to her."

There was a loaded pause, and then the girls completely freaked out. Yrma turned and started to walk away. Nina covered her eyes with her hand and shook her head. Kara leaned into the nearest locker, head resting on her forearm like it was all too much.

"What?" Bobby asked. "What'd I say?"

He looked to Tucker for help, but Tucker had no idea what was happening. Then Yrma turned sharply on her heel and came back to them.

"THAT WAS ME, BOBBY. The really sad girl was me. That's how I met Nina. I had just moved here from El Salvador."

Bobby was adamantly shaking his head.

"Nope. Don't believe it. There's no way you ever cried at school."

Yrma did her best to look mad while Bobby kept voicing his doubts, and then he was joking with her, apologizing while she forgave him. Nina watched Bobby the whole time, and when everything had subsided, she leaned toward him.

"Did you hear from Maryland yet?"

"No, not yet. You?"

"No."

Standing on the sidelines of it all, Tucker was struck by a

feeling that Bobby was going to be fine when he got to college. Totally fine.

As for himself, Tucker still wasn't sure. He worried that Michigan was too big and too far away. He worried that his roommate would be some bro and they'd hate each other. He worried that he'd end up having sex again when he maybe still wasn't ready for it . . .

Tucker hated worrying so much, when it seemed like everybody else couldn't wait to finish senior year. He wanted some way to quiet all this college anxiety for good, and he was looking at this weekend like kind of a test run, a way to prove to himself that he would be okay in the fall, that he was ready. Trying to have a mature conversation with Erika about what was going on with them—that was part of it. He wanted to feel like he was moving toward next year with a clear head.

As for his dad—he had time to deal with that.

Tucker and Bobby were quiet as they left through the big double doors, spilling out with the crowd of kids, weaving their way to Tucker's mom's car. It always took forever to get out of the parking lot with everybody leaving at once, so Tucker didn't try to rush. He settled in and turned on the music, loading the directions in his phone.

When he finally spoke again, he tried to keep his voice neutral.

"That would be cool. If you and Nina both went to Maryland."

"Shut up."

"You know I love Destiny, but she's probably going to end up in Atlanta like her sister, right? I'm thinking there's a long game here . . ."

"Seriously shut up and give me your phone. Your mom made me swear I would hold it and not let you text while you were driving. She doesn't trust that app."

Tucker laughed and handed the phone over. Bobby started to put it away, but then it beeped.

"Um, you have a weird text from Frank?"

"What does it say?"

"It says: *I got nervous that you might need some gum, so I put some gum in your backpack. I didn't get a chance to ask your mom first, but I'll definitely have to tell her, so that should be interesting.*"

Tucker and Bobby stared at each other, and then Tucker grabbed his backpack from the seat behind him. He dug around until he found a plastic bag from CVS. He opened it, then blinked several times at the box of condoms.

He showed it to Bobby.

"Frank is such a stud," Bobby said.

"Never say that again."

Bobby couldn't stop laughing, and Tucker was trying to laugh, too, but really he was thinking that even Frank expected more of him than he could deliver.

Taking a deep breath, Tucker did his best to ready himself for the road ahead.

# 24

## ERIKA

"I owe you big for this," Erika said. "So big."

"*You* owe *me*?" Salma asked. "I'm getting free coffee, free pastries, and free drama. You owe me nothing."

"Oh my god, there's not going to be drama. This is probably going to be boring as hell."

"Chem classes are boring as hell. Listening to you and my boyfriend talk about *Game of Thrones* is boring as hell. Sitting next to you when you meet your dad's pregnant fiancée for the first time is the opposite of boring as hell."

Erika sank down in the booth, looking nervously around, as if she could have somehow missed her dad walking in with a woman who was ready to pop.

"I can't believe they're driving out here to sit in a stupid coffee shop," Erika said.

"Well, you're the one who told them dinner was off the table."

"Tucker is going to be here by dinner. I don't need those worlds colliding."

She looked over at Salma, who had a wicked smile on her face.

"I hate you," Erika said.

"Can I see his picture again?"

"NO! I told you, it's not like that."

"Then why do you seem all weird and nervous?"

Erika drummed her fingers and didn't know how to answer. Last week, when he'd asked about coming, she'd said yes right away. She was dying to see him. She wanted to show him how happy she was, how she was finally building a nice life here at school. And she wanted to support him, while he dealt with all that was going on with his dad.

And maybe he needed her to hold him. Maybe other things would happen if she did.

That idea still made Erika nervous, because of how much she liked him and how vulnerable that made her feel. She told Salma pretty much everything these days, but when she tried to talk about her feelings for Tucker, the words got trapped in her throat.

What if this weekend didn't go well? Better to fail in privacy, not have all of her friends cooing over her, asking if she was okay.

"To be clear," Salma said, her voice suspicious, "when he

meets Jacob, you think that will be cool?"

Erika started gnawing on her thumbnail, inwardly cursing Salma for bringing up the one thing Erika did not want to think about.

"I told Jacob I was busy, because I had friends visiting. I'm not going to see him."

Salma paused. "That's . . . quite interesting."

"Jacob and I are *not a couple*. We've been very explicit about that. He's graduating in May, so we're not anything serious. You know that."

"But he has a pet name for you."

"Oscar the Grouch is not a pet name! It's just . . . an apt description."

"I thought he made a point of telling you that he's not hooking up with anyone else?"

Indeed he had, a couple weeks ago. And Erika had casually added that she wasn't either.

As she was starting to feel particularly grumpy and under-caffeinated—her thumb chewed down to the quick—the bell on the door jingled. In came her dad and Jennifer. He had his polo tucked into his jeans, and she was in a dress with leggings and boots, her stomach an enormous arch, her big, curly hair shining. Erika watched her gaze scuttle nervously around, but her dad spotted her first, waving curtly, businesslike. Jennifer finally saw her then, and her eyes went wide and a little wet, and *oh my god*.

The woman was terrified. Absolutely terrified.

She shuffled Erika's way and was smiling so big, the corners of her mouth twitching. Erika stood up, feeling overly formal as she did, and Jennifer came right for her and wrapped her in a hug, the baby straining there between them.

"Oh, it's so nice to finally meet you. Oh, gosh. You must have much better things to do on a Friday."

Jennifer seemed to be breathing heavily, but maybe that was a normal pregnant thing.

"I'm so sorry," she added.

Theoretically those words referred to being a buzzkill, but they seemed a little too heavy for just that, the way she'd said them. Erika and Jennifer hadn't let go of each other yet, and Jesus, it didn't take much—did it? Erika went completely soft. She kind of wanted to tell her dad to fuck off, and Jennifer could hang out with her and Salma.

Instead she hugged Jennifer's shoulders a little tighter. She thought about telling her that no one around here parties this early anyway, but there was zero chance of her saying that in front of her dad. Zero.

"It's fine," Erika said, more stiffly than she wanted. "Don't worry about it."

Jennifer let her go, and her dad came in for a briefer hug. Was he nervous, too? He seemed a little nervous. He mumbled *you look good, you look good* in a casual way, but his eyes were casing the room suspiciously. As he did, Erika remembered that the last couple times they'd gotten together in DC, she'd picked weird hipster places to make him uncomfortable, and now she felt mortified.

*I'm not a brat anymore. I'm not a screw-up. I'm a college*

*student with good grades and nice friends, and I'm in charge of a whole floor full of girls.*

She introduced them to Salma, and then her dad was asking what everyone wanted and heading to the counter to order. Jennifer carefully lowered herself into her chair, staring at the girls perched across from her in the booth.

"Whew, I feel like such a mess. Can you believe I'm teaching high schoolers about contraception and STDs while I look like this? Yikes! Although in a weird way, it might be helping? I swear the girls look increasingly terrified, the bigger I get."

Okay, that was actually kind of hilarious, but Erika could barely manage a smile because she was still feeling too awkward, too uptight. Luckily, Salma did her duty and came to the rescue.

"That dress is from Target, right? I accidentally took it to the dressing room the other day. I didn't realize it was from the maternity section. It's really cute."

Jennifer laughed then, and—thank god—no longer looked like she was going to cry. She started talking about Target, Salma chiming in, while Erika sat there tensely. *Why aren't you talking?* Erika liked Target. Who didn't like Target? It was the world's best neutral ground. The last time she was there, though, she'd bought lip gloss and underwear and tampons, and every single one of those things seemed suddenly obscene and unspeakable, which she knew was ridiculous.

An incoming text beeped on Erika's phone, and she nervously checked it, afraid that somehow Tucker was already here, but no. It was Jacob, sending her some silly meme.

"Everything okay?" Salma asked.

Erika jumped a little, then said it was nothing, putting her phone back in her pocket and doing her best to tune back into the conversation without staring at Jennifer's stomach. Meanwhile, Salma—blessed, perfect Salma—was asking about baby names now.

"We haven't really told anyone, what names we're thinking. Paul doesn't want to because he says it's nobody's business, but I'm actually too afraid to say them out loud until the baby is, you know. Here and healthy. I know that sounds stupid and superstitious."

But it didn't, not to Erika. She thought it sounded perfectly sane. *Despite historical evidence to the contrary, I am a cautious creature, Jennifer. I completely understand.*

Jennifer drummed her fingers on the table. "I'm almost forty, so the risks are a little higher . . . I don't know why I'm talking about this, sorry! Anyway, I would tell you about the names, if you wanted to know. Of course I would tell you."

Jennifer was looking right at Erika, who swallowed and glanced anxiously around. Where was the goddamn coffee?

"Oh, no worries," she finally said. "You don't have to."

Erika didn't want to put any pressure on her—that's why she'd said that—but it came out like she didn't care. Now Jennifer was nodding too much and Erika's dad was back and complaining about something he'd ordered, and why, why, why was Erika doing this again? Why did she think this was worth a try?

Because Tucker had convinced her that it was. She'd asked

him if she should agree to this, and he'd said of course.

*You would be a great big sister.*

She'd wanted so badly to believe that was true.

Salma diligently continued to fill the air with chatter, talking now about Will, how long they'd been together. Jennifer looked over at Erika and smiled.

"Are you seeing anybody?" she asked.

Erika shook her head, not daring to look at her dad's face, turning her eyes down to her mug instead. Chugging her coffee, she let her eyes drift to the clock in the corner, counting the hours until Tucker would be here.

# 25

## TUCKER

Tucker's entire being shifted into a new gear the moment they stepped on campus. It was mild for early March, a tease of spring in the air, and everything was how he'd pictured it, exactly like it looked from Erika's Instagram. Green expanse and stately brick. All these kids deep in conversation as they walked to who knows where. Tucker couldn't quite see the Bay, but he could smell it—brackish and choppy, full of crabs and jellyfish.

"This place is cool," Bobby said. "I could never go somewhere this small, but I like it."

"I know," Tucker said. "Me too."

"You're a hundred percent going to Michigan, right?"

Tucker took a breath. "Like ninety percent. I'm almost totally sure."

Bobby stopped to look at a campus map and adjusted their course, leading them down a brick pathway.

"So . . . are we going to see your dad?"

Tucker watched kids pouring up the steps that led to the cafeteria, shouting and laughing. Ready for the weekend.

"I don't want to go. I don't think we should go."

"It's up to you. I'm just asking."

"Let's forget it and have fun this weekend. It's fine."

Bobby nodded and changed the subject to baseball, their last season together. Tucker chimed in here and there as they made their way to Erika's dorm, passing through a tunnel that ran beneath the humanities building. There was a long line of bulletin boards, and Tucker took in the flyers for a cappella concerts, poli-sci seminars, flag football.

There was a bright pink sheet of paper that said "YES, YES, YES" in enormous letters, and then underneath, in smaller type, "Consent is sexy."

There was also a notice about an upcoming meeting of the Social Justice Society, with a note about discussing the campus assault. The news had just come, Tucker knew, that there would be a trial in a couple of months. He and Erika texted about it all the time.

As the boys were about to emerge from underground and back into the sun, Bobby called over to Tucker.

"Here comes Erika."

He looked up and there she was, jogging toward him in her boots and little leather jacket, with a girl he recognized from her photos as Salma.

Tucker got a rush, seeing her again, but he was nervous, too. He'd thought a lot about this moment, about how he should say hello . . .

He didn't have to do a thing. Erika fell into his arms and hugged him for dear life.

"How was everything with your dad?" he asked, saying it quietly into her ear.

"Awkward but not torture, I guess. How's everything with your dad?"

Tucker paused, unsure how she was going to interpret the fact that half the reason for this trip was suddenly gone. But then he plunged forward.

"I don't think I'm going to go."

"I totally get it," she said. "We can talk about it later."

Her breath tickled the skin on his neck, a feeling that made its way down his whole body. She finally released him, and then she went to hug Bobby. At the same time, Salma stepped toward him, introducing herself.

"C'mon," he said. "I know who you are."

She nodded, pressed her lips together. "Ditto."

Now the four of them were standing in a circle. Erika was explaining that Tucker and Bobby would crash two floors up from her, in Salma's room, since Salma would be staying with her boyfriend, Will, that night.

"It's a single," Salma said, "so my apologies. One of you will be stuck on the crappy air mattress, which is definitely going to deflate."

Without discussing it, Bobby and Tucker turned to each

other and did Rock, Paper, Scissors. Bobby won, and Tucker cursed under his breath, though even as he did, some part of him wondered if there was a chance he was going to need the air mattress at all.

Erika shushed the two of them and put her hands up dramatically.

"Forget sleeping, all right? Who cares about sleeping? We need to start our fairy-tale college weekend that I've planned just for you jerks. First, we drop your shit off, then we'll get you some gross pizza from the only place that delivers to this forsaken wasteland, and then—THEN—we'll take a boat ride to a stupid, overthought theme party."

Erika looked at Tucker expectantly. "Sound good?"

"Magic," Tucker said, smiling. "It sounds totally magic."

"I fully realize that I look like an asshole," Will said. "For having a boat. But people buy boats all the time and then don't want them, so you can get them for practically nothing, especially if you know how to fix them. And the school has a dock, and they rent space super cheap . . ."

As Salma unlooped the rope that kept them tethered to the shore, Erika grabbed a spot on the two-seater bench closest to the bow. Tucker followed her, settling carefully and quietly into the seat on her left. It had been ages since he'd been on a boat, and already he loved the feeling it was giving him—something about the gentle rocking, the view. He was suddenly looser, freer.

Erika turned to him, her mouth twitching into a smile. "So what do you think of St. B's?"

Before he answered, he watched her, backlit by the setting sun.

"It's beautiful. I love it. Seriously, I do."

She started pointing out things she wanted him to see. The bright collection of boats that belonged to the school's sailing team. A house on a distant cliff that she fantasized about living in. The crumbling lighthouse that the town and St. B's were trying to come together to save.

"So . . . do we ride this home in the dark?" Tucker asked.

"Oh hell no," Erika said. "Will doesn't drink and boat. It'll be a mile or so walk back to campus, so not too bad. It actually takes way longer on this thing, it's just a lot prettier. You'll be on a lake next year, right?"

"Not right on it or anything, but it's not that far from campus. I'll go visit it for sure. Then we can pretend we're looking toward each other."

"Definitely. I'll wave to you and everything."

"I'll wave back. That will be a great way to make new friends. By being the weird guy who waves at lakes."

She laughed and elbowed him. Their shoulders were touching now.

"Okay!" Will called. "I'm gunning it. Is everybody ready?"

Salma clapped and cheered. As soon as Bobby took a seat, Will revved the engine. And then they were off, slicing their way into the Bay, flying, flying.

Away from the shore.

Away from everything.

Away, away, away . . .

Tucker hunched against the cold, taking the spray against his face and laughing at nothing, at just the speed and the sun and the bounce that came as they met each wave. Bump and splash, bump and splash.

The day no longer felt so mild when they were out there being beaten down by the wind, and Salma opened the trunk and took out a couple blankets. Will and Bobby said they were fine, so she kept one for herself, tossed the other to Erika.

Erika spread it over her lap and then stretched it out in Tucker's direction. He slid over as close as he could get, the two of them warming each other under the wool. They passed the lighthouse, both of them looking up at its impossible height and its dying façade, bricks cracked and falling.

"How long until we get there?" he asked.

"Not long. Ten minutes. You aren't seasick, are you?"

"No, no," Tucker said. "Not at all. I was kind of hoping it was going to take longer."

Erika elbowed him again. "Right? I'm so excited to finally show off this damn boat to somebody."

"You still haven't asked Marissa to come for a weekend?"

The wind was howling in their ears now, and Erika had to lean her face right next to his so that she could be heard.

"Not yet. Things are still weird. I mean, we 'made up' or whatever, but I feel like we barely ever talk."

"That's why you need to invite her, so she can enjoy the boats and booze. Boats and booze fix everything."

"Yeah, yeah. Maybe. And listen—I'm really glad that you're here. If you're not going to see your dad or whatever . . . I'm happy you still decided to come."

She was looking right at him now, and her eyes were impossibly bright.

"I'm happy, too," he said. "I'm happy to see where you live. And . . . mostly I'm happy to see you."

Tucker hadn't meant to come on quite so strong, certainly not this early, but the sun and the wind and the speed—all of it was making him feel a little reckless.

They hit a whitecap, and the boat launched high into the air, crashing back down and tossing them together.

His arms were around her; his lips felt dangerously close to her ear.

He waited for her to pull away, but she didn't.

"Got you," he said quietly.

The boat kept flying forward, and he wondered if she'd heard him, or if she was ignoring him maybe—but then she rested her head on his shoulder.

"Got you, too."

# 26

## ERIKA

Will docked the boat near what were known as the Half-Way Houses—a small cluster of rundown townhomes occupied almost entirely by St. B's upperclassmen, who were desperate to get off the main campus.

Erika knew they'd be early, since Will wanted to catch the tail end of daylight for the boat ride, so they'd come prepared. They spread the blankets out on the dock and made themselves comfortable while Salma passed out beers from the cooler. She and Will started taking turns telling their most ridiculous college stories, the worst of their drunken shenanigans—some of which now included Erika.

Listening to them, Erika couldn't believe she'd been here almost two years, that so much of her time here was gone. She'd wasted some of it—she knew that—but she was so ready to make the most of what she had left.

Bobby had discovered that Will was a math major, and they were entering some almost-impossible-to-understand discussion about that, while Salma loudly begged them to stop. Tucker seemed like he might be lost in thought, but now Will was handing him another beer and trying to pull him back in.

"Do you know what you're going to study? Obviously you don't have to know, and obviously this is an incredibly boring conversation, so no need to answer."

Tucker took a drink of his beer, then put it down and leaned back on his hands.

"I think I want to do elementary ed."

"Oh wow, that's cool," Will said. "I remember every single one of my teachers from elementary school. Mrs. Garcia was my favorite—first grade. She was very supportive when I was going through this weird phase where I would rip off my shirt and try to escape over the fence during recess."

"*What?*" Salma said. "Please tell me you're joking."

"We had just moved for the third time! I was going through some shit."

"Uh, that's fine, but if you were going to run away, why would you want to be half-naked?"

Bobby broke in with a story about him and Tucker getting in trouble on the playground, and with Will and Salma busy laughing at that, Erika scooted closer to Tucker.

She poked him in the knee.

"I didn't know you wanted to be an elementary school teacher."

Tucker was smiling down at his beer, fiddling with the tab.

"Yeah, I don't know. It's something I just started thinking about, but I've never actually said it out loud. To anybody."

"Really?"

"I thought I'd give it a try and see how it felt."

Erika poked his knee again, more gently this time. "So how did it feel?"

He quit messing with the can and smiled at her.

"Good. It felt good."

Erika was suddenly so happy. Maybe it was silly, but she got a little flush of pride, knowing that she'd created the moment for him to say something important out loud. Wasn't this proof, that there was something between them?

She leaned toward him, took her voice down low.

"So when I was at my therapy session today, Elisabeth had an idea for me."

"What's the idea?"

"She wants me to apply to this women's leadership program? It's at Smith College, in Massachusetts, this summer. She thinks maybe St. B's would fund me to go. I would never think to apply for something like that, but if the lady I cry in front of on a regular basis thinks I can do it, then maybe I should give it a shot, right?"

She looked up, and he was watching her, his eyes wide.

"That sounds incredible. You'd be perfect for that. It's . . . is it *all* summer?"

"Pretty much, yeah. That part's not so great."

Erika hadn't really had time to process the whole idea, but

hearing Tucker get excited about something had made her want to be excited about something, too. And now here they were, the tips of their shoes touching while the last of the day's light sank down into the Bay. She'd been so worried about him, about everything with his dad, but now it seemed better not to ask. Why should he go, if he didn't want to?

He deserved to have fun this weekend. They both did.

Erika crawled over to the cooler and grabbed two more cans, then came back and gave one of them to Tucker.

"So what's up with this party tonight?" he asked. "We have a pretty good track record, when it comes to parties."

Salma leaned over, purposefully invading Tucker's space and their conversation.

"Wait, Erika didn't mention that she's taking you to prom?"

"Um, no," Tucker said, laughing. "She definitely did not."

He looked at her, waiting for an explanation, and now Erika was the one fiddling with the tab on her can.

"Tonight's this goofy fake prom thing, in three connected houses over there. Like, girls can wear a fancy dress if they want to, and some guys are buying ugly thrift-store suits or whatever. There's going to be different music in each one. Nineties, Aughts, and Now."

"Uh, was I supposed to bring something to wear?" Tucker asked.

"No, no," Salma said. "Half the people don't really participate in this kind of thing. Will is wearing normal clothes."

"I guess you're not participating?" Tucker asked Erika.

He said it like it was a joke, because right now she had on jeans and a sweater. Embarrassed, Erika shrugged.

"Salma and I dropped our clothes off yesterday, on our way back from the thrift store. I'm going to change inside."

"Oh! I wasn't messing with you, I swear. I just didn't know."

Erika finished her beer, set the can down carefully, and stared at it.

"I like dressing up, you know? And I never went to my real prom, since I was kind of a walking PSA. Not the girl to take pictures with in front of your mom."

She'd said it lightly, but now Tucker's eyes were brimming with something she couldn't quite identify. He broke their mutual gaze, looking over at Salma.

"My mom loves Erika."

Now Erika's cheeks were flaming, while she mumbled that Tucker was being ridiculous. But it was true, wasn't it? Every time Erika had been to Tucker's house over break, Janet had fussed over her.

Meanwhile, Salma's eyebrows were sky-high.

"Perfect, then. We'll take a picture of you two tonight, and then both your moms will have something for their fridge."

Erika's face had not calmed down. It was still on fire. Her fear of getting close to Tucker—it was still there. But as she drank her beer, as she looked over at the houses and thought about the party, she was starting to get very tired of being so damn cautious.

# 21

# TUCKER

Salma said they'd go to the Nineties house first, since it belonged to their friends Grace and Hailey, and since their thrift store bags were waiting there. She and Erika walked in without knocking, entering a room where all the blinds were closed and a cheap strobe light was flashing, streamers and balloons hung haphazardly in a joyful, if half-assed, joke. A bowl of slightly scary-looking punch sat next to boxes of wine.

Snoop Dogg was playing, and a few people were starting to dance, but most people were just talking, lingering, drinking. Erika went upstairs to get changed, while Tucker and Bobby hung out on the perimeter, taking everything in.

Why did it feel so different from a high school party? It was something about the proudly ratty furniture, the utility and water bills tacked on a board by the door. The whole place had an alien energy, a vibe of both carelessness and ownership. It seemed impossible to Tucker, that this would be his life soon.

"Do you think this is what it will be like for us next year?" Bobby asked. "Or do you think big schools are totally different?"

"I don't know," Tucker said. "I'm still having trouble picturing it all."

Bobby started talking about what his cousin had told him about UVA, but he stopped suddenly, gave Tucker a little punch on the shoulder.

"You know what I just realized? This is our first college party. We're at our first college party together."

That made Tucker smile. "You're right! Wow."

Just as Tucker was going to add that they should go get another drink, maybe do a toast, Erika walked down the stairs.

She was wearing a sequined dress. Silver and loose, it hung from her shoulders and stopped at her knees. When she got to the first floor, Grace and Hailey came over to *ooh* and *ahh*. She held the skirt out for them to examine, letting their fingers test the material's shiny intricacy.

"Okay. Three to one," Bobby said. "That's Destiny's current prediction."

"What?"

Bobby held up his phone. "Destiny's been requesting updates, on your little situation here. We're doing odds on whether you'll actually be staying with me, in Salma's room. Right now, Destiny says it's three to one."

"You guys are the worst. I'm seriously not eating lunch with you anymore." Tucker's eyes flicked over to Erika again. "Wait—three to one in my favor or against?"

"In your favor, of course. But tell me more about how you and Erika are just friends."

Bobby had a smartass look on his face now, and Tucker tried his best to act pissed, but he was having trouble pulling it off. He was kind of delighted that Destiny had so much confidence in him.

He needed that right now.

Tucker had thought that he and Erika would have the whole summer to see what might happen. If they didn't, that put a lot more pressure on him to make something out of this weekend, to make something out of tonight. But he could do it, couldn't he? Already, this whole experiment was going well. He loved being on campus. He loved Erika's friends, and he loved having Bobby with him, too. He was talking about next year in a way that felt honest, hopeful.

Tucker looked out at the dance floor, which was now officially rumbling to a start. He was a little surprised to see Erika already in the thick of things with Salma and Grace and Hailey, all of them very dedicated to doing the Macarena.

He tried not to be too obvious about watching her, but god she was cute when she got like this. And of course she would like to line dance—it was the same side of her that liked Christmas—and he loved seeing her that way, when she could just be silly.

Wasn't that what was so great about the two of them? That they brought that out in each other?

Tucker took stock of himself, trying to figure out if he had it in him right now, to do the Macarena.

He definitely did not.

"Hey, look," Bobby said, grinning. "A big-ass coffee table."

Tucker glared at Bobby. "That's a strong no right now."

Bobby snickered, then repeated the words *right now*.

# 28

## ERIKA

When the Nineties house became unbearably crowded, they moved to the Aughts house, which belonged to boys and was more dilapidated and less decorated than the last. Erika was already a sweaty mess, but it was one of those nights like a wedding or a real prom where you couldn't help it, where everyone was a sweaty mess and nobody cared. Erika had only had one drink since the dock, but she was buzzing anyway because tonight was feeling like the pinnacle of all the work she'd done to put herself out there, to make friends, to have fun again.

Maybe it was a little silly, to describe that as *work*, but that's what it had been like, getting to this point. Now "Paper Planes" was playing, and she was dancing like a dork, not caring who was watching, surrounded by girls she cared about and who cared about her.

"Oh my god," Hailey said. "Look at the boys, over there by the wall. They're still in boy mode, where they can't quite cut loose yet."

"Don't you feel bad for them?" Salma asked. "Being all bottled up like that, putting on an act all the time. What a sad, sad way to live."

"Pathetic," said Grace, who managed to keep dancing while also fixing her hair. "And to be clear, Tucker's friend is taken? Because I'm not above cradle robbing."

Erika scoffed. "Oh my god! Two years is hardly cradle robbing."

The defensiveness in her voice was so painfully obvious—all three of the girls turned to look at her, grinning. Then Salma burst out laughing.

"Shut up," Erika said. "You're all the worst, and I wish I never met you."

Now they were all cackling, but it was with warmth, with love, and Erika felt the last bit of armor she'd been wearing around them fall off.

"Fuck, I really like him," Erika said. "I don't know what to do. He lives two hours away! He's in high school! He's about to leave for freaking Michigan! I haven't told him about Jacob!"

"That's a bit of a hot mess, no doubt," Salma said. "But so is the two of you pretending like you're just good buddies."

Hailey poked her in the arm. "Look, whatever happens, I totally give you permission to grind on him on the dance floor. I mean, you're only human. Also, this is slightly drunk me talking, so take my advice at your own risk."

"Speaking of being only human," Grace said, "M. I. A. is on, and I cannot listen to this song without smoking a joint. Who wants to come outside?"

Salma and Hailey said they were in, but Erika felt too keyed up and said no thanks.

As the girls walked away, Erika took a breath and headed Tucker's way.

"This party isn't too stupid, is it?"

"What? No! Erika, this is so great. Seriously."

He was still windswept from the boat, and she had an urge to run her hands through his hair. Somewhere in the back of her mind, she could hear Marissa's voice saying the word "yummy."

"You're not dancing," she said. "So I wanted to make sure you're having fun."

"I am, I am." Tucker reached out and tugged very gently on her sleeve. "This is nice."

She scowled at him. "Don't make fun of my dress."

"Why would I make fun of your dress?"

"I know it's a little ridiculous. Sometimes I like to wear ridiculous things. So don't make fun of me."

Very slowly, a smile took over Tucker's face.

"Is this about the Christmas tights? I think we had a misunderstanding that night. I really liked the tights."

Erika's heart started going fast-fast-fast. Tucker was watching her, and she knew she needed to say something, but it was too dark, the music was too loud, she was starting to sweat.

And then "Single Ladies" burst out of the speaker.

All over the house there was shouting, cheering, to the point that Erika covered her ears with her hands and Tucker followed suit, the two of them looking into each other's eyes and laughing. Right away, people started rushing the dance floor, and it filled up so fast that everyone had to start dancing wherever they were. Tables were moved, rugs shoved out of the way, heels kicked off. The cheap laminate floor was shaking under their feet, and then someone emerged from the kitchen with a tray of Jell-O shots.

This was it, right? The moment when the night officially took a turn, when the party-that-was-going-to-be-just-okay got kicked up a notch, and there was no turning back.

Tucker shifted toward her an inch.

"I know a good portion of the routine from this video," he said, "but I don't really want to explain why."

She looked up at him, lips pursed.

"Frankly, I would only want an explanation if you *didn't* know the moves from this video." She put her hands on her hips and looked at him pointedly. "So where are they?"

"Where are they?"

"The moves from this video."

Tucker pulled back then, laughing and shaking his head.

"Uh, I'm not quite there yet."

"But it's my prom, Tucker. MY ONLY PROM."

She was sure that would do it, but no. His eyes drifted to a far wall, and he crossed his arms.

Erika took a step back, feeling embarrassed. Had she read him totally wrong? She mumbled that she needed to find her friends and turned to go, but then he reached out and grabbed her elbow.

"Erika, hang on! Don't walk away."

She looked up at him, waiting. They were hovering right on the edge, weren't they? Tucker took a deep breath.

"It's not that I don't want to, it's just . . . I used to like dancing—not because I was good at it, but because I liked goofing around or whatever. But then it seemed like girls were always saying it was 'cute' or people were laughing at me, I don't know. I can't seem to do it anymore."

His face was so open right now; it made her chest go tight. She was touched he'd felt comfortable saying that to her, but also he was getting self-conscious. He was in danger of turning back into the kid who didn't want to be a puppy dog, a Hufflepuff.

She couldn't let that happen. Getting him on the dance floor right now was a chivalrous act of duty.

"Tucker, you know being goofy is the best part about you, not the worst. You know that, right?"

He didn't say anything. Erika reached out and tugged on the bottom of his shirt.

"Look, if we go dance, it won't be cute. It will be the opposite of cute, like borderline offensive. If there are any baby animals in the vicinity, they'll die if they look at us."

Tucker didn't say a word, didn't move a millimeter. A gulf of quiet opened between them, and as Erika was about to collapse on the floor, dead from mortification, he spoke.

"I need to get a Jell-O shot. And then I'll come find you."

Erika managed to carve out a modicum of space on the dance floor by pushing a much-abused armchair farther into the corner. It wasn't much room, but they wouldn't need much, would they? Not the way they were planning on dancing.

Some part of Erika's brain was trying to whisper to her, about how getting close to him like this was scary, but screw that part of her brain. A bigger part of her wondered if she had it in her to kiss him in the middle of all these people . . .

Probably no on that last point. Erika was light-years better than she'd been back at the beginning of the year, but sucking face in the middle of a crowd was still out of her current comfort zone.

And then someone was right behind her, talking into her ear.

"Hey, there. You look very sparkly tonight."

Erika jumped, even though she knew the voice. Of course she knew the voice.

She whirled around, eyes wide.

"Jacob, shit. I mean, hi. I didn't know you were going to be here."

"I didn't know *you* were going to be here. How, uh, how's

your weekend going with your friends?"

He was smiling, but she could still see it all over his face, how much she had hurt his feelings, and all in an instant she felt like an absolute and total piece of garbage.

What was wrong with her? She'd essentially told Jacob that she was going to be hanging out with people she liked, so he should stay away.

"It's good. It's been nice, so far. Just standard college fun times."

Okay, she was clearly unable to form meaningful words. She needed to escape this situation as quickly as possible. *Fuck, fuck, fuck.*

"Did you finish your Yeats essay?" he asked. "I was sending all my good vibes your way. Fifteen pages is no joke."

"Yeah, yeah. It's done. Must have been the good vibes for sure."

Ugh, why was he so nice? Ditching him would be infinitely easier if he would say something dumb or obnoxious. Erika's eyes were jumping around, both desperate and afraid to find Tucker. She considered a trip to the cooler, to the bathroom, anything. As she was about to make a run for it, "Single Ladies" ended. In its wake, she heard the opening strains of that goddamn Adele song—the impossibly sad one.

"One dance?" Jacob asked. "Just if you want to. It's cool if you don't want to."

His hands were in his pockets, he was smiling down at her, and Erika was officially a walking pile of shame. Yes, this thing with Jacob had a shelf life, but he'd been sweet and kind when she'd very much needed sweet and kind, and had she ever told him that? She'd never tried, not even a little.

"Of course," Erika said, swallowing hard. "Let's dance."

She moved toward him first, and then they were holding each other—close, but not too close—swaying gently. Erika kept her eyes on the ground, and as she stared at the stained rug and Jacob's tacky sneakers, she told herself that everything was fine. The night was still in her control, wasn't it? She and Jacob were having a nice little moment, and he would probably go to one of the other houses any minute. He'd be gone from her life for good in a matter of weeks. There was absolutely no reason for Tucker to know a thing about him.

Yes, she could have handled all this better, and right this second, things were a bit of a mess, but what could she do? It's like Hailey said: Erika was *only human, only human, only human.*

Adele was ending, and over Jacob's shoulder Erika could see Salma looking at her, both amused and confused. She was also gesturing to the door, to the next party.

It was almost time to move on.

# 29

## TUCKER

Tucker watched as that guy, whoever he was, let go of Erika. He did it slowly, his hands seeming to linger.

Tucker told himself to relax, not to be some psycho, possessive creep, staring at her while she had a friendly slow dance with some kid who she probably knew from class or whatever.

Still, Tucker's heart was puddled down at his feet.

When they'd been out of Jell-O shots by the time he'd gotten over there, he'd decided that he didn't need one, that he could dance without the extra courage. But then Adele had come on, and he'd never gotten a chance.

Tucker felt a hand on his shoulder. Bobby was standing behind him.

"Destiny wants updates. She's dying."

Tucker wanted very much to be annoyed, but the truth was,

he could use some help. He sighed loudly, waiting for Bobby to get his phone out and his thumbs ready.

"We literally made a weird promise to dance all over each other, but then she slow-danced with some other guy instead."

"Which guy?"

"The one in the hat."

"Whatever—he's walking away. She's not even watching him go. It's all good."

And it was, right? Everything was fine, it was going to be fine. Who cared about that guy?

*You need to chill and stop freaking out.*

Bobby's phone dinged.

"Destiny's not worried."

"Really?"

"Yeah, yeah. She thinks you're still on track. Now she's saying nice shit about you . . . Blah, blah, blah—you can read it. This is seriously her worst quality, how much she likes you."

Tucker gathered himself, then looked out at the dance floor. Salma and the other girls had returned, and Tucker had to move a little to the left, to get a better view of Erika—her hips swinging, her flushed cheeks and sweaty hair.

He watched the sequins of her dress, the way they took in and gave back the light.

"I'm not trying to just make out with her or whatever. I really like her. Way more than I've ever liked anybody."

Bobby stared at him, then wrote another text. They waited, waited, waited.

*Ping.*

"Destiny says that if you actually tell Erika that, your odds will go through the roof."

Tucker took a deep breath.

"I'm almost ready. I need a few more minutes. Maybe one more beer."

Bobby gestured out at the room. "Well, we've got plenty of minutes, tons of beer. And music, lots of loud-ass music."

Tucker nodded, thinking that, in fact, that last part might be what would officially push them over the edge. A song would come on, and it would have the perfect chords, a magic melody.

It would remind them how beautiful life could be.

Finally they made it to the Now house.

The hour was growing late, but the crowd was still thick. The boy and two girls who lived here had cleared out all the furniture, and they had a better sound system and a keg. On the living room wall was a big Harry Potter poster labeled with the names of which roommate went with which character, and Tucker was thinking how important it was to find people who knew who you were and loved you for it.

Taylor Swift was playing, and of course that meant Erika was on the dance floor, jumping up and down. Lots of people were jumping up and down—it had reached that point in the evening when everyone was letting go.

Tucker loved parties.

He suddenly knew that, in some deep part of his soul. He loved nights that were full of the unknown, all that possibility. He loved music and staying up late and making people laugh.

Most of all, he loved having a story to tell the next day.

Tonight would be a story worth telling, wouldn't it?

Maybe he could try talking to her, right here and right now. He should tell her how he felt. Despite the heat and the chaos and the noise, that was the best way.

Tucker looked back to where he'd seen her, then realized she had left the dance floor and was digging through her purse. She covered her lips in shiny, pink gloss, then ran a finger delicately around them.

*Okay, fuck talking, fuck the best way. Just go.*

Erika started walking toward the dance floor, and Tucker cut in from the other side, dodging his way through the horde. He was following the flash of her dress, and right before he reached her, *that* song came on—the one that was completely inescapable right now. It played on the radio every hour, in the background of three different commercials. There were endless videos on YouTube of people singing it in their cars, and Tucker had definitely caught Frank humming it the other day while he did the dishes.

> *When you see the screen glow—you know.*
> *I'm checking on you late night,*
> *Not to fight, thought we might,*
> *. . . You know.*

As the first verse blasted from the speakers, fake prom hit a whole new level, the dance floor a mass of tangled bodies.

In the middle of it, Tucker found Erika.

They stood facing each other. She looked happy but nervous, and Tucker knew that he probably did, too.

He also knew exactly what to say.

"So, on the surface, it seems like this would *not* be an Erika song, but the secret thing that most people don't understand is that it's actually *such* an Erika song."

Her hands were on her hips and she was making that face— the one where she was pretending to be pissed when she wasn't.

"Oh, really?"

"Yes, really."

She nodded. Her foot started to tap.

"So, it's possible that I have a running mix right now and this is the first song on it *and* the last song. Possibly it also shows up once in the middle."

He nodded. "Well, I happen to love this song, too. So I'm ready when you are."

She ran a hand through her hair, trying to arrange it but just sort of sticking it up in too many directions. A smile was twitching on her lips. "Look, I was being kind of pushy and weird before. About dancing. If you don't want to, it's seriously fine."

"Is *this* seriously fine?"

The coffee table dance—it came back to Tucker like the most natural thing in the world. And as soon as he began, Erika's face transformed.

She was all lit up. She was laughing so hard, her head tipped back and then she was grabbing his hand, pulling him to her. They were right on beat, right on rhythm, legs intertwined.

And yes, it was a silly, seventh-grade type of dancing, but that felt perfect, and it certainly didn't change the fact that his arms were wrapped around Erika's waist, his thighs were touching Erika's thighs.

Someone bumped into them, and they were knocked apart, Erika tripping backward into the couch. He asked if she was okay, but she didn't answer, just stood up and hopped onto the middle cushion.

She put her hand out for him and mouthed *c'mon*.

He let her pull him up, and now they were dancing for everyone, dancing horribly, because it was so hard to stand up there without falling over, but that didn't matter. People all over the room were screaming, and Tucker looked out at their smiling, laughing faces, and then he spotted Bobby in the corner, with his phone out, standing right next to a whiteboard.

He picked up the pen, then slowly wrote something in very large script before quickly erasing it.

*D says 100%*

Erika started to fall, and Tucker reached out and grabbed her, pulling her toward him. She sank into his arms, and the happy music was still going, still washing over them.

"I know it wasn't your real prom," Tucker said, speaking right into her ear, "but was it okay?"

She burrowed farther into his shoulder.

"Perfect," she said. "Just perfect."

# 30

## ERIKA

Erika, Tucker, and Bobby were the only ones going back to her dorm. It was a chilly walk, but Erika smiled the whole way. She couldn't stop thinking about how it felt to dance with Tucker on the couch.

A few times, the memory of Jacob flickered back into her mind, what a close call that was, but then she would bat it away.

It was no big deal, right? Everything was fine.

They boarded the elevator, and Erika pushed three for her floor, five for Salma's. They were silent as they rode up, and then the door opened with a ding.

"Super Smash Brothers?" Erika asked. "My room?"

"Sure," Tucker said.

He got off the elevator and Erika followed—then they

looked back at Bobby.

"I'm good," he said. "Destiny is begging me to call her right now."

Bobby clicked the button to close the elevator, stared up at the ceiling, and then was gone.

*This is it, this is it, this is it, this is it.*

Erika took out her keys, then dropped them. Her lock was finicky, and like always she had to fumble and jiggle for a minute to get it to work.

Tucker was standing very close to her while she did.

"Erika . . . I wanted to say that I'm really glad that we found each other again this year. I feel like I'm happier because we did, you know? Like you helped me figure out some important things."

She paused, the door handle cold in her palm. She stared straight ahead, not daring to look at him.

In that moment, she knew that she'd screwed up.

Erika wanted something with Tucker tonight, but she wanted it to be real. There was no way to have something like that unless she was more honest.

*Impossible. It would be impossible to explain this Tucker.*

But even as Erika had that thought, she knew it wasn't true. She was afraid—afraid that Tucker would be a jerk about it, that he would be judgmental. Worse than that, what if some deep, sad part of her agreed with him? She'd thought she'd moved past all that, and she'd certainly come a long way, just not quite as far as she'd like. The *s*-word was still waiting for her like it always was, a hibernating snake in the back of her mind . . .

But Tucker wouldn't be like that. She was sure that he would understand. She just needed a little bit of time, to get her courage up. To find the right words.

"That's . . . that's really nice, Tucker. Thank you for saying that. I'm Pikachu, all right?"

The hallway felt stuffy. She still hadn't opened the door.

"Of course," he finally said. "Sounds good."

She changed into a pair of pajamas in the bathroom of her suite, with the door firmly closed. She came back out and turned on their game. They both sat on their own corners of the bed, like at Ryan's, except this was a twin, so they weren't quite so far apart this time.

They played one round, and then another, and another. The hour grew late. Tucker took off his shoes to get more comfortable.

When Erika had lost three in a row, she decided that she was done with this little charade.

"So," she said. "Do you think the air mattress is deflated yet?"

"Oh, it deflated before we even left for the party," Tucker said. "But I'm, uh, really tired. I'm sure I'll go right to sleep."

Erika's heart careened. She knew she wanted him to stay. One way or another, this was officially happening.

"Just sleep here. It's fine. You can't sleep on the floor."

"No, no, no. Don't worry about me, seriously . . ."

Erika got up and dug through her drawer, pulled out the biggest T-shirt she had.

"Not your size, I know. But it's at least as big as the one you wore to the party at the Cave," she said, tossing it toward him.

He silently took it and disappeared into the bathroom. While he was gone, she turned out the lights and crawled into bed, trying to slow her pounding heart.

The bathroom door opened a crack.

"Um, do you want me to sleep in my jeans? I mean, I can, it's no problem . . ."

Erika pulled the comforter over her head.

"No, no. Take off your stupid jeans, Tucker. It's fine."

A minute later the door squeaked, and then she felt his weight settling in next to her. He was being careful not to touch her, but she crawled toward him, curling up as small as she could and burying her face in his chest.

He wrapped his arms around her, and she felt warm then, and safe. One of her legs slipped between his.

"Uh, good night," he said. "Hopefully Pikachu worked and we'll fall right to sleep."

She was too nervous to laugh, and now they were quiet, pressed against each other. Decision time was here. Either she could tell Tucker how she felt about him and also what was going on with Jacob, or else she could silence all those thoughts and let go. Have fun.

But try as she might, she could not go with option number

one. It was just too scary. And option number two still didn't feel right.

*Okay, fine. Maybe this* isn't *happening. Fall asleep and then figure it out in the morning. Sleep, sleep, sleep. Sleep, sleep, sleep.*

As she was rolling that word over in her mind, a regular game of hers, an idea came into her head, a completely mad idea.

Her pulse started going harder.

*Oh my god no. Absolutely not. Who even does that?*

But she wanted to. She couldn't think about anything else, with him so close. She shifted up so her mouth was by his ear, because if she was going to suggest this, it was definitely going to be in a whisper.

*You can't say this. How will you even say this?*

But she already knew.

"If Pikachu doesn't work, we could try the other way."

There were goose bumps on his legs—she could feel them.

"I could put myself to sleep," she said. "And you could put yourself to sleep."

There were three long seconds of pure silence, when neither of them moved.

"Really?" Tucker asked.

She didn't answer, and he coughed, let his arms go a little looser.

"Okay," he said.

*Now what, now what, now what, now what.*

"I've never done this with anyone before, so you have to start," Erika said.

"I've never done this with anyone before either, so you *definitely* have to start," Tucker said.

Erika let a giggle escape, then recovered. She thought about doing a countdown or something, but then she decided she needed to just go or she would lose her nerve, so she went, and he went, and they were going, going, going . . .

Tucker was in the bathroom, cleaning up, and Erika's heart hadn't slowed yet—her breath was still coming short and fast. She realized she was scared out of her mind.

She was suddenly convinced that he would come back, announce how weird that was, and leave. Or he'd wait until she was asleep and then text Bobby. *You won't believe what she wanted to do.*

As he walked back into her room, she shut her eyes. He got into bed, pulling her to his chest and sighing into her hair.

Then he started laughing.

"I'm sorry, I'm sorry. That was kind of intense," he said. "That was intense, right?"

Erika laughed, too, the tension inside her uncoiling. She was very ready to fall asleep, and then maybe wake up and do that again in the morning. Except with kissing. She would figure out a way to talk to him, he would totally understand, and then they could do that with kissing, or maybe do other things with kissing . . .

Then Erika's phone buzzed from across the room with a call. She sat up quickly and got out from under the covers, immediately on edge, the lateness of the hour making her think of Makenzie, of the stairwell. By the time she'd made her way across the room and dug her phone out of her purse, there was a message from Angela, the RA one floor up. She had some kind of situation with some kids on her floor and was hoping for backup.

Erika started hustling around, grabbing clothes from her drawers.

"So this is terrible timing, but the RA upstairs needs help with something, not really sure exactly what. Who knows how long it will take, so don't feel like you need to wait up."

Disappearing into the bathroom, Erika glanced only briefly in the mirror at her flushed face as she got dressed and made a half-assed attempt to smooth her hair and fix her fading makeup. By the time she came out, she was still a little afraid to really look at Tucker and had to take a deep breath before she turned to him to say a quick goodbye.

He was propped up on his elbow, looking at her wide-eyed.

"Are you okay?" he asked. "You seem kind of nervous."

"Oh, it's nothing. I mean . . . I was nervous for a second, because middle-of-the-night things still freak me out. But if it was something serious, she would have told me or called security or something. I'm sure it's fine."

"But I can at least walk you up there . . ."

"Nope, nope, nope. You're not wearing any pants, for starters.

I'll see you in a few, okay?"

She put all of her attention on her shoes, and almost fell over as she yanked them on. As she was finally ready to leave, Tucker called to her.

"Erika, can we talk? If not tonight, tomorrow?"

She paused and kept her eyes on the door in front of her.

"Yeah. Yes. Of course. I know. I know we need to talk. We'll talk soon."

# 31

## TUCKER

There was zero chance, zero, that Tucker could fall asleep right now. He couldn't even sit still. Kicking his way out of her bed, he grabbed his phone and started mindlessly clicking while he paced the room, trying to make sense of everything that had just happened.

He'd been so close to kissing her, through all of it, but he felt like he wasn't supposed to, and now he didn't know what this was, what was going on with them. It was so clearly past time to be open and honest.

She'd said they would talk, and he wanted to be ready. Tucker had started writing a speech in his head, back at the party. Now he put on the finishing touches, saying it to himself a few times.

*I know that it doesn't make sense to have anything right now, when we're going to be so far away from each other, but I don't know how to ignore what I'm feeling. Every night we've spent together this year is a night that I wished would never end. I want more of them if you want them too.*

He needed her to get back quickly, before he lost his nerve. Perched on the edge of her bed, he went to her Instagram page, lingered on the photos she'd posted from tonight. The two of them on the boat, the two of them clinging to each other at the party—seeing their faces together made his heart swell.

Then he started scrolling back further, looking through pictures that were familiar to him, all those images that had given him a glimpse into Erika's life these past few months. He paused on that picture where she was piled on a sagging futon with a bunch of her friends, because he'd always loved how happy she looked in that one, how much she was laughing . . .

But that's when he saw him. The guy from the party. The slow-dancing-to-Adele guy.

Tucker had never noticed him before, and the guy wasn't tagged, so Tucker still had no clue who he was. But looking at the picture anew, it seemed like he was awfully close to Erika, and that might have been his arm around her. Tucker kept scrolling, and there he was again and again, always with that stupid look on his face. Cocky. He looked cocky, right? He had on a St. B's Swimming T-shirt in one picture, and he looked like a swimmer, he had that build. Was he older maybe? He seemed older. Tucker went back to the photos of himself and Erika on the boat, and suddenly felt like a little kid.

With a very deep breath and conscious effort, Tucker closed out of Instagram. He looked at the time, counting the minutes since Erika had been gone, and now it seemed like a mistake that he was sitting here.

Why had he let her walk out? He should have insisted that he walk her to where she was going. She'd flat-out admitted she was nervous, and he'd let her go—what was wrong with him?

Tucker started fumbling around in the dark for his jeans, trying to decide the best thing to do.

# 32

## ERIKA

Erika felt like the smell of vomit was going to be following her for the rest of the weekend. Oh god, that had been a mess, an absolute mess; everyone had been written up, although they could go in front of the discipline board and apologize, take one of those classes, and redeem themselves.

There was one more thing she had to take care of.

Erika stood there in the hallway next to Eliot, the only boy who'd been partying in room 405 that night. Or not partying exactly—they'd been watching *The Great British Bake Off* and playing some kind of drinking game, which had apparently destroyed them.

Now Eliot was crouched on the floor, trying to stop the spins.

He had begged to be let go with just a warning, so that he

wouldn't get kicked off the swim team. Erika had told him that she couldn't do that, but she promised to at least stick up for him, tell the coach he'd been cooperative. Still, the kid was really upset and completely freaking out, so Erika had called for help.

The elevator dinged, and there was Jacob.

Erika stood up and awkwardly smoothed out her clothes, took a quick second to check on Eliot, and then made her way down the hallway.

"Hey, hi. I am—god. I am *so* sorry to do this, but he was about to cry, and I asked if he knew you, and I thought maybe you could talk to him, calm him down . . ."

"It's fine, it's fine. I'm happy to do it. Eliot's the best. I mean—maybe not right now. Right now is not his finest moment."

Jacob had his hands stuck in his back pockets, a tight smile on his face. "This stuff happens a lot. He'll get in trouble, but I doubt he'll get kicked off the team. I'll explain it to him."

"Jacob . . ."

"Look, it's late, and I want to get him back to his room and get him some water. So I should probably start moving."

Erika nodded very quickly.

"Yeah, yeah. For sure. Um, I can go call the elevator?"

From down on the floor, Eliot gave a pitiful groan.

"Elevators make my tummy feel weird. Elevator yuck, yuck."

Jacob ran a hand down his face, then walked over and offered Eliot a hand. He pulled him up slowly, then did his best to keep him from collapsing as they headed for the stairs.

"I'll help, I'll help," Erika mumbled. "I can open the door for you."

As she walked alongside them, she noticed that Eliot had indeed calmed down and was now looking adoringly up at Jacob.

"I want to be like you when I grow up."

"Oh my god," Jacob muttered.

Eliot gave a little gasp and stopped in his tracks. "I just had *the best idea*. Let's be on a reality baking show together. As a team. You can be the handsome one, and I'll be the funny one."

Jacob sighed.

"Eliot, you're plenty handsome. Now, can we please keep moving?"

"WHAT? REALLY? Okay, let's have our own baking show. We can bake in our Speedos."

"No."

"WHY? We'd get so many girls. And make so many cookies."

As they all started walking again, Erika let a laugh escape, though she tried to cover it up by coughing into her elbow. Jacob wanted to laugh, too, she could tell, but instead he shook his head and pretended to be disappointed.

"You should really be taking this much more seriously."

"I'm sorry, I'm sorry," Erika said, grinning. "I'm just really excited about the cookie show."

Eliot leaned closer to Jacob. "The hot RA is *totally* not mad at me anymore."

Jacob stuck a finger in Eliot's face. "Watch it, okay?"

"*Oh my god,*" Eliot said in a deranged whisper. "*Is she your girlfriend?*"

"No, she's my friend. And you need to chill, regardless."

Eliot nodded, then sank back down to a crouch, a few feet short of the stairwell. "I can chill. I will chill. Just . . . I need to do it down here. For one more minute."

As they waited for Eliot to get a hold of himself, Erika and Jacob stood facing each other. He seemed more relaxed than when he'd first arrived. His expression was gentler.

"Thanks again," Erika said. "You're, um, you're a really good friend."

She was relieved when that made him smile.

"I'm glad you called me, really. You're a good RA."

Erika felt her cheeks go pink. "Thanks. I try to be."

"I'm going to miss you next year, Oscar."

Jacob put his hand up for a high five. Smiling, Erika gave him one.

"I'll miss you, too."

"Have I even explained to you why this happened?" Eliot called from the floor. "THIS IS ALL BECAUSE OF THE RASPBERRY DRIZZLE CAKE."

Jacob took that as a cue to haul Eliot back to his feet. Erika got ahead of them, stepping forward to open the door to the stairs.

Before she could, it flew open from the other side. Tucker was standing there, hair messy, eyes wide.

"I was coming to check on you. I thought . . ."

And then his eyes floated behind her, to Eliot. To Jacob.

Erika could feel herself starting to sweat. She fumbled for the right words, the ones that would get Jacob and Eliot on their way as quickly as possible . . .

But then Tucker turned and—without saying a thing—headed up to Salma's room.

"Tucker. *Tucker*. Where are you going?"

He was still striding toward Salma's door, and it seemed that he was going to walk right into her room and not say one word to Erika. At the last second, he turned around and started pacing back and forth.

"What's up?" Erika asked. "What's going on?"

She was disgusted, though, saying that, because of course she already knew.

"I asked if you wanted me to come, if you wanted me to help," Tucker said. "I don't understand why you told me no, and then you called . . . some other guy. That other guy."

Now was the time to be honest—it was past time—but she wanted so much to avoid the discussion that she was having a pure, physical reaction. Fight or flight. Her heart hammered in her chest.

"He's on the swim team, and the kid who needed help is also on the swim team."

She still hadn't said his name. She'd never said his name around Tucker, as if that could save her somehow.

As Erika was about to ask Tucker to come back to her room,

to just go to sleep and they could talk in the morning, the elevator gave a loud ding. A pile of girls in fake prom dresses tumbled out of it, cackling and chanting about shots as they made their way down the hall. Erika did her best to avert her eyes and her ears, because technically she wasn't on duty and she certainly couldn't deal with anything like that right now, there was no way . . .

But then a tall girl in a pink princess gown stopped right next to her and gave a little squeal.

"OH MY GOD. IT'S COUCH COUPLE."

Her friends stopped and turned around, and yes, this was actually happening. All of them were clapping. Tucker was staring at the floor, so Erika was stuck taking this on alone.

She turned to them with the most strained of smiles.

"We're kind of busy."

"YEAH THEY ARE!" the girl in the princess gown shouted, and then—mercifully—they were all heading down the hall.

Erika waited until they disappeared into a room, the door slamming behind them. She clasped her hands together and tried to calm her pulse, but she couldn't. She kept thinking about tonight, the party, how this all could have been beautiful and right if only she hadn't screwed everything up.

"Who is he?" Tucker asked quietly. "Are you seeing him?"

She wanted to deny it. She could feel the words forming in her mouth. *No, no—it's nothing*, and oh god. She could not believe she'd almost said that.

"He's Suzanne," she finally said. "He's just my Suzanne."

A horrible silence descended, one that had contour and depth.

"You're sleeping with him?"

"Not that, but . . ."

"Never mind, never mind. I don't know why I asked that. It's not my business."

Erika couldn't stand the broken look on his face. Her hand went to her mouth and trembled.

"I never wanted this to happen. I was going to end things with him and explain things to you, but it got messed up. *Fuck.* This was bad timing, okay? This isn't me. You know that, Tucker. All of this . . . it's not me."

"Cheating's not you?" he asked.

The hallway's fluorescent light flickered and buzzed.

Three words. It was just three words, but they were sarcastic and thick with history. Clearly, he knew more about the video than he'd ever let on. He hadn't forgotten whatever sordid little details he'd heard, back at the Cave.

Was it only now that they were bothering him? Or had they bothered him all along?

Erika lowered her voice.

"You've always acted like you didn't care, about any of that. Like you were above it. I should have known that was bullshit."

Tucker took a step toward her. For a second she thought he might take her in his arms.

"No, no. It's not bullshit. I *don't* care about it. You know that I don't. I'm so sorry I said that. I'm just upset. I'm just—"

The stairwell door banged open behind her. Erika shut her eyes, silently begging the universe that it wouldn't be more people from the party. Then she turned to look, and *oh no*.

*No, no, no.*

Jacob and Eliot were limping together down the hall.

"Dude, I know you're pretty out of it, but how did you forget what *floor* you lived on?"

Jacob paused to rearrange Eliot's weight, and as he did, he looked up, his eyes flicking back and forth between Erika and Tucker.

He kept watching her, carefully, as he shuffled Eliot down the hall. Erika stared at the wall, afraid to look at him, conscious of how palpably tense the air around her and Tucker was, both of them standing there so stiffly.

*Please walk by, please walk by, please walk by.*

And they almost did. Jacob was so close to passing them without a word, but then he paused.

"Erika, are you okay? Is this guy bothering you?"

Tucker scoffed, loudly. Erika did her best to ignore that and keep her voice steady.

"No, Jacob, no. He's not bothering me. We're . . . I'm sorry, but I can't talk right now. Okay?"

"Are you sure?"

"I'm harmless," Tucker broke in. "Totally harmless. Don't worry about me."

This was turning into a total and complete nightmare. Erika could not believe that Tucker was being such an asshole, and she could not believe that she'd made such a goddamn mess, one that was getting worse by the second.

"Jacob, I'm sorry, but I need you to go."

He lingered for another moment, then got Eliot the rest of the way down the hall, opening the door to Eliot's room and helping him inside.

Erika and Tucker stood there in silence, and then Tucker finally spoke.

"Was this all a joke to you? What happened tonight, in your bed. Was that some kind of joke?"

Erika was starting to feel dizzy. When her voice came, it was hoarse.

"No! Of course not."

"But why say all that stuff, about what you like best about me? Why put on a big show and pretend like you care?"

"Of course I care! That's why I'm upset right now, don't you get it?"

Tucker's eyes had gone dark, and then he was looking at the floor, at his half-tied shoes.

"No, I don't get it. I think I'm just someone you text when you're bored. When you're not busy with somebody else."

Erika was shaking. Her heart was in shreds.

"Fuck you, Tucker. Fuck you."

She turned and walked to the stairs as quickly as she could.

# 33

## TUCKER

Tucker gave Erika a chance to get away from him, and then he walked back to the stairwell and sunk down to the floor. He put his head in his hands and took deep, ragged breaths.

*Every night I've spent with you has been a night that I wished would never end.*

He couldn't believe that he'd actually been planning to say those words. He was still a total puppy dog. A complete, pathetic loser. He'd been on the verge of pouring out his soul to Erika, and meanwhile, she was just in college mode, hookup mode. So she was messing around with that other guy and messing around with him and it was all whatever.

Tucker tried to silence all the awful thoughts running through his mind and focus on something practical instead. He had to pull himself together and go back to the deflated air mattress, then explain to Bobby why they had to leave first thing in the morning.

He wasn't ready, though. Not yet. He needed a minute to himself, to be miserable here in the hallway.

His stupid phone was in his pocket, beeping, but when he went to turn it off, he realized that it was his mom. She was texting him repeatedly and saying that they needed to talk, that it was important.

Tucker gathered himself as best he could, then called her.

"Hi, hon, hi. I'm sorry to bother you. I hope— How is everything? Are you having fun?"

He shut his eyes and tried to stay calm.

"It's fine. What's going on?"

His mom exhaled loudly. "Can you please tell me if you've been drinking? This is not about me being mad. I just need you to be honest."

"I had like three beers, but that was hours ago. I'm totally sober."

She was silent for a moment, the connection crackling. "This is important, Tucker."

"I'm being a million percent honest. What's going on?"

"Your aunt Maggie got in touch with me. Your dad's in bad shape. The hospice nurse—she thinks he must have developed a tumor in his liver, and that it's bleeding out. He could be gone by morning."

The news went through Tucker like an electric shock—a pure, undeniable sensation that took away everything else.

It was amazing how he thought he was ready, when in fact, he wasn't ready at all.

"Are you telling me this so I'll drive over there and say good-bye?"

"I wouldn't have called, but you're so close—I wanted you to know, so you could make your own decision."

His mom was crying. He couldn't even begin to imagine what his mom was feeling right now. Tucker's mouth was dry and his heart was going much too fast.

"I don't think I have anything to say. And he never has anything to say."

For a few seconds, he couldn't hear a thing, no motion, no breathing. When she came back, her voice was still unsteady.

"Listen—your uncle Nate and your aunt Maggie? They are kind, lovely people. They tried, very hard, with me. When you were first born, they tried to be part of my life and your life, even when Ray wouldn't. I pushed them away because . . . because I was young. I was young and I was scared and I was angry. By the time I grew up a little and realized that was a mistake, I felt like it was too late to fix things."

Now she was crying again, worse than before.

"Both of them are at the farm too, and I know it would mean a lot to them if you went. So maybe you could do it for them, and for me. Maybe it's not fair of me to ask that, but I'm asking you anyway. Because I believe that you're up to doing this."

Tucker started sobbing, curled into a corner on the cold, dirty stairs.

"Let me think for a minute," he managed to say. "I'll think about it, and I'll let you know."

# 34

## ERIKA

She escaped into the common room. Hunched in a chair in the corner, she unfriended him, unfollowed him. Bobby, too, and Nina. A couple people from the Cave. Anybody who might bring some news of him into her life. Then she sat there and tried to think what in god's name she should possibly do now.

She could go see if Jacob was back in his own room yet. Ask if he had any condoms.

She could go get Salma, but Salma was with Will in another building, maybe quite literally *with him*, right this minute, and it would be way too pathetic, banging on his door. Besides, Salma knew about the video, but she only knew the very basic story. There was so much more that Erika would have to explain, and she wanted to talk to someone who would understand without Erika having to give all the awful details . . .

She didn't think, just made the call.

Marissa answered on the second ring.

"Drunk dial? Please say it is. I've had a long week, and I'm very sober. I could use this."

Erika started crying.

"Oh my god, E—what's wrong? Are you okay?"

"I'm fine, but I'm not fine, because of a whole bunch of garbage that just happened. I know this is insane, but can I drive there right now to see you? It's only an hour, right?"

There was a pause, and she listened to Marissa breathing, shifting around.

"Is this about Tucker? I saw pictures of you guys on a boat . . ."

"Yeah, it's about him, but it's complicated."

"Have you been drinking?"

"Barely anything, and it was forever ago. I'm wide awake."

"Okay, here's what we'll do. You'll drive here and keep your phone on speaker the whole time. Then I'll know you're not dead on the side of the road, and we can catch up."

"Thank you."

"No driving until you stop crying!"

"I promise, I promise."


Over the phone, they started with apologies and confessed how much they missed each other. Marissa demanded to know everything about these new people clogging up Erika's Instagram feed, and then had to recap all of her recent roommate drama. Erika told Marissa about coffee with Jennifer, and Marissa told Erika more details than she really needed about the vagina ring Marissa had gotten from Planned Parenthood. Erika started laughing (what a miracle that was), and Marissa yelled at her to focus on the road.

When she was about ten minutes from Maryland's campus, Erika finally stopped stalling. She told Marissa about Tucker, all their texting, the party tonight. Her room and what happened after.

"M, there's something that I never told you, about the video. Dana . . . she went and erased it off both their phones. She did that for me, even after everything. I didn't tell you because I wanted you to hate her still, for that stuff she said about me."

There was a pause, a small one, before Marissa spoke again.

"Okay, cool. She wasn't just a worthless shit-talker. I'll file that away with my high school memories."

Erika choked out a laugh and told her to stop, at the same time that she was pulling into the visitors' lot that was right behind Marissa's dorm.

"Okay, I'm here," Erika said. "I'm parking."

"I'm running toward you," Marissa said. "It's very dramatic and romantic."

Erika shut off her car. She took a deep breath, looking out the window into the dark. She was almost to the end of what she was trying to say, and she wanted to finish it while she was still technically alone.

"When I was in the middle of it, with Grayson . . . I knew

it was a mistake. I didn't want to be doing it, but I felt like I couldn't stop. Like it was too late or something."

Marissa let out a sharp breath. "It's never too late. You can always stop. I see your car, by the way. I'm almost there."

Erika looked out her window. "I felt so scared and sick and alone as soon as it was done—I couldn't sleep that night. I kept thinking it was going to haunt me for weeks or months, and then, *then*, everything got infinitely worse."

"Do you see me?"

Erika leaned her forehead on the window, raised her hand in a wave.

"It's been so hard, trying to get past it, but I've been so much happier lately. I don't want to backslide because of what happened tonight."

"You won't, I know you won't."

Marissa was outside the car in her pajamas, her hair a big, glorious mess, staring in through the glass. When Erika opened the door, they finally hung up their phones and put them away.

"I'm sorry," Erika said. "I was such a bitch at Christmas."

"Who cares? Let's pretend you were on your period or something. Also: you're my favorite person. Don't tell Marco."

Marissa crammed herself into the front seat, and the girls were safe in each other's arms.

# 35

## TUCKER

Tucker was frightened when he arrived because the farm was so powerfully dark at night. He drove down the dirt road with no streetlights to guide him, then parked in a clearing near Grandma Ruth's.

Lamps lit every room on the first floor, casting a stark divide between the bright interior and pitch-dark outdoors.

Tucker shut off the engine and sat alone in his car, letting the minutes tick by. He was glad that he could see so little because he didn't want to remember the difficult days he'd spent here.

He had not been to the farm since the crash.

The more time passed, the more Tucker could pretend that none of this was real, and the more he began to consider turning around and leaving. But then the front door swung open. Nate and Maggie were there on the porch. She was leaning on him, weeping, and couldn't see Tucker.

Did they hate him, because he hadn't been there to see his dad? Did they hate him because of the accident?

Tucker wouldn't have blamed them if they did. But he pushed that thought away and made himself step out of the car.

Nate and Maggie heard his footfalls, and in perfect unison they looked up and saw him.

They walked out and met him with open arms.

Tucker's visits to the farm were always spent almost entirely outdoors, and it felt strange, being in his grandmother's home. She had embraced him, though, when he walked in. Now she sat at the kitchen table, staring at a glass of water without taking a sip.

Tucker learned that Ray had been living in a room on the first floor for weeks now, and so far, Tucker had caught only glimpses of it—the corner of a hospital bed, an IV pole, the flash of someone in scrubs.

Nate came over and gently touched Tucker's arm.

"He might not be able to talk, when you go in there. He might not really be awake. We don't know. But we'll ask the nurse to step out, and you can have a few minutes alone with him."

*No.* Tucker wanted to say no, but already this plan was in motion, and what reason could he possibly give, except that he hated the person on the other side of that wall?

The nurse came out, and Tucker walked in.

There was Ray.

He was laid out beneath a sheet, needles piercing his skin, plastic tubes shoved up his nose. The bandanna was gone, and his flesh was more sallow and wasted than ever. His arms looked thin enough to snap.

Tucker couldn't believe how far Ray had fallen in the weeks since he'd seen him.

He approached the bed carefully, looking at his father's face. Tucker thought he might be asleep or something worse, but no. He was awake, if only just.

Ray peered at Tucker without moving, then took a labored breath.

"Look who made the long trip."

Tucker felt like this was a dream, a movie. No, it felt like he was high. He was expanding and then floating. Up, up, up.

Simple words came out of him, and they felt weightless too.

"It wasn't a long trip. I was down the road, visiting a friend at college."

"A friend?"

Tucker paused. "The girl from the diner."

His dad tried to move—to shift or to sit up, Tucker wasn't sure. Whatever it was, he gave up right away, pooling back down into the bed.

"Well, now I feel bad. That you left that for me."

Tucker was still floating. He had taken up residence somewhere near the ceiling, as far from these proceedings as possible, untouchable.

Words continued to come from his mouth.

"I screwed things up with her anyway. So it was no big deal."

Was his dad laughing or coughing? It was impossible to tell.

"I would say that you got that from me, but I don't think you got much from me."

Ray's eyes were fluttering, fluttering. Shutting.

"Good for you, on that front."

And with that, Tucker crashed back down to Earth.

This was not a dream. Not a movie. He was not high or even slightly drunk. He was very sober and he was here, in the present, in this horrible moment in which he did not know what he could possibly say.

*I love you. I forgive you. I'm sorry.*

None of those were right, none of them.

He should sit here, being stoic. That's what men did, right, in situations like this?

Tucker realized that Ray was asleep now. Not a peaceful kind—one that was all sickness and drugs. Tucker had to do something, so he stepped forward and touched his father's shoulder. It was so thin that it felt like a bird's wing, and Tucker jerked back, afraid that even the weight of his hand might be enough to hurt him.

When Tucker's heart had slowed a bit, he tried again, resting his fingers as lightly as he could on his father's wasted body.

Then he whispered goodbye and walked out the door.

Tucker sat at the kitchen table with Maggie, Nate, and his grandmother. He stayed where he was while the three of them took turns being at Ray's side. Then the nurse came out and told them that she thought it would be very soon.

There was space only for the one chair in the makeshift hospital room, but Maggie said it was fine, they would all go stand by the bed. Tucker felt shaky, but also sure that he could do this. He just had to stand there, right? Stand there and breathe.

Then came the sound of feet padding down the stairs. A scared little face peeked around the corner.

*Riley.*

In all his panic and exhaustion, Tucker had completely forgotten that Riley was living here, too. He watched as the little boy slipped into the kitchen, his Star Wars pajamas rumpled, hair messy with sleep, eyes wide with confusion.

Riley smiled.

"Hi, Tucker."

Maggie immediately tried to usher him away, murmuring that he needed to go back to bed. Riley said no, no, no—they were being too loud and he wasn't tired and why was everyone here, what was going on?

"I'll take him outside," Tucker said quietly. "We can go sit outside."


"Put your hands out like this, okay? With your palms up. Now I put mine on top and you try to slap them, before I can pull away."

"Like this?"

"Yeah, yeah. But you have to be *way* faster. I'm incredibly good at this game, so don't feel bad if you . . . OW! Okay, okay.

That was beginner's luck."

Riley laughed. "Again?"

"Okay, I'm ready. But this time you'll never . . . OW! How are you doing that? Now I'm embarrassed."

On the next two rounds, Tucker yanked his hands free before Riley could get him, hoping if he did that, the game would truly seem real. And it was working, wasn't it? Riley was licking his lips, looking determined.

"Okay, last time," Tucker said. "You have no chance, none at all, I'm . . . AHHH! All right, you win. You're freakishly good at that."

"Since I won, can I have more Altoids?"

"No! I can't believe you actually like them. They taste terrible!"

They'd been on the porch for almost an hour, and Tucker had run dry on jokes and stories. He was starting to feel exhausted, but at least it looked like Riley was, too.

"Hey," Tucker whispered. "How's your leg doing?"

"My leg?"

"You know, the, um, the one that you hurt? The one that was in a cast?"

"Oh. The cast was really itchy. And I wasn't allowed to go in the pool."

Tucker looked down at his shoes and nodded quickly. "That sucks. I'm really sorry about that—really sorry."

They sat quietly, listening to the crickets. Riley looked up at him with wide eyes.

"*Now* can I have more Altoids?"

"No! Listen, have you seen the Harry Potter movies? Or has anybody read you the books?"

"Not yet."

"Okay, how about I tell you the first story?"

Riley mumbled "okay," but a second later his head was on Tucker's shoulder and his eyes were flickering. Tucker was barely two sentences in when Riley fell completely asleep. After a minute, when Tucker was certain he was out for good, he took the little boy in his arms and turned, ready to carry him back to his room.

Then he saw Maggie standing in the doorway.

She was smiling, but there were tears rolling down her cheeks, too. Tucker made his way up the steps, and stood there holding his cousin, looking at his aunt through the ratty screen door.

"Didn't mean to spy on you," she said. "It was just so nice, to listen to the two of you. I needed that right now."

"I'm sorry," Tucker said. "I never said I was sorry about the accident . . ."

Maggie shook her head and told him to stop. "You're so good with him. You always have been, and I know . . . I know . . ."

Tucker clung harder to Riley, while Maggie seemed to fall apart right in front of him. Then she opened the door and came outside, her face growing harder as she looked Tucker in the eye.

"You never met our father, and I don't have much to say

about him, but you should remember this—your dad was the oldest, and the oldest bears the brunt. You hear me? The oldest bears the brunt. I know an only child must, too, but I'm not sure it's quite the same, as when you're trying to hold back the load from other people. Other children."

Tucker's throat swelled, and he could not speak.

There was a part of him that wanted to pretend this was news, what she'd just told him. But hadn't he always known? Even if no one had said it to him so directly, it was something that he sensed from the stories he heard, and from the ones that were never told.

Tucker knew then that he'd made a mistake, trying to be stoic.

He should go back to the side of the bed and be himself. He should cry if he wanted to, maybe tell his dad a story—the one about beer tasting ugly, that would be perfect. Ray might even laugh, if he told that story.

"Can I . . . will you take Riley, so I can go back in and see him?" he asked.

Maggie pressed her lips together and shook her head.

"Oh, Tucker. He's already gone."

Tucker stayed out on the porch, trying to pull himself together as he stared at his phone.

He thought it would be easier to talk to Bobby first, but Bobby didn't answer and was surely asleep, so Tucker left a long rambling message. It ended with him saying that Bobby was one of the best people he knew, and that he felt like he was a better person because the two of them were friends.

When that was done, he stalled as long as he could before he called his mom. Frank answered after half a ring.

"Tucker, hi. She's . . . listen, don't tell her I told you this, but she's outside smoking."

Tucker choked out a little laugh. "What? She still does that?"

"Only like twice a year. When she's really stressed. Are you okay? Where are you?"

"I'm at the farm. He's . . . it's over."

"Oh god, Tucker, I'm so sorry."

Frank kept talking, but Tucker blocked out the words, because they were too much right now. Instead, he watched the sun edging up on the horizon. It was bringing the land into view and reminding him of the accident.

His mom had been a wreck that day. And she'd had to cry her eyes out next to Tucker's bed, alone.

"I'm really sorry," Tucker said, cutting Frank off. "That I didn't want you in my room at the hospital, that day when I got hurt. I was . . . I was scared. And I was ashamed."

Frank gave a little cough.

"You were also in a lot of pain, Tucker. You don't have to apologize for anything."

"No, I think I do. And I screwed up your wedding. You had to put off your wedding."

"That was fine. That was nothing. It was just going to be a party in the backyard. We had that day at the courthouse instead, and that was perfect. I think about it all the time."

Tucker covered his eyes with his hand. He was shaking.

No one could undo what his father had done. And no one could fill the void he'd left. Tucker would have to carry with him a store of darkness, one he'd be fighting his whole life.

He would need all the light that he could get.

"Thanks for buying me that suit, for the wedding. I really like that suit."

"Of course, of course."

"And thanks for buying me gum, even if I didn't need it. I mean—it's not because this happened, that I didn't need it. I just don't really need it yet."

"Sure, sure. I was just worried about you. And for the record, I didn't need it either, when I was your age. There's nothing wrong with that."

Tucker was thinking again of Erika, of the awful things he had said. He tried to imagine some different version of tonight, one where she was here with him. That might have helped, being able to curl into her arms, but it wouldn't have been enough to change anything.

Tucker used to think falling for someone meant entering a private world, a place where you didn't need anybody else. Now he felt like that wasn't true at all—if anything, it reminded him how much he needed other people, other kinds of love.

He wiped his eyes and stared up at the stars. They were so bright here, so beautiful.

"Did you find anything for Mom's birthday?" Tucker asked.

"Oh, not yet. Striking out again."

"Are you upstairs?"

"Yeah, I am."

"There's a bag on the desk, in my room. I saw it and thought it might work, so I picked it up for you."

That wasn't actually true. Tucker had bought it for Erika as a little joke, then forgot to bring it. But now this felt better, this felt right. When he heard the rustling of plastic, he pictured Frank staring at the bottle of Taylor Swift perfume.

"Tucker, this is so stupid. She will never, ever use this. Thank you."

"You're welcome. And I love you."

"I love you too. Can you hold on, just for a minute more? Your mom is coming. Here she is, here she is."

A
FEW
MORE
PARTIES
FOR
THE
ROAD

# 36

## ERIKA

Erika's mother had begged to come for support, but Erika wouldn't let her—Salma was with her, and that was enough.

Erika had never been in a courthouse before. In a way, it was like the movies, the long halls lined with massive wooden doors that led to cavernous rooms. In another way, everything was old and sterile and dull, government issue. A bigger version of the DMV. That was weirdly comforting, to think of this as the DMV. Something that you had to do, so shut up and do it.

It was Friday. Finals were over, her papers were in, RA duties wrapping up. Now she just needed to get through this, drive home tomorrow morning, and smile her way through the stupid party Saturday night.

Salma patted her knee.

"Hey, girl, hey," she said, giving her a tight smile. "You doing okay?"

"Yes," Erika said. "I swear I'm fine. Thank you for coming."

"Listen, I'm here for you, but also here for this, you know? This is important."

It was important, she was right, and thinking about that made Erika's heart thump. Why had she gotten here so early? She wondered if Makenzie was here yet. She'd heard that Makenzie got to sit in a private room with her parents, so there was no way to know.

"Talk to me about something, anything," Erika said. "It's too damn quiet in here."

"No problem," Salma said. "I actually have a real, no-bullshit question for you. Are you dreading going to your dad's tomorrow?"

Erika groaned. "I don't know. I really don't."

Her dad and Jennifer were having a little party at their house to celebrate everything—the marriage and the baby and the new place back in the suburbs, not so far from Erika's mom. Erika had said she would go, and Jennifer had been so grateful, considering all that Erika had going on. Court today, and then leaving first thing Sunday for Smith . . .

Erika had toyed with the idea of bailing on the summer program. She'd even let herself dream of a relaxing summer at home with her mom, not living several states away trying to be some kind of leader. The Erika of a year ago—she would have ditched for sure, gotten her old job at Applebee's.

Erika of today was going—she was just nervous as hell.

Looking up at the ceiling, she sighed.

"Who wants to have a party six weeks after a damn baby is born?"

Salma elbowed her. "Jennifer, of course! *Oh gosh, I know this is a bad idea, but I just really wanted to do it. It'll be fun, right? I think it will be fun.*"

Erika side-eyed her.

"That was seriously spot-on. Have you been practicing or something?"

"I haven't, I swear." Salma was watching Erika carefully, biting back a smile. "And I like her, for the record. Hope that's okay to say."

Erika crossed her arms, leaned back against the wall.

"I know, I know. I like her, too. I just never know what to say to her."

Erika had called on FaceTime to see it—an angry, squishy face inside of a blanket. Were they always so red in the cheeks? Erika didn't have much experience with creatures that small. She guessed it was a cute-enough baby, though she needed to stop saying "it."

She was Tessa. Tessa Green.

"I don't know how you've held out this long without meeting her," Salma said. "I'd have driven the two hours to their house for the baby cuddles. Baby cuddles always hurt my ovaries, but in a good way."

"You're so weird," Erika said. "My ovaries don't have the same urges as yours."

Salma was about to say more, but then Erika grabbed her

arm, because here came the prosecutor, Rebecca.

She was short and all shoulders, wearing her usual uniform of a generic-looking black suit with the lowest and boxiest pair of heels you could imagine. The girls watched her coming toward them. *Clunk, clunk, clunk, clunk.*

Erika had not hesitated the first time she'd sat across from her, several weeks back. She'd said *I might not be good witness material* before she'd even said hello.

Rebecca had listened, blank-faced, while Erika had explained. When the story was done, Erika had folded her hands on the table in front of her, her heart pounding the whole time. Rebecca had made a couple notes on her laptop, then announced that it was fine. She didn't think any of that would come up, and if it did, she'd try to object. But she couldn't make any promises.

Erika had said she understood, and Rebecca had nodded. *Good girl*, she'd said.

Now here Rebecca was, marching down the hallway, her focus straight ahead so that she didn't notice Erika until she was right next to her. When she saw her sitting there, she stopped short.

"You're off the hook."

Erika and Salma both stood up. Erika's purse fell to the floor, but she left it there.

"What do you mean?" she asked. "What happened?"

"He took the plea at the last minute. The judge accepted it. Three years' probation. One-year jail sentence, suspended."

"Suspended," Erika said. "Does that mean he doesn't go at all?"

"Not unless he screws up in the next three years," Rebecca said.

Erika looked at Salma, whose eyes were wide, her mouth open.

What had happened that night? Erika didn't actually know, because what had she really done, except tell Makenzie that she was sorry, that she would believe her, that she wanted to get her to someone who could help? There was almost nothing specific in the paper. The whispers in the dorm told a little more. That Makenzie was drunk and no one should have been touching her. That she didn't remember how she got into the room with him. Erika knew that people had seen her stumbling out, limping, and hadn't said or done anything, because it couldn't be what it looked like, right?

The bruises. Erika had heard that they'd photographed the bruises on her wrists, other places, and she was shaking now to think of it. She turned to Rebecca.

"I'm confused. Is this *good*?" Erika asked.

"It's good. I know it might not feel good, but these cases are hard, so this is a win."

*A win.* There had to be a better word for this. Erika was swallowing again and again.

"It doesn't feel like a win," Salma said.

Rebecca nodded, shrugged.

"I know it doesn't, believe me—I know."

Someone called to Rebecca from the other end of the hall. She put a hand on Erika's shoulder before she walked away.

And that was it. It was done.

Erika thought about screaming. Instead, she kicked the bench and hurt her foot, which was clad in a pair of cheap Target flats to go with this cheap Target dress that was supposed to look respectable.

Next to her, Salma was fuming, mumbling things that Erika couldn't quite hear. She tried to reach for Erika, but Erika shrugged her away and faced the wall, looking at a portrait of who-the-hell-cared, some old white dude. She covered her mouth with her hand.

She was thinking of the tangle of Makenzie's hair, when she had found her. She would never forget that.

She was thinking of her own hair, too. The fluorescent shine that used to frame her face. The bright lipstick that she liked to wear to match it.

She hadn't worn lipstick for a year, after everything. She didn't like calling attention to her mouth. And her hair— these days, Erika liked how her short, brown hair looked. But when she'd first changed it after high school graduation, it was because she never wanted to look like that person again. She never wanted to be that person again.

But it was impossible, of course, to really leave things behind. To be somebody different. Erika knew that.

Lots of girls knew that.

"I'm going to sit," Erika said. "Just for a second."

She lowered herself onto the hard bench. Salma settled beside her and put an arm around her, murmuring nothing words. Then she gave her shoulder a squeeze.

"I think somebody's here to see you."

Erika's head snapped up, and she sucked in her breath.

"My car died, and I needed a ride," Marissa said. "Marco's busy with his stupid internship."

"Are we too late?" Nina asked. "Oh my god, we got here as fast as we could."

Erika stood up and hugged them both tightly. The four girls stood in a circle, while Erika began to explain what had happened. She'd only gotten a few words out, though, when Salma grabbed her arm and turned her slightly, directing her gaze down the hallway.

Makenzie was there, behind two people that Erika assumed to be her parents. Her father was holding the door open, and they were about to leave, while Erika stood frozen, watching them.

Maybe Makenzie could feel their eyes because she looked in their direction, paused there on the threshold.

She was wearing black dress pants and a white button-down, a low ponytail.

*In a moment, she will turn and run this way. Her hair will unfurl, go flying behind her. My arms will be open and she'll fall into them.*

All that happened, though, was Makenzie put her hand in the air, the smallest wave, her face neutral.

Erika swallowed hard and then she waved back. As soon as she did, Makenzie slipped out the door and was gone. The door slammed behind them, echoing loudly.

"Are you okay?" Salma whispered.

"Yes. No. I don't know."

Erika sat down again, waiting for her heart to calm, sorting through all of the emotions that were knotted in her chest.

She hated what had happened here, she hated it down in her soul. But all the bravery she'd been gathering in the long months leading up to today, all the strength—she would hold on to that. There would be times, she knew, when she was going to need it. When the women around her would need it. And on the days when she struggled the most, she would think of Makenzie and what it must have taken for her to be in this building today.

Erika looked up at her friends, gave them a shaky smile.

"I'm so glad that all of you are here."

# 31

## TUCKER

The race was ending in the park he used to come to when he was a kid—a big swath of green that had seemed vast and tinged with magic back then. It had a fountain, an iron gate that led down to a flower garden. There was a building on the property, too, an old estate where people liked to get married. He remembered once when he was little, he'd been dashing down the path and almost run right into a bride and groom in the middle of a photo shoot. His mom had gotten teary, and when he'd asked why, he didn't understand her answer.

At the time, he didn't know why someone would cry because they saw something beautiful.

Today, there was no wedding, of course. Instead, it was tables of water and Gatorade. Free T-shirts. Paramedics standing by just in case. He could see it all as he crested over the hill for that last quarter mile, and it was the kind of Saturday morning that made you glad to be alive—blue sky, gentle breeze. He was still too far away to pick out his mom and Frank, but he knew they were there waiting for him.

The race had in fact been Frank's idea, a way for Tucker to raise money for cancer research. Frank had done a triathlon, the year after his first wife, Ann, had died, and he'd said it had helped, having some way to channel his feelings. That made sense to Tucker, so he'd started a page and promoted it online, and that meant everybody he knew—not just the few people he had told at first. He'd made some money and gotten a lot of unrequested sympathy, and now here he was, running faster than he'd ever run in his life.

Tucker had been quick enough all those years of playing baseball, but he'd been training hard now for two months. He'd made mixes that were all bass and speed, and he'd pounded his way through the neighborhood, sweating and straining until he was almost too tired to think.

Erika did pop into his mind sometimes when he ran; he knew she'd done track and that she could still crush a mile pretty good. He always shut that down as quickly as he could, because it was better for him to not think about her.

The morning after his dad died, he'd returned early to collect Bobby, then texted Erika to tell her that they were gone, that he was sorry, that he wouldn't bother her again.

He didn't tell her about his dad, and she'd never responded. They hadn't spoken since, not one word.

*Almost to the end. Go, go, go.*

Someone was screaming through a bullhorn. A guy in a tiger suit was jumping up and down, cheering everyone down the last stretch. The air was warm and Tucker had run hard, maybe a little too hard; his breath was coming ragged now, his side stitching up as he took those final steps across the finish line and then found a space where he could collapse.

Seconds later, his mom was hovering over him, face scrunched and concerned.

"My god, how are you done already? Are you okay?"

He smiled and told her he was fine, sitting up as she was sitting down, the two of them next to each other in the grass.

"Where's Frank?"

"He told me it's annoying, when people try to talk to you right away."

"And yet here you are," Tucker said, unable to keep the smartass smile off his face.

She acted like she was going to hit him on the head with the water bottle, then handed it to him instead.

"Well?" she said. "Are you glad you did it?"

"I am. For sure."

"Good, good. So do they sell last-minute tickets to prom?"

He rolled his eyes, and she put her hands up, conceding the point, keeping her mouth shut.

"It's just prom," he said. "It's not a big deal. I'd rather go to the farm."

His mom was watching him carefully.

"I'm happy that you want to do that. I really am. But listen, I called Maggie this morning, to say hi and make sure she knew that you were coming. Tucker—she told me this is the last time everyone will be together there. Grandma Ruth is moving into an assisted-living place in September. And then they're selling the land."

The news made Tucker's chest go tight. He was going to lose one of the only places that he could remember ever spending time with Ray, one of their only connections.

Then Tucker looked up sharply at his mom. "What about Riley?"

She sighed. "Nate's getting transferred to New Jersey next month, and his wife hasn't found a job there yet, so things are complicated with them. Maggie's planning to move Riley in with her family as soon as she can, but she has to get a new schedule first, to make it work. Plus they need a bigger place."

Tucker stared at his shoes. "Maggie has five kids."

"I know, hon, I know."

Tucker thought of Riley and Grandma Ruth, alone on the farm all summer, counting the days until it was gone. He untied and then retied his laces for no good reason, then cleared his throat.

"What if, um, what if Riley came and stayed with us for the weekend?"

"You mean *this* weekend?"

"I could watch him the whole time—you wouldn't have to do anything. He can sleep in the guest room, and we can take the Metro to the zoo or something. He likes monkeys, and I thought . . ."

"Tucker, relax. I think that's a great idea, I just . . . let me call Maggie, okay? I'll call her and let you know what she says."

"Thank you, thank you," Tucker said. "This is going to be awesome."

Ignoring her protests, he gave her a very sweaty hug.

# 38

## ERIKA

"Nina, I can't believe prom is tonight, and you're *here*. Shouldn't you be at the spa or something?"

Nina rolled her eyes.

"Erika, I told you. I broke up with Theo weeks ago, and I'm just going with Kara. I'm going to get ready in about five minutes."

"It's kind of too bad," Marissa whispered. "Because Theo was a total smokeshow."

Salma giggled at that while Nina mumbled *oh my god* and went back to her breakfast.

After the courthouse, Marissa and Nina had come back to the dorms with Erika and Salma and had ended up crashing there, eating pizza and watching terrible movies. Now the four of them were at the Daily Grind, and with most of the St. B's students gone, they had it almost entirely to themselves. They sat together at a big table, finishing their bagels and clutching giant plastic cups that were more whipped cream than coffee.

Erika sighed. "I'm still so bummed to hear about Kara and Yrma."

"Tell me about it," Nina said. "This is what my mom always warned me about. *They're your best friends, and someday they'll break up, and then what are you going to do?*"

"So it really is that bad?" Erika asked.

"Kind of. It's just fresh, I guess. I think everything will be okay."

They were all quiet after that, drinking their coffee, lost in their own thoughts.

"They're dropping like flies," Erika finally said. "I guess it's that time of year, but c'mon. How's a girl supposed to believe in love anymore?"

"Um, by basking in the glow of me and Marco? By imagining the insanely beautiful children we'll be making someday?"

"Ew," Nina said. "Can you at least say *having* instead of *making*?"

Salma leaned closer to Marissa. "Hey, I still haven't seen a picture of him. I want to imagine the beautiful babies."

Marissa happily took out her phone, and Erika waited until she and Salma were fully distracted. Then she reached out and touched Nina's arm.

"I don't think I ever said thank you for yesterday, for coming to the courthouse. And skipping school! I know I didn't actually have to do anything, but I'm really glad that you guys were there, and I'm glad you hung around. I think I needed the company this weekend."

Nina gave her a little smile, but it was a pained one. "Are you kidding? This was important. Even my mom was cool with it. But Erika . . . when I was driving Marissa up here, I mentioned something that I assumed she knew, and that I assumed *you* knew, but apparently neither of you did know about this kind of big thing?"

Marissa stopped chatting with Salma then. Meanwhile, Erika went still, waiting to hear more.

"We were trying to figure out the right time to tell you, and yesterday just didn't seem . . . anyway. I guess we should tell you now," Nina said.

Marissa gave a little cough. "So, E, I know we agreed never to speak his name again, but do you think enough time has passed?"

*Tucker.*

Erika had been trying her best not to think about him these past few months, and she'd certainly had plenty to distract her. Last night, she kept wondering if Nina was going to bring him up, some part of her hoping that she would. . . .

But now Nina and Marissa both had troubled looks on their faces, and Erika raised her eyebrows, silently asking them to go on.

"Let's start with the kind of smaller thing?" Marissa said. "Just as an FYI, he's kind of around the corner."

The back of Erika's neck tingled.

"What do you mean, he's around the corner?"

"He's not going to prom because there's some party this afternoon, for his dad's family," Nina said. "I guess he goes every year, and he didn't want to miss it?"

Tucker was going to the farm today. Erika took a moment to consider that. He hadn't been since the accident, had he? The thought of him being there again set off an ache in her heart.

"Okay," she said. "That's fine. It's, whatever. What's the rest?"

Nina and Marissa exchanged a glance, and then Nina sucked in her breath.

"Erika, Tucker's dad died."

The bell on the front door jingled. The espresso machine screamed. Erika almost insisted that Nina was wrong. The words were on the tip of her tongue.

*I'm sorry, you must be mistaken. That asshole was supposed to be around until the end of the year.*

Erika willed herself not to chew on her nail and tried her best to make her voice steady.

"Did it just happen?"

Nina shook her head, her face crumpling.

"No, it was months ago. Bobby told me it happened that weekend they were visiting you."

After a couple of minutes alone in the bathroom, Erika returned to the table, where her three friends were all staring at her in concern.

"I'm okay, seriously. Or sort of okay. I guess I'm worried about him."

Nina sighed. "He definitely hasn't been himself, but he seems better than he was at first. I think he's hanging in there."

Erika nodded, then changed the subject, asking what Nina was wearing tonight. They looked at dressing room pictures on Nina's phone, and then Salma and Marissa were reliving their prom night antics while Nina laughed.

Erika was distracted through it all, too many thoughts churning in her head. Then she felt Marissa's foot poking hers.

"So are you packed?" Marissa asked. "You ready to meet the baby?"

"Yes to the first part. I guess to the second."

Marissa's lips were pressed tightly together, and she was watching Erika carefully. "So you're going to go grab your stuff from the dorm, then head out?"

Erika drank the last of her coffee and set the empty cup delicately on the table.

"That's the plan. I've got a party to go to, right?"

# 39

## TUCKER

*If I lived here, I would never forget to look up.*

That's what Tucker thought after he'd parked his car next to the others and stepped out into the bright day, the clouds overhead grand and slowly moving, moving. The grass was high as he walked through it. He remembered that this was a point of discussion, the year before—that the land was going wild. His grandmother hadn't had the means or the money to control it, and so everything had grown unchecked. The creek flooded; trees fell.

Did that matter? Tucker had no idea. He didn't know much about this place, how it worked, what it was worth.

He did think it was beautiful. The tragedy of losing it—he felt that in his heart.

As he walked into the party, Maggie spotted him right away

and came to smother him in a hug.

"Your mom called me. Riley is so excited, thank you. I have a booster seat to put in your car. And don't be surprised if he crawls into bed with you around three a.m. There's more, but I'm going to put it in an email and send it to you and your mom, okay?"

"Okay, cool. Yes. Thank you, for letting me do this. I really wanted to do this."

Maggie was about to say more, but then Tucker was almost knocked down when Riley crashed into his legs. Tucker made a big show of falling to the ground, letting Riley crawl all over him, letting the grass tickle his skin as he stared at the sky.

He wanted to commit the feeling of this place, this day, perfectly to his memory.

Tucker hugged his grandmother, then Nate and his wife, then Maggie's husband. He shook hands with some of his dad's cousins. Everyone was saying how nice the weather was, but of course there was a shadow over the day because Ray was gone, and soon the farm would be, too.

Tucker had seen everyone at the official service, but that had been such a strange, terrible day. The funeral home was so cold and impersonal, and Tucker had stuck close to his mom, finding it hard to talk to anyone else, his relatives looking unfamiliar in their dark clothes. Now everyone was back in their T-shirts, his cousins joking and laughing, talking about their summer jobs, their swim meets. Bill was holding up a bat and a Wiffle ball, asking Tucker if he wanted to start a game.

Riley appeared again, clinging to Tucker's leg.

"Will you take me to Chuck E. Cheese this weekend? I love Chuck E. Cheese."

"Maybe. You know I used to work at a place a lot like Chuck E. Cheese. But it was even better."

"TAKE ME THERE! Let's go there."

Tucker felt an ache then, in his chest, and found it almost hard to answer.

"I wish I could. It's closed for good."

Riley put on a cartoon-like pout, and Tucker laughed, releasing him. He was about to offer to pitch, but then he saw that Bill had dropped the ball and bat and was heading over to his grandmother's porch. Everybody was. Tucker walked over, too.

Nate was standing with a beer in his hands, his eyes tearing up a bit as he said that they should do a quick toast. He came up with a few vague but heartfelt words—how it had been a long couple months without Ray, that he would be missed. People bowed their heads, and the quiet seconds stretched out. Tucker thought that was going to be it, but then Maggie stepped forward and said she had a story.

"Does everyone remember the table?"

There were groans, laughter. One of his dad's cousins threw a hand in the air and pretended to walk away, but Maggie kept talking.

"Ray built a little furniture, here and there. Simple stuff. You all know that. I asked him to build me a table, oh god, twenty years ago? I had the wood! I paid him! And still, the whole time he was making it, he complained that I was going to get to keep it. He finished it, brought it to my house, and every damn time he came by, every time he talked to me, he would say again that he shouldn't have given it to me. I got so sick of it that I finally put it in the back of Nate's truck. Nate, you helped me. You remember. Ray had just moved to that apartment in German-town, and I drove it all the way there, left it in the lobby. He came down and got it, but never said a thing, never thanked me, just ate on it for years."

People were laughing now, and Tucker felt himself smiling a little.

"I bet you think you know where this is going, right? Well, no. You're wrong. He didn't leave me the table. I have no idea what happened to that table, but wherever it is, I hope some-one's enjoying it, because it was lovely, it really was."

Now people were laughing harder. Someone started clap-ping and others joined in, a gentle, tentative applause. Maggie had a beer in her hand, and she raised it in the air.

"A toast to the disappearing table, and a toast to Ray."

She looked at Tucker, and he wondered if he was supposed to be raising a drink, but he didn't have one. Instead he smiled at her and nodded.

Maggie nodded back, kept her eyes on him.

"He was a difficult man," she said, "but he left behind some beautiful things."

* * *

Tucker needed a few minutes to himself after that, but when he felt steady again, he went and found Maggie. He stood with her under a magnolia tree, its branches making delicate, complicated shadows all around them. He told her the story about beer tasting ugly, and she laughed so hard, wiping tears from her eyes.

Tucker wanted to laugh, too, but he was feeling troubled.

"I was going to tell him that story, you know . . . that night. But I never got a chance to. I didn't say enough to him. I wish . . . I wish I'd done better."

Leaves rustled overhead, and Maggie grabbed his arm, giving it a gentle shake.

"You did fine, okay? I'm sure you did fine. I know I said some tough things to you that night, but Tucker—I wouldn't have blamed you if you hadn't come at all. I know, okay? I know what he was like. I know how much he failed you."

Tucker managed to say *okay* but nothing else.

"And you know what?" she added. "Whenever I think of that night, I'm going to remember you on the porch, with Riley. So I'll always have something beautiful to think about, even when I'm feeling sad."

Both of them were quiet then, and eventually Maggie said she needed to go bring out some more food. Before she went, she straightened Tucker's shirt collar and gave a flick to his hair. She mumbled something about him being too cute for his own good, but then she stopped, her gaze focused over his shoulder.

"Who's that?"

When Tucker first turned, he was staring into the glare of the sun. It took a moment for him to focus, to be sure that it was really her.

# 40

## ERIKA

She took a big breath of the clean spring air, trying to keep calm despite the fact that she'd walked right into a party she wasn't invited to.

She'd almost changed her mind a dozen times on the short drive here, but there were some conversations you couldn't have over the phone. There were some conversations that couldn't wait.

Her eyes jumped around, taking in all the people who were staring at her. She was suddenly worried he might not actually be here, or that she'd been wrong and this wasn't the place. She was so sure, though. He'd showed it to her once on a map, and she always thought of him when she drove by . . .

And then she saw him, jogging toward her.

She liked watching him, the athletic way he moved.

She liked having this chance to take in his face, the naked, questioning look there.

He arrived at her side, but she didn't know what to say. She'd had all that time in the car to prepare, and now she'd lost her words.

"Hi," Tucker said.

"Hi."

She wanted to hug him, but it seemed too soon, and there were so many people watching. Besides, Tucker's expression was strange, and for a second she thought that he didn't want her here at all.

"I saw that he took a plea," Tucker said. "I'm not stalking you online or anything. I set up a news alert, so that I'd hear when something happened. I just saw it an hour ago."

She'd forgotten her sunglasses, and she put her hand up against the brightness of the day, grateful for an excuse to hide a little.

"I'm told it's a win," she said. "Even if it doesn't feel like one."

The sound of birds and wind and insects filled in the space between them.

"That seems like bullshit," Tucker said.

"Yeah, it's bullshit for sure." She swallowed and looked at her feet. "As for being a stalker, I think I probably take the cake today . . ."

He didn't laugh, and that's when she decided that she didn't care. She hugged him, collapsed into him.

"I didn't know he was gone, Tucker. I didn't know until today."

Tucker asked if she wanted to go for a walk, and so they headed for the woods, following a wide, hard path that was full of fallen branches and stones. Tucker reached up and plucked a leaf free, then let it flutter to the ground. He told her what had happened that night, getting a phone call from his mom, driving to the farm.

It broke her heart, the thought of him enduring that alone.

He was looking up as they walked, and Erika looked up, too, admiring the trees etched against the sky.

"I know that I apologized in a text," Tucker said, "but that obviously wasn't enough. I should have said more, but I was . . . well, you know. A little overwhelmed by everything. But I'm so incredibly sorry, about what I said to you, how I acted. I got all possessive and competitive and it was not okay, any of it."

Tucker stopped in his tracks and turned to her.

"I'm been thinking a lot today, about my dad. My whole life, I felt like I was the total opposite of him, nothing like him at all. And maybe that's true, but still . . . All the insecurities I have from the times I was around him, those aren't just going to disappear. And there are so many people in the world that can make me feel the same way, if I let them. I'm more aware of that now. I think I'm in a better place, where I can really fight against it. But I wish I'd figured that out sooner. I wish I'd never said those awful things to you. I can't stand the thought that I hurt you."

Erika pressed her lips together and took her time before she spoke, wanting the words to be right.

"I should have apologized, too. I'm so sorry, you have no idea. I was purposefully keeping things from you, and implying how much I cared about you, but then I was afraid to really go there."

"I understand. And I forgive you. Obviously, I forgive you."

"I forgive you, too."

The two of them slowed their pace as they came across a fallen tree. Erika hopped up and sat on it, and Tucker followed. The bark was rough under her legs, but she liked being up here, getting to take in all the green around them. When she turned to look at Tucker, though, he still looked anxious.

"Erika, I hope you don't feel like you have to say all this, just because I lost my dad, or because you're worried about me. I don't want you to be here, forgiving me, because of that. If that's why, I don't deserve it."

Around them, insects hummed, squirrels chattered. The air was warm, and the sunbeams were golden, coming in shafts through the trees.

"That's not why, I promise," she said. "That night, at St. B's—when you told me you were happy that we found each other again? I felt the same way. I still do."

He nodded slowly. Overhead, a pair of birds let out a sweet, warbling song.

"I'm so glad you're here," Tucker told her. "I'm happy that you get to see this place, meet my family. And . . . I really missed you."

"Me too. I missed you, too."

The two of them sat quietly, their hands so close but not quite touching.

# 41

## TUCKER

Tucker took Erika to meet Maggie first, so of course Erika was smothered in a hug and told how welcome she was and how pretty she was, except too skinny, so what did she want to eat?

Erika admitted she was starving, and so they hit the buffet table, and then she had to meet a dozen more people while clinging to a flimsy paper plate that was wilting under the weight of an overcooked hamburger and a pile of Doritos, plus potato salad, Jell-O salad, pasta salad. "All of the salads that aren't really salads," Tucker called them, and Erika said that's why they were the best ones. Nate patted her on the shoulder when she said that and announced she was a keeper.

Tucker started stammering, trying to explain that she was just his friend, but Erika waved at him to stop, mouthing *it's fine*.

The two of them retreated to the steps of his grandmother's

porch, eating quietly, taking in the scent of charcoal undercut by honeysuckle.

"I'm going to Michigan," Tucker said.

"That's great. I'm really happy for you."

"You're done with your semester?"

"I am, but . . . I'm leaving. Tomorrow morning. My mom's driving me up to Massachusetts. I start the program at Smith on Monday."

"Are you excited?"

Erika's plate was empty, but she was poking at it with her fork.

"I *am* excited, but I'm also freaking out a little. I hate being away from my mom. And I'm nervous to be around a bunch of, I don't know, super-accomplished, confident girls."

"I am positive your mom is painfully proud of you and has told the entire hospital all about this. And you *are* a super-accomplished, confident girl."

Now Erika graduated to full-on stabbing the paper plate, filling it with a constellation of tiny fork holes.

"There's another problem. We all have to come with a plan for an individual project to do while we're there. Mine was supposed to be writing an essay, about my experience testifying. I filled out a whole stupid sheet about it, saying what the thesis was going to be and how I was going to try to pitch it to BuzzFeed or Jezebel or whatever."

"I think that sounds great."

"But there wasn't a trial. I didn't do anything. And besides—it doesn't feel right. I feel like I was going to try to tell some story that wasn't mine."

"You'll think of something else. I'm sure you will."

Erika nodded, mumbling *sure, sure* as she finally set down the fork.

"What about you?" she said. "What are you doing this summer?"

"Oh! Uh, Ryan's family has a beach house. In Bethany? Me and a couple other guys are going to stay with him. His dad's a partner in this new crab house that opened last summer, so we can all work there."

"Wow. That's really cool, Tucker."

Was it really cool? Tucker had been pretty excited about it for the past month, ever since the plan had come together. He thought it was exactly what he needed. An escape from his difficult year, from losing his dad. A summer to remember.

But then he'd come here today. He'd walked inside his grandmother's house, which had always been spotless but was now half boxed up, dirtier than it should have been. He'd watched how slowly she was moving now, trying to imagine how she could possibly keep up with a six-year-old . . .

Right then, Riley came screeching up from the creek, clutching a frog.

"Is that him?" Erika asked gently.

Tucker smiled. "Yeah. I'm actually about to take him to my house for the weekend. Do you want to come by and say hi?"

\* \* \*

Riley was immediately sprinting around the house, taking stock of every room, confused about the lack of toys but very excited about Tucker's Xbox.

Meanwhile, Erika was back in Tucker's kitchen for the first time since Christmas break, perched on that same stool at the breakfast bar that she always sat in, drinking a can of the mango seltzer that she liked. The sight of her there was so familiar, yet also a reminder of how much had changed in the last few months. It gave Tucker a bittersweet pang.

Frank and Janet had just gotten home, and they were unloading a bag of groceries—kid food, Tucker realized. There was peanut butter and chicken nuggets, Goldfish and macaroni and cheese.

"Are we going to start the movie?" Frank asked. "Because I am so ready."

Tucker turned to Erika, a pleading look on his face.

"You have to stay. Please. Riley has never read a word or watched a second of Harry Potter, so we're starting with the first one tonight."

Erika spun herself around on the stool, letting out a frustrated groan.

"I would *love* to do that. But I have a thing I really have to go to. My dad and his new wife are having a party, and I need to meet my baby sister. Or half sister. Is it me or does *half sister* seem sort of rude, like why make that distinction? I should just say *sister*, right? Shit, I'm really nervous. And now I said *shit* in front of a kid. Twice."

"Ray said *shit* all the time," Riley announced, while trying to balance his stuffed Spider-Man on top of his head.

Erika caught the doll as it fell, then handed it back to him.

"Well, thanks. For letting me off the hook. But yeah, I should split. I'm going to run to the bathroom, and then I'll take off."

As Erika headed for the front hall, Frank called to Riley from inside the pantry, asking him to help pick out the snacks.

Janet appeared at Tucker's side.

"Did you want to go with her?"

"What? No. She didn't ask me, and I told you, I was going to do everything this weekend. I'm taking this seriously, I swear . . ."

"I know you are, Tucker, I know. But we're just going to watch a movie and put him to bed. I think we can handle it. And besides, you have truly, truly watched Harry Potter too many times."

"Yes, but sharing it with people you love is different. It's kind of a monumental occasion."

Janet pressed her lips together, then reached out and messed with his hair.

"That's great and all, but this is literally your mother telling you that you're an enormous nerd and you need to leave the house."

Tucker rolled his eyes.

"Mom. To be entirely and completely clear? They do not sell last-minute prom tickets, and I'm not taking her."

"Okay, I'm not *that* obsessed with you going to prom. And I'm not trying to match-make, either. I think you've spent a little too much time by yourself, since your dad died. It would be nice if you got out."

Tucker knew that was true. Just hearing her say those words—*your dad died*—was painful to him. He had to take a moment to center himself, to push away the desire to run to his room and sink into his bed.

A party might do him some good.

"Okay, yeah. Thanks. I'll see if she wants me to come. To be honest, I kind of messed up earlier this year. With Erika. So it would be nice to have a chance to be a good friend."

"Well, okay then. Go be a good friend."

# 42

## ERIKA

"There it is," Tucker said, slowing the car as he spotted the right address. "That's the place."

Erika stared out the passenger window, taking in her dad's new home. The house was small but stately, with pretty white shutters and a cherry tree in the yard. There were cars lining both sides of the street, and Tucker had to park half a block away.

He turned off the engine, but Erika stayed where she was, her seat belt still buckled.

"I honestly have no idea if this is going to be boring or totally uncomfortable or what."

"How are you feeling in general?"

Erika peered back at the glow of the little house, as if she'd magically be able to see inside.

She sighed. "I'm not very good with kids."

"Just do your best. Or maybe it will be different, because it's your sister."

Still not used to the word, Erika repeated it quietly to herself a couple times.

"Okay, *sister* is definitely better than *half sister*," she said. "And I do like the name Tessa."

"So are you ready?"

"I suppose."

"That's the Erika Green spirit I know."

"Shut your stupid face, Tucker."

"Okay, okay, but listen—I know you said you didn't want to stay long, but we can be here as late as you want."

Erika's lips twitched. "I should try to get some sleep. My mom and I are getting on the road really early."

Tucker looked down at his lap. "Right, right. I keep forgetting that."

Erika finally unbuckled her seat belt, then told him she was as ready as she'd ever be.

Laughter and chatter were coming from the backyard, so the two of them headed that way. Tucker pushed open the gate and they walked through. There was a small crowd gathered on a patio, flanked behind by a garden in bloom and above by little white lights strung all through the trees and across the fence. Erika spotted a couple people she knew and waved awkwardly. She was looking for her dad, but it was Jennifer she saw first.

She was wearing a long, loose dress that billowed as she hurried to Erika.

"Oh, you're here, you're here!"

Erika blushed, mumbling that she was sorry they were late, but Jennifer didn't seem to be listening. She was too busy hugging Erika so hard it almost hurt.

"You look really nice," Erika said. "And this is my friend Tucker. Hope it's okay that he came."

Jennifer's eyes went wide, and then she wrapped Tucker in her arms, like he was a gift brought just for her.

"Your dad's trying to get Tessa to sleep, but I don't have high hopes. Can I get you a drink?"

She swept them inside, into a pretty, yellow kitchen that was still full of unpacked boxes. Jennifer held up a bottle of wine, and Tucker declined, but Erika said *yes, please*, so Jennifer poured two glasses.

From there, she led them to a little side room that was occupied almost entirely by a piano. Erika and Jennifer sat on the piano bench, while Tucker hovered in the corner of the room. Down the hall, they could hear the baby crying.

"Whew. Sorry," Jennifer said. "I needed a small break from people. And I wasn't sure if you were in the mood for a party, after everything that happened yesterday."

"Oh, it's fine," Erika said. "Really. I'm . . . I'm happy to be here. And besides, he took a plea. I didn't have to do anything."

"I heard, I heard. From your mom. Did she tell you that I ran into her at the salon before Tessa was born? And I asked her weird pregnancy questions and now we text each other? Oh my god, your mom is so cool. Don't you think your mom is cool? Anyway, she told me what happened, but still—I'm sure it's been very stressful."

"We don't have to talk about it, seriously. I want to hear about Tessa. Also, I want to know if childbirth is more or less terrifying than it is in the movies."

As Jennifer was about to respond, the wailing from down the hall grew louder. Erika's dad appeared in the doorway with a screaming bundle.

"Oh! Hey. Didn't know you were here. Uh, I'm not sure I can walk in circles anymore. And my arms feel like they're going to fall off. Sorry."

Jennifer gave a deep sigh, and then she and Erika both stood and headed toward Paul, Erika glancing nervously at the baby, while Jennifer mumbled that she was sorry they were meeting like this. The crying grew somehow louder than it already was, and Erika started to feel nervous, sweaty.

Then Tucker appeared at Paul's side.

"I can take her," Tucker said. "I can walk in circles."

His eyes were on Erika, asking her if she wanted to stay there and keep talking.

She smiled at him and mouthed *thanks*.

Twenty minutes later, Erika and Jennifer were still in the piano room, and had moved from talking about babies to talking about the courthouse.

Erika sighed. "It's weird, I spent so much time being worried about what would happen, when I was on the stand. If they'd bring up that stuff from my past. You . . . you know about it, right?"

Jennifer kept her face neutral and nodded.

"Okay, so I spent all this mental and emotional energy, getting ready to relive it. And then it didn't happen. I never had to talk about it. Maybe this sounds stupid, but it feels like kind of a waste."

Tessa's cries had finally subsided, and Erika could hear people chatting in the kitchen. She could feel Jennifer gearing up to say more to her, but Erika suddenly felt bad, keeping her here, making her miss her own freaking party.

"Um, anyway. Thanks for listening. I should really go find Tucker."

Erika stood first and then Jennifer followed, smoothing out her dress and stretching out her back. As they were walking out, Erika noticed two framed baby photos on a little table in the corner.

One was her and the other was Tessa. Delicately, she reached out and picked both of them up.

"Oh, oh," Jennifer said. "I should have asked before I put yours there, but I wanted both. Is it okay? I had to ask your mom for a copy, because Paul—he's so unsentimental! He hardly has any pictures."

When Jennifer said that, Erika had to take a moment to compose herself. Very carefully, she set the pictures back down and managed to keep her face pleasant.

When her dad had lived in his DC apartment, he'd indeed had almost no photos—but there had been the one, of Erika when she was five. She was chubby-cheeked, still blond. All sunshine.

Right after the video, that picture had disappeared.

Maybe that had been some kind of coincidence, but she didn't think so. There was a time when just thinking of its absence from the shelf had made her so sad, so angry, so bitter . . .

Right now, it made her feel protective. Of Tessa. Of Jennifer, even if Jennifer was a grown-ass woman who could make her own decisions.

Erika thought it might be a good thing, if she was in their lives.

"I don't mind at all," Erika finally said. "Look at me, I'm cute as hell. Now let's go party."

Jennifer smiled. "Yes, let's. Whew. You know I'm really sorry about the plea, but I am glad you didn't have to sit there and talk about anything you didn't want to talk about. Although I wish someone *would* come and talk to my health classes about that stuff. There is nothing in the curriculum about, you know. I can't use the word *sexting*, it's too stupid. But whatever, there's nothing about it. All we have is that god-awful assembly every year—all the schools in the county do it now. *It Doesn't End . . . Once You Press Send.* That's actually what it's called, can you believe it?"

Erika went completely still.

*Unbelievable.* That horrendous assembly that those women on the PTA had developed in the wake of her humiliation— not only did it still exist, it was spreading to other schools.

She wanted to scream at the absurdity.

"That thing is awful," Erika mumbled. "Can't somebody come up with something better?"

And as soon as the words were out of her mouth, she knew.

Yes, somebody could come up with something better.

*Massachusetts, here I come.*

# 43

## TUCKER

After many minutes of walking Tessa back and forth through the hallways, bouncing her the whole time, Tucker had finally gotten her to calm down. He thought she was asleep, but as he was getting ready to look for her crib, she started cooing.

Very carefully, he peeked at her face. She smelled like sour milk, and her eyelashes were perfect.

Paul reappeared in the hallway, looking sheepish.

"Hey there," he said quietly. "Sorry to abandon you for so long."

"It's no problem," Tucker said. "I'm happy to do it."

Paul nodded, taking that in, while Tucker stood there, considering the man before him.

He was short and broad-shouldered. Square-jawed. Paul yawned, and Tucker noticed that the bottle of beer in his hand was still full, like he'd forgotten to drink it.

"Apologies in advance if I barely know my own name. Babies are no joke. Don't have one before you're ready, and maybe don't have one when you're forty-six either. Sorry, that came out wrong. This is all very exciting, just very exhausting." He cleared his throat. "So, um. Where did you and Erika meet?"

He sounded a little suspicious on that last question. Tucker instinctively held Tessa tighter.

"We worked together a couple years ago."

Paul nodded absentmindedly, then started asking Tucker about school, which turned into a nonstop barrage of questions about what Tucker was interested in, what he wanted to study, what his ultimate plan was. Tucker was happy about his answers, though he wasn't sure if Paul was impressed. Because that's what this was about, right? Sizing him up?

But then Paul sighed, rubbed his temples.

"You know, I'm actually glad you're here. I can only take so much of . . . you know. *This.* The endless conversations about breastfeeding and where to order diapers online. Enough already."

As Paul started rambling about baseball, Tucker considered him with a frown. He realized that Paul hadn't been feeling him out at all. He was just one of those men who preferred to talk with other men. Who only knew how to talk to other men.

How strange that seemed. How pathetically sad.

Paul was going on and on about the Nats and their bullpen problems, but Tucker ignored him and broke in.

"I'm really excited for Erika," he said. "About this summer. I think she's kind of downplaying what a big deal it is. I know she's going to be great."

Paul suddenly seemed to remember his beer. He took a couple slow swigs. When he was done, he pointed it at Tucker.

"So what about you? Big plans for this summer?"

"Sort of. My friend's family has a place at Bethany Beach. His dad's a partner in this new crab house on Coastal Highway. It's kind of by the water tower, on the Bay side? I'm going to work there."

Now Paul was smiling. "Excellent. I did a summer at the Jersey shore when I was in college. Whew. Did I get into some trouble."

*Trouble.* That was a fine idea, wasn't it? Tucker still wanted some trouble in his life, for sure. Ryan had officially declared this the summer of bikinis and beer, and Tucker liked bikinis. Beer was growing on him.

And yet he was suddenly full of doubt and restlessness. Because the whole time he'd been bouncing the baby in his arms, all he could think of was his own family back at home.

"Can I hand Tessa back to you? I need to make a quick call."

Standing alone in the corner of the garden, Tucker tried, as calmly and rationally as he could, to convince his mom that he should stay home for the summer, so that Riley could stay with them, too.

"I can go to the beach next summer. It's not a big deal. This is really important."

"Tucker, he seems like a very healthy, happy little boy, so I don't know why you think—"

"You weren't there today. I caught Grandma Ruth sitting at the table, breathing heavy, and she made me promise not to tell Nate and Maggie. I think even a few more weeks is too long. This will be so much better for him, until they figure out what's next. Until Maggie moves or finds a way to rearrange her place or whatever."

His mom was silent on the other end, and Tucker did his best to keep his mouth shut and let her think.

"I appreciate what you want to do here—really I do. But it's so much more complicated than you're making it sound. Who has legal custody of him? How hard did they really look for his mom?"

Now Tucker was the silent one.

"I think Grandma Ruth has custody? And I'm not sure about his mom."

"This is what I mean, okay? This is not some simple little thing. It's not as easy as saying you'll take care of him during the day. You need to make some money before next year, so you'd have to work at night."

Tucker stared at the twinkling white lights that lined the fence. He smelled the basil growing in the big blue pot at his feet. He listened to the drone of the cicadas.

"I'm sorry," he said, his voice breaking a little. "I knew it was too much to ask. I just thought I'd give it a shot."

As Tucker was struggling with how to say goodbye, his mom sighed.

"It's not that it's too much to ask, hon. I need time to think. I obviously have to talk to Frank. And then I'll make some calls."

Tucker shut his eyes and clutched the phone tighter in his hand.

"Thank you. You have no idea how much this means to me. And he's going to totally love staying with us. I mean, assuming it works out. But I really think it will. He's going to be so happy, you'll see."

Another silence stretched out between them, and then his mom spoke to him gently.

"Tucker? I love your big heart, but I'm worried that it's giving you some big ideas right now. I don't want you to get ahead of yourself, okay? We are talking about the summer. And it's still very complicated."

Tucker felt a pang in his chest then, because his mom knew him well. In a secret corner of his mind, he had been thinking big. The idea of Riley staying with them forever hadn't been there at first, when he'd asked about the weekend. But over the course of this day, all those emotional moments on the farm, Erika reappearing, meeting Tessa, the possibility had been planted inside him.

If Tucker had just asked his mom and Frank straight out, of course they would have said no. He knew this was no small idea, what he was thinking, and it certainly wasn't something to be decided spontaneously or lightly. But after they'd spent some time with Riley, maybe they'd feel differently. Maybe this would start to feel right for everybody—he thought there was a chance that it would.

Still, he knew he needed to take this slow, not to get his hopes up too much. No matter what, he'd stay in Riley's life, and that's what mattered most.

"I hear you, Mom. Seriously. I understand what you're saying."

"Okay. I was just making sure. We'll talk more tomorrow?"

"Yeah, yeah. For sure."

They said goodbye, and two seconds after he'd hung up, his phone pinged.

His mom had texted him a picture of Riley curled up in Frank's lap, watching the movie.

Now Tucker couldn't stop smiling.

Special nights could change things—he still believed that. Maybe it was a little innocent, a little childlike, to put his faith in that idea, but that's who Tucker was.

It was who he always wanted to be.

# 44

## ERIKA

Tessa was sleeping when Erika finally held her. They were alone in the nursery, and Erika examined her as gently as she could.

Tessa's cheek was impossibly soft to the touch, and her tiny fingers were curled around the edge of a thin muslin blanket. Her mouth made a sucking motion, even as she slept. It was very silly and very cute, and god—she was vulnerable. What a terrifying thing, to bring something so vulnerable into the world.

Still, Erika noticed that Tessa had heft. She was solid and healthy and strong.

Erika hummed to her, very quietly. Then she kissed her head, set her in her crib, and told her that she'd see her soon. As she tiptoed out of the room, her arms tingled and felt heavy, remembering the weight of her sister.

* * *

Erika slipped into the bathroom and looked in the mirror. She was feeling very fierce. Very happy.

There was something she wanted to do.

Heart beating fast, she took out her phone and got ready to type. She had to dig deep to come up with exactly what she wanted to say.

**Hi Dana. I wouldn't be surprised if you got rid of my number, so . . . this is Erika. I never said thank you, for what you did. So I'm saying it now, two years late. Thank you for tracking down those assholes' phones. Thanks for erasing it. I hope you're well.**

That last line sounded kind of ridiculous, didn't it? Too late, it was sent. As Erika was about to get up and walk out, a call came through.

She barely managed to keep from dropping the phone in the toilet. Her hands shook as she answered.

"Um, hello?"

"Hi, Erika."

"Hi."

"This is so weird. I usually only make phone calls when something is horribly wrong. Or when I just painted my nails, and I don't want to mess them up."

Erika took deep, slow breaths. This was going to be okay. Everything was going to be okay.

"That is entirely and perfectly reasonable. I approve of those parameters."

"Right? This is a little different, obviously, but I didn't want to type this, so here we go. Thanks for saying thanks. That was . . . very nice of you. But also, I was awful in high school. Like, the worst. I'm sure you heard the stuff I said about you. I guess I didn't know any better? No, ugh. That sounds like a cop-out. How about 'I know better now.' Let's go with that."

Erika stared down at the fuzzy pink bath mat. "Well . . . thanks again, I guess. For saying all that."

There was a long silence on the line, and then Dana exhaled.

"Now what do we talk about?"

"I have no idea," Erika said.

"Uh, how's things? You good?"

Erika looked up and took stock of her surroundings, reflecting back on this very strange day. She'd spent yesterday in a courthouse feeling defeated, but also like she knew who she was—a fighter. She'd spent the afternoon in a field of green, lifted high by the feeling of giving and receiving forgiveness. All of that had led her to having a few moments of real connection with Jennifer and Tessa, and then to this conversation she'd been wanting to have for a long time.

"I think I'm weirdly good?" Erika said.

"Cool, me too. We don't have to hang out or something now, do we?"

"No offense," Erika said, "but I hope not. I mean, if I ever see you at a party or something, I guess we can hug?"

"Yes. I will totally hug you someday at a party."

"Great," Erika said. "It's a deal."

Erika went and found Tucker, and the two of them shared some whispered words about the phone calls they'd made, all the ideas that were swirling in their heads. They were both happy, a little bit giddy. She told him that they should get going, that she needed to get some rest tonight, but first she had to say goodbye to Jennifer.

They walked inside, and Erika spotted her right away, huddled by the fridge with a little pack of women that Erika had met earlier, when they'd left the piano room—they were Jennifer's friends from college and her sisters, Beth and Cori. Right now, they were all drinking wine out of plastic cups, cackling about something. When Jennifer saw Tucker and Erika, her eyes lit up and she called them over.

Jennifer introduced Tucker to everyone, then touched Erika's arm lightly and pointed to an elaborate display of cupcakes behind her, taking her voice down low.

"So, I told your dad I was going to pick up a sheet cake from Costco, because I love sheet cakes from Costco, but he insisted on getting these from some place in Bethesda."

"They probably cost a fortune," Beth muttered.

Jennifer swatted at her and kept talking. "So he brings them home, and when I unpacked them, I asked if he'd gotten, I don't know, licorice flavor or something. He looked at me like I was nuts and said no, vanilla. But, oh my god, they're awful.

I think there's something wrong with them."

"Smell one," Cori said. "I swear, it's like an ashtray."

"No, no," Beth said. "Don't be ridiculous. They smell more like old, burnt coffee from a gas station."

Erika started laughing, and Tucker—peering around like he was a spy undertaking a secret mission—grabbed a big pink cupcake. Standing next to Erika and leaning back against the counter, he held it carefully under his nose.

"Well?" Jennifer asked.

"It's not that bad," Tucker said.

"*Really?*"

"No, I'm kidding. This thing is a nightmare. It smells like Donald Trump's soul."

At that point they all started laughing so hard that Jennifer had to plead with them to be quiet, not wake up Tessa. Tucker handed the cupcake to Erika, and she held it at arm's length like it was a bomb, because yes, the thing was as bad as everybody said.

Beth was cranking open another bottle of wine, considering Tucker carefully as she did.

"So. Where did Erika find you?"

"Oh!" he said. "We're, um, just friends. But she found me about three years ago, when we worked together at a crappy arcade."

The women were smiling and watching him like they were waiting for more. Tucker glanced Erika's way, as if he were considering how much he should say.

Erika bumped his shoulder with hers.

"Tucker was fifteen. Through a series of elaborate lies, he managed to get scheduled for all of the same shifts as me."

"Smooth," Beth said. "Very smooth."

Tucker had a big, goofy smile on his face now.

"Whatever," he said. "She was definitely into me, too. I think it was the braces. And the zits."

Now everybody was cracking up again, and Erika was feeling a little embarrassed, but in that good, giggly sort of way.

"And you two have been friends ever since?" Jennifer asked.

Tucker met Erika's eyes for a second, both of them struggling to come up with the right words.

"No, no," he finally said. "We didn't see each other for a long time, but this past year . . . we keep seeming to end up at the same parties. And they're always really good parties."

"Tell us about the parties," Cori demanded. "We're old and we need this."

"We so do," Beth added. "Especially because this one is pretty boring."

Jennifer scoffed. "Um, it's a party for *a baby*. Was I supposed to have a keg or something? And I'm pretty sure Erika and Tucker don't want to recount their nightlife for me."

Jennifer leaned her head on Beth's shoulder, and Erika could see it then—that they'd all had a teeny bit too much to drink. They looked so happy, though, and she kind of wanted to give them what they were asking for, a good story. She could tell the PG versions, couldn't she? She just had no idea how to begin.

Then Tucker cleared his throat.

"Last summer, there was a secret party at the shut-down arcade where we used to work. We snuck in with a bunch of people and played mini golf, jumped in the ball pit. Also Erika made everybody dance to Taylor Swift because she's obsessed with Taylor Swift."

Jennifer straightened up, her eyes bright. Everyone perked up, in fact, and Beth started chanting *more stories, more stories, mores stories.* Erika's heart was thumping a little harder as she started talking.

"Last Christmas, we went to a party at the house—you know the one in the Kentlands, with the decorations?"

"Oh my god!" shouted one of the college friends, her mouth hanging open. *"You've been inside that place?"*

"Yes! There was a band and a DJ and a Santa. Tucker and I crushed everyone in a Harry Potter Trivia contest, and then we went to the secret video game room, and I completely slaughtered him at Super Smash Brothers. Absolutely destroyed him."

Erika stared down at the monstrous cupcake, fiddling a little with the wrapper.

"He was cool about it, though. He still took me out and bought me pancakes."

"See?" Cori said, poking Jennifer in the arm. "Didn't we need this?"

Everyone was looking at Tucker now, so Erika did, too. She expected him to have a smartass smile on his face, but he didn't. His face had gone a little serious, a little shy.

"I went to visit Erika at St. B's in March," he finally said. "She took me to a fake prom party, and we danced on a sofa to 'You Know' while everybody cheered."

And it came back to her then, all in a flash, exactly what that moment had been like.

She remembered the music and their bodies pressed together. The tickle of his breath when he'd whispered in her ear. That had been the two of them at their very best, when they made each other feel free, feel light. And the fact that she'd been on display and that felt good, for the first time in so long . . .

Erika had tried hard to forget about that party entirely, because of everything that had happened at the end. But the night had been so good before it had been bad, had it not? Now that she and Tucker had made amends, she could remember it without flinching. She could embrace the parts that were beautiful.

The women were still grinning at them, still sipping from their cups.

"Oh god," Beth said. "*That song.* I wish you hadn't mentioned it. It's going to be in my head all night now."

Jennifer covered her eyes with her hand. "Okay, I have to confess. I secretly love it."

This set off a loud debate among all the women—half of them swearing to loathe "You Know," the other half reluctantly admitting to liking it. Erika was too embarrassed to share how strongly she felt about this particular issue, so she stayed silent, her cheeks going a little pink.

She realized that Tucker was checking on her, gauging her reaction. Then he interrupted everyone.

"Hey, hey!" he yelled. "There's nothing wrong with that song! I happen to love that song."

"You love that song?" Beth asked skeptically.

"It's a good song! I would defend that song forever. Until I die."

"Until you *die*?"

"Yes! It's the perfect soundtrack for . . . basically everything. Dancing. Driving. Running. Definitely good for running."

Now that smartass look was creeping onto his face, and Erika waited for him to say more, to give her up, but he didn't. She took a breath, ready to make a confession of her own, but she was too distracted by Tucker's stupid smile, by how maddeningly adorable he was.

Erika shoved the cupcake in his face.

She'd done it in an instant, utterly without thinking. Tucker's nose and his cheeks were now frosted in pink, his mouth hanging open in shock. He moved as quickly as he could to grab another one from the counter behind them, and she did her best to dodge him, only half succeeding.

Now Erika had sprinkles all over her chin, and the thing really did smell like an ashtray. Crumbs were raining from her face down onto the floor, and as they did, she came to her senses.

*Oh my god, you're making a mess of their new house, not to mention acting like a five-year-old.*

She turned wide-eyed to Jennifer, and started stuttering out an apology, but then Jennifer grabbed a cupcake and smooshed it into Beth's cheek.

"That's for calling my party boring."

"JENNY!"

Two seconds later, cupcakes were flying everywhere, and everyone was screeching and laughing, Cori crying out that the things were poisonous and they were probably all going to die. One got Erika right on the nose, and she squealed in disgust.

"What in the . . . what are you *doing?*"

Erika whirled around to see her dad standing in the doorway of the kitchen. She desperately wanted to peg him in the face, but the cupcakes were no more. Jennifer was handing out paper towels, and everybody was still laughing, ignoring her dad as he continued to stand there and ask what was going on before finally throwing his hands in the air and disappearing.

Erika walked over to the sink and did a half-assed job of cleaning her face. Tucker came over and stood right across from her, smiling. Very slowly, he reached out and wiped a bit of frosting from her nose with his finger.

"Now what?" she asked him quietly.

Tucker looked surprised, his face a little flushed.

"Um, I know you have an early morning. I thought you said you needed to go?"

That had been her plan a few minutes ago—to get home, get some rest. But somewhere in the course of recounting all those parties, Erika had officially stopped caring about that.

"One night of not enough sleep isn't going to kill me. I'm covered in toxic frosting. It's barely past ten. I can't go home yet. *We* can't go home yet."

Tucker nodded, smiling.

"Okay. I did hear from Bobby about something we could do."

"I'm listening."

"It's really dumb."

"Spill, Tucker."

He sighed. "Bobby's girlfriend, Destiny, could get us into after-prom, if we wanted to go. But it's that stupid one the school puts on at Dave and Buster's. You know, the thing they do to keep kids from drinking in hotels. Once you go in, you're not allowed to leave, so . . . it's probably not a good idea. We'd have to stay until the end, which is, Jesus. I don't even know. Three in the morning?"

He wanted to go, badly—it was written all over his face. He wanted a few more hours of acting stupid with her, didn't he?

It was exactly what Erika wanted, too.

"We're going."

"Are you sure?"

"Yes, yes, yes! Get your keys."

Erika turned to give a final wave to Jennifer and the others. As she did, she saw that they were all watching her and Tucker go, looking at them a little wistfully.

"Don't do anything we wouldn't do," Beth called. "No, wait.

I don't mean that. Do all the things we used to do, before we got old!"

The last thing Erika saw as they hustled out the door was Jennifer laughing and punching her sister in the shoulder.

# 45

## TUCKER

Destiny was in charge of the after-prom committee, which is how Tucker's and Erika's names had gotten on the official list. A couple of parent volunteers were waiting at the door, and they checked Tucker's and Erika's IDs, made them sign the paperwork with the night's rules, and then let them in.

As soon as they entered the main room, Destiny spotted them. She waved wildly, then started up a modified version of one of the school's cheers. "We've got Tucker, yes we do." A couple other girls took it up, too, and just as everyone was staring at them, Destiny switched over to Erika's name.

Erika squealed and hid behind him, refusing to emerge until the chanting finally ended. Her face was pinker than he'd ever seen it.

"Sorry," Tucker said, though he wasn't actually sorry at all and couldn't stop smiling. "Destiny is the head cheerleader."

"Yeah, I can tell," Erika said. "I think I need a drink after that."

"You *do* remember that not drinking is kind of the entire point of this thing?"

She gave him a little shove, then spotted Nina and ran off to say hello. A second later, Destiny popped up at Tucker's side, with Bobby in tow. She wrapped Tucker in a hug, while Bobby patted him on the shoulder.

"Uh, thanks for that greeting," Tucker told her. "And thanks for sneaking us in tonight."

"Oh, I put you both on the list a month ago. I just had a feeling."

Tucker tilted his head, disbelieving. "Really? Cause the odds were pretty long, a month ago."

"We had faith in you," Bobby said.

"*We?*" Destiny said, giving him a pointed look. "You said there was zero chance."

"Shhh. Don't tell him that." Bobby put an arm around her, then turned to Tucker with a more serious look. "You okay? How was the farm?"

"It was good. Riley's at my house. He's finally seen the first Harry Potter."

Bobby shook his head. "Older cousins are supposed to introduce you to cool shit, not turn you into a dork."

"Harry Potter *is* cool."

"Whatever you say. Now I want to kick your ass at air hockey."

Tucker said he was in, but then he saw someone and stopped short.

He told Bobby to hold on one second—he had one more thing he had to do.

"Hi! You look great, really great. That's kind of like a fancy version of a tennis dress."

"That's exactly why I bought it."

Tucker had not seen much of Suzanne this year. Their schedules were not aligned, they didn't go to the same parties, and of course she'd been very busy.

Tucker glanced nervously around, as he tried to figure out where to begin. "I heard you're playing at Northwestern next year. Congrats."

"Yeah, I worked my ass off—so thanks."

"You're welcome."

She stared at him, her stark, pretty eyebrows raised as high as they would go. He'd forgotten how intense those things were. They were able to convey complete, cohesive questions.

Right now they were asking, *What exactly is the point of this little chat?*

"Are you, uh, having a good time?" he asked.

She shrugged. "Actually, I'm pretty bored. I beat my date at like four different games, and now he's over there pouting. But it's totally my fault for coming with such a tool."

Tucker followed her gaze to the corner of the room.

"Oh god, you came with Adam? To say you're too good for

him is the understatement of the century. I apologize on behalf of our entire high school that it could produce no one better to take you to prom."

She was smiling at him now, but barely. Tucker fumbled on.

"Listen, I wanted to say how sorry I am, about how things ended last summer. I know I sort of said sorry before, but I didn't do a very good job. Okay, I did a terrible job."

Around them, games were pinging and beeping; lights were flashing. Tucker spotted one of his baseball friends triumphantly walking around with a giant stuffed M&M that he'd won from the prize counter. He did his best to block all that out and gather his thoughts.

"I was in kind of a bad place, back then. I was pretty down on myself, and I kept hoping you were going to suddenly, magically want to be my girlfriend. Because you're so amazing, and if you wanted to be my girlfriend, then I thought that would really say something about me, you know? Prove what kind of guy I was? Anyway, maybe you don't care about any of this, I would totally understand if you didn't—I just wanted to explain."

Right over Tucker's shoulder, there was a very intense game of Dance Dance Revolution happening, and for a moment Suzanne acted like it was much more interesting than this conversation. Then she looked back at him, her expression a little gentler.

"It helps a little. I'm glad you told me. And I'm really sorry about your dad."

"Yeah, thanks for your note. That was really nice. And thanks for giving to my fundraiser."

She stepped forward with her arms out, then gave Tucker a very delicate hug.

"I'll see you around, okay? And good luck in Michigan. I hope you're happy there."

"Yeah, yeah," he said with a smile. "I really think I will be."

Tucker and Erika ate too many snacks and drank too much soda. They played a drag-race game against Bobby and Destiny, losing horribly, each insisting the other was to blame. They whacked moles and threw darts and started pooling their tickets, debating which terrible prize they would take home and which one of them would get to keep it.

Every time someone asked Erika what she was doing this summer, her face lit up as she told them. And she was having an absolute blast, playing all these silly games—Tucker loved seeing that.

Just now, she and Kara had agreed to play that ridiculous wrestling game—the one with the enormous padded suits that people wore as they tried to knock each other down. As soon as the girls pulled the suits on, they realized they were one-size-fits-all, and they were both entirely too short for them. When they tried to square off, they couldn't actually wrestle, and had to settle instead for a competition of who could successfully walk toward the other. Neither managed more than a couple steps, and finally they were both lying there like bugs.

As Tucker watched Erika, prone and laughing hysterically, he couldn't help imagining some different world, one where they had gone to the same school, been the same age. They might have been best friends. Maybe something more, who knew. But right now, with the way things were . . .

He ran over to help her out of the suit. Grabbing onto both of his arms, Erika slowly emerged, sweaty and disheveled. Once she was free, she smiled up at him and didn't let go.

"How'd I do?" she asked.

"So good. Incredible. I sent a video of it to my mom."

"TUCKER!"

She finally released him, then did her best to fix her hair, but it was sticking up everywhere, and she looked so damn cute.

Erika pointed at her head. "How is it?"

Tucker frowned. "Awful. Just awful."

She flipped him off, and that was what did it—that's what brought to bear all that he'd been struggling with since the farm.

He had to let it out, what he was thinking.

"Can we talk? For a second?"

As soon as he said that, her face fell a little. Tucker turned and made his way to the quietest corner he could find, over by the pinball machines. She followed, then stood across from him, waiting.

"Erika, this should all be perfect right now, and in a way it is, but it's also the worst, right? All day I've been thinking *what if*, but there's no way, is there? You're leaving, and then I'm leaving, and . . . oh, wait." Tucker stuttered for a second, felt his face go red. "I shouldn't have assumed you were thinking the same thing. You might not have been thinking *what if* at all . . ."

Erika put up her hand, telling him to stop. Her lips were pressed together, and her eyes were big and teary. She ran her hand through her hair a couple more times, then stared at the floor.

"I was thinking *what if*, too. But you're right. We're on the edge of all this *stuff*, and we don't have any time, and . . ."

Her voice had gotten shaky, and she let her words trail off.

Tucker looked out at the bright, loud room. Then he closed his eyes and tried to focus on the things that really mattered— on what was best for her. For him.

"Okay. I'm glad we said all that. And I feel like such a jerk, complaining. It's been a really hard year, but I think I'm good and you're good and we're ready for what's next and that's what's most important. You're about to take off and go do something amazing, and I'm really happy for you. I don't want to mope or whatever. We should be celebrating."

Erika swiped at her eyes and managed a tiny smile.

"You're right. You're absolutely right. That's why we should make tonight count."

She reached out and squeezed his arm, directed his gaze to the left.

"C'mon. Let's get a souvenir."

\* \* \*

Erika pushed him into the photo booth, then crawled in after him, and Tucker was immediately struck by how little room there was. He could have done a whole bit about how the person that designed this thing totally did it on purpose . . .

He couldn't quite manage to say all that, though—not with Erika half on his lap, one of her arms around his shoulders.

"You know I could have taken a selfie of us for free, instead of paying *five dollars* . . ."

"Shut up, Tucker! It's not the same."

"Okay, okay. But you better make a really stupid face. If I'm going to keep this forever, I want your face to look as ridiculous as your hair looks right now."

In front of them, a clock was clicking down, preparing them. Five, four, three . . .

"Sorry," Erika said. "I didn't come in here to make silly faces."

"*What?*"

The camera flashed, with Tucker laughing at Erika while she looked decidedly away.

"So we're going to take *serious* pictures, in the photo booth?" he asked.

"It's not that, it's . . . I'm a little overwhelmed, okay? I'm pretty freaking upset that this is how things have to be, but I'm also really, really glad we're together, for a few more hours."

On the screen in front of them, the clock once again started to tick.

"Okay, okay," Tucker said. "I get it. I will take a very solemn photo with you to commemorate this sort of shitty, sort of awesome night."

Three, two . . .

The camera flashed just as Erika made a fist and held it in front of his nose.

"*Tucker*. Listen to me! We've been to all these amazing parties this year, right? And we're in the middle of our last one! Even if we can't be together, I want a little extra something to remember it. Do you know what I mean?"

"Yes, I do. I definitely do. That's why I paid *five whole dollars . . .*"

"TUCKER!" Erika was laughing, covering her face. "I don't want a picture! I want *something to remember*."

The third countdown was starting. The very last flash was on its way. She was looking right at him, and finally he saw it, what she was asking with her eyes.

His heart went wild in his chest. "Really?"

"Yes!"

As the camera clicked, he took her face in his hands and he kissed her. It felt like years of *yes* said all together in an instant.

# 46

## ERIKA

She crawled onto his lap and kissed him until her lips stung, not caring how obvious it must be to anybody walking by what was going on in the photo booth. Her hands were in his hair and his arms were circling her waist, and she never wanted to stop.

Except they had to, of course. His elbows were banging into the walls, and her head was bumping the ceiling. He kept laughing, and she kept chiding him, and finally they had to come up for air.

She wrapped her arms around him and buried her face in his neck, breathing him in. Leaving him would be harder, having had this little hint of what it could have been like, but she still thought this was worth it. They were both going into it open-eyed, honest. She didn't have a shred of guilt or shame about it.

Also, Tucker was a really good kisser.

"I can't believe this is it," he said. "I can't believe, after all this time, and now . . ."

"It's the fucking worst."

He was running his finger up and down her back. She curled into him as far as she could and sighed.

"We probably have to get out of this photo booth," Erika said.

"I know, I know. This sucks. I mean, everything we just talked about—that epically, royally sucks. But you know what else sucks? This party."

Erika barked out a laugh, then leaned back to look at him.

"What? I thought you were having fun! This has been so much fun!"

"I know, I know. I am glad I came, that I saw people. But this seems like a crappy way to say goodbye, you know? It's not up to our usual standards. If we can't have . . . you know . . . what we want to have, then we should at least have one more awesome night."

Erika thought for a second, then carefully drew back the curtain on the photo booth a couple inches. She glanced out at the loud room with all its neon colors, its clean carpet.

"I see what you mean. This is, like, a corporate version of the Cave. Not as much grime, but not as much charm either."

"And we can't even leave."

Erika scoffed, then poked him in the chest.

"Oh my god, there's no way that's really true! I'm twenty

freaking years old. What are they going to do, block the door?"

"That's a good point," Tucker said. "Screw this. Do you want to escape?"

Erika leaned forward until her forehead touched his.

"Yes," she whispered. "The escape begins now."


"I want to help, but there's nothing I can do!" Destiny said. "If you say you're sick, a parent has to pick you up. And if you leave, you can't walk at graduation—it says it on the form you signed."

Tucker turned to Erika. "Graduation is boring. Let's go."

Erika punched him in the arm. "No way! What about your mom? Don't tell me your mom doesn't care about graduation."

"Oh, Tucker's mom cares," Bobby said. "She cares big-time. She cried the other day just *talking* about it."

Tucker rolled his eyes. "Okay, okay. We can't leave by the front door. We'll have to sneak out."

Destiny put a hand in the air. "Officially? I heard none of this and had nothing to do with it. But *unofficially*, I'm going to point out that there are four other exits, each guarded by a pair of teachers. You need to find the weakest link."

Bobby nodded. "Yes, definitely. We need to find the weakest link. But also, to be clear, this is Dave and Buster's, not Alcatraz."

Destiny scoffed and told him not to ruin the fun. Then she and Tucker began a fierce debate about which door was their best bet, while Erika scanned the room, trying to think. As she did, she spotted Nina surveying the prize counter. Erika went over and took her by the elbow, whispering that she needed her and steering her quickly back toward the huddle.

"Tucker and I are breaking out of after-prom. It's all hands on deck."

"Are you kidding?" Nina asked. "Please tell me you're kidding."

"Not kidding! You know you want to help us!"

Nina kept insisting this was a terrible idea, but by the time they'd arrived back to where Tucker, Bobby, and Destiny were waiting, the operation was in full swing.

"Okay," Tucker said. "We definitely want to go for that far corner. There's almost nobody hanging out over there, and it's Mrs. Donovan and Miss Beckett at the door. They're both total softies, and Miss Beckett is the tennis coach, so . . . I've got a plan for getting her away. Now we just need to get rid of Mrs. Donovan."

Nina sighed very loudly, then started tapping her foot.

"I am probably going to regret this, but . . . I know for a fact that Mrs. Donovan loves Yrma. So I think this might be a good excuse to force my incredibly annoying friends to speak to each other again."

Tucker and Erika were crouched behind a ludicrously enormous claw machine game, one that was full of three-foot-tall stuffed animals. It was the perfect vantage point from which to make a run for the door, as soon as it was clear—and already they were halfway there. Suzanne had led Miss Beckett off to a little alcove by the bathroom and was now talking with her very intently.

Erika peeked around the corner of the claw game to watch, but her stomach dropped as she did.

"Oh my god. Suzanne looks like she's about to start crying. Is she . . . is something actually wrong? Do you think she's okay?"

"She fine, she's fine," Tucker said. "That's her tennis coach, but the tears are fake. She said she'd never fake-cried before, so she wanted to try it."

Erika whirled back to watch again, just in time to see the tears rolling down Suzanne's cheeks. "Holy shit. That is . . . impressive."

"She told me this was the best part of her night."

"*What?*"

Tucker shrugged. "She likes a challenge?"

Erika was wishing that she was a little closer so she could hear the full performance. Meanwhile, Nina was standing off to the left, coaching Kara and Yrma. Erika whispered that it was time, and Nina hauled the girls over.

"Okay," she said. "We're all set. The two of them are going to stand by the Skee-Ball machines and start yelling at each other. They'll be close enough to Mrs. Donovan that she'll be the first to spot them, but far enough away from the door that you guys should be able to make a run for it without her seeing, once she's been lured away."

Kara and Yrma both had their arms crossed, and they were very deliberately not looking at each other.

"Uh, thank you," Erika said. "I really appreciate you doing this, you know. For us. This is . . . this is cool, right?"

Yrma arched an eyebrow. "Oh, *I'm* totally fine. This is no big deal. At all."

Kara let out a single, loud laugh. "Um, I'm *also* totally fine. I'm not even sure I can pull this off, acting mad. Because I'm so over it."

Nina sighed very loudly, rolling her eyes so hard it looked like it hurt. Just as she was about to give the girls their final orders, Yrma held out her hand, nonchalantly examining her nails.

"I mean, I can provide some ammunition, Kara. If you want."

The atmosphere around the claw machine grew very tense. Erika's eyes were darting back and forth between Kara and Yrma, and she was getting more nervous by the second.

Kara crossed her arms.

"Ammunition?"

Yrma smoothed out her hair, shook out her shoulders.

"That day that we met? On the soccer field? You were right. I totally said . . . you know. That word."

Kara's eyes flashed. Very slowly, she started nodding. Erika glanced sideways at Tucker, who mouthed *uh-oh*. For one horrible moment, she was terrified that they'd started an actual problem, all because of this stupid plan, except . . .

She wasn't entirely sure if Kara was mad or really excited to be right.

"*I. Fucking. Knew it.* Can we talk about the fact that you were just learning English but somehow knew *that word*, of all words? Why? How?"

"Wouldn't you like to know?"

Kara started poking Nina aggressively on the shoulder.

"I told you she said it. Didn't I tell you?"

"Yes, yes. You freaking told me! *Nine million times.* Now can you please have your stupid fake fight where I told you to?"

Nina grabbed both their arms and began dragging them to the appointed spot. The girls obeyed, but spent the whole walk whispering conspiratorially at each other over Nina's head. Once she had deposited the two of them by the Skee-Ball, they started yelling.

"This was all your fault and you know it!"

"It was all your fault and *you* know it!"

Tucker started giggling and Erika kicked him, told him to get ahold of himself. She peeked back around the claw machine again, her eyes on the girls, waiting to see if Mrs. Donovan would take the bait.

But as she watched them, she groaned and kicked Tucker again.

"Oh my god. They're *laughing.* Both of them! They don't look like they're fighting at all—this is never going to work!"

But right then, Mrs. Donovan jumped out of her chair. She hustled toward Kara and Yrma, waving her hands, pleading with them to calm down.

"Let's not end the year this way, ladies. Please, let's not? Ladies? *Ladies!*"

Erika felt Tucker grab her shoulder and give it a squeeze.

"Now or never?" he whispered.

"We've got this. Let's go."

Walking fast, but not so fast that they'd attract attention, they made their way to the door. Erika kept glancing over her shoulder, worried they'd be spotted, but Mrs. Donovan and Miss Beckett were both fully distracted, and the room was so crowded. Ariana Grande was pounding from the speakers; lights were flashing everywhere. No one could possibly notice them, right? Erika scurried faster, and there it was—the door. They were golden. She fell into it as hard as she could.

It didn't budge.

Erika tried again, then whirled around to look at Tucker.

"*It's locked.*"

"No," Tucker said. "No way."

He swiveled around to check the room, then tried the door himself, softly cursing when it didn't give way.

"Why are they guarding the damn door if it's locked? How is this not, I don't know, a safety code violation? Okay, forget this, they won't kick me out of graduation, there's no way— we're just leaving through the front door."

"No! I can't do that to you. Or your mom!"

"C'mon, who cares?"

Erika sighed and grabbed his arm, ready to pull him back

into the room, to try to convince him they could have fun here . . .

And then she saw it, right there at eye level.

"Tucker."

He turned to see what she was pointing at, then whipped his head back, eyes wide.

"No way."

"Yes way. I'm doing it."

"You wouldn't!"

"But what if I did?"

"You wouldn't. You *seem* cool on the surface, but you're a total rule follower. You're such a Hermione."

"Hermione always broke the rules when it mattered!"

Tucker bit his lip.

"That thing about the ink—that's an urban legend or something, right?"

"We're about to find out."

A second later, Erika's hand was bright blue and the fire alarm was screaming in their ears.

# 41

## TUCKER

Everyone had evacuated to the parking lot, which was threatening to descend into chaos, though the teachers and parents were making a pretty impressive effort of rounding everyone up and keeping them from disappearing.

Because the fire alarm had automatically unlocked all the doors in the building, Tucker and Erika had been among the first out, and had managed to hide behind a low wall of bushes on the lot's far right before any of the chaperones had exited. Now they were stuck staring woefully at Tucker's mom's car.

"Who is that leaning on it?" Erika asked. "A teacher?"

"It's the vice principal."

"*The vice principal?* Oh my god, we're never getting out of here."

"No, no! We'll figure something out."

Tucker took stock of their surroundings. Dave and Buster's sat alone off the highway. The parking lot was fenced, with one entrance, a paid gate.

"We just need to wait for everyone to go back in. Or if that takes too long, we call an Uber and then sneak out to the road. We can probably make it without anyone seeing."

Turning toward Erika, he looked down at her hand, feeling half-elated, half-horrified.

"Oh my god, I seriously didn't think . . . *how is that real?* I didn't think the ink thing was real!"

"What am I supposed to do about this?" Erika asked, but she was laughing, thank god she was laughing.

"Will it be weird if you show up to your summer program wearing one glove? That would be fine, right? It can be your thing."

"How about I touch your face, and then you can show up to graduation wearing a mask? That can be *your* thing."

"Hey, hey! You know my mom would be devastated, and then I'd have to tell her it's all your fault. You broke the law and made me flee a school function."

"I *made you?* That's an interesting take on how that all went down. Very interesting."

"Look, we can play the blame game later, after we get out of here."

"I'll text Nina. You go find Bobby."

"I see him right there! Are you cool crouching here for a couple minutes?"

"Yes, yes. It's fine. Leave me here with my incriminating blue hand."

Tucker had been on the verge of creeping from the bushes, but he rocked back on his heel.

"I feel like there is some kind of obvious joke I should be making right now, but I can't quite come up with it . . ."

"Oh my god, shut up and get out of here!"

Tucker emerged as stealthily as he could, slipping toward Bobby, who was busy talking and laughing with a bunch of people from his calc class, commiserating about the final. When Tucker gave him a tap on the shoulder, he jumped. The two of them retreated to a spot a few feet away where they could talk quietly.

"*How are you not gone yet?*"

"We came out of that door over there, and we had to hide! And do you not see who's leaning on my mom's car?"

Bobby whirled around. "Shit. Uh, just so you know, Destiny talked to one of the managers and he said that nobody's going back in until the fire department gets here and clears the building. He said an hour, at the very least."

Tucker cursed under his breath. "Uh, by the way, how mad is Destiny?"

"Officially? Super mad. Unofficially, she is loving every second of this, but expects you to report all the details to her, and she wants them to be good."

"Okay, okay. Yeah. We'll get out of here somehow. It's going to be a little tricky. I need a second to breathe. And think."

Tucker sat down on the curb, and Bobby sat down next to him. They looked out at the crowd, lit from on high by the glow of the parking lot's lights. There was a buzz in the air, a whole new energy. The a cappella club had gathered together and launched into their Disney medley. Two people were making out behind a minivan. Mrs. Donovan was still standing between Kara and Yrma, continuing to mediate their "fight."

Bobby started laughing. "You kind of made this a wild night for everybody. I know you'll be around a couple more weeks or whatever, but this wasn't a bad way to say goodbye, before you take off for Bethany."

Tucker laughed. "Oh my god, I didn't tell you. I'm not going! Or probably not. I asked if Riley could stay with us for the summer, and I think it's going to happen, so I'm staying, too. Which means I need a job ASAP."

Bobby punched him in the shoulder. "Work with me—at baseball camp! They told us last week that they still need a couple more counselors."

Tucker sighed and shook his head. "I wish I could, but I can't. This is only going to work if I watch Riley during the day."

"He's six, right? You can sign him up. There's still room."

"Seriously? Oh my god, that's so perfect."

Tucker leaned forward, elbows on his knees, and took a deep breath. He was feeling overwhelmed by relief, by happiness—because this was exactly how he wanted to spend the coming weeks. He was ready for college, he knew he was, but he wanted a little more time to bask in the familiar, in the people he loved and the places he knew best. He wanted to layer new memories on top of the old ones, let them shore him up for his departure, for this next stage of his life.

He glanced over at Bobby. "Hey, listen. I'm sorry I didn't come around much this year. It was hard for me, being near my old house. But I don't think I'll feel like that anymore. It won't be sad, or if it is, it'll be like that happy-sad feeling, you know?"

"Sure, sure. You should definitely come around more. My parents would be, you know. Happy to see you more."

They were both staring out at the highway, the one that led right back to the neighborhood where they'd grown up together.

"Do you know what I was thinking about the other day?" Bobby asked. "When your dad gave you that old knife and we hid it in my room, because you knew your mom would never let you keep it?"

"And then your mom found it and completely freaked out," Tucker said.

"And then my dad said it was actually pretty cool, and I thought she was going to kill him."

That story hit Tucker right in the chest, but the pang that he felt—it was harsh, and it was complicated, but it wasn't all bad.

"I kind of wish I still had it," Tucker said. "The knife."

"Your mom might have kept it. I could see her doing that."

"Yeah, yeah. I'll ask. I could show it to Riley. I mean, not to play with. Just to show him."

"You can pretend it's magic, like that one Sirius gives Harry."

At first Tucker laughed, but then he sat up straighter. Mouth agape, he turned to look at his friend.

"BOBBY."

"What? You know I read those stupid books."

"I know, but that's a very specific reference. I feel so close to you right now. Do you know that Sirius Black is the death that Erika finds the most emotionally devastating? Mine is obviously Dobby."

Bobby covered his face with his hands.

"You two are the worst. Seriously. You totally deserve each other."

"Thank you! I think so too, but the timing is all messed up. We did kind of make out in the photo booth, though."

"Yeah, I noticed. Lots of people noticed."

As Tucker was preparing a response to that, Nina came rushing over to them.

"Hey, hey! Destiny is about to get up and give some kind of speech, to distract everybody. When she does, Erika's going to sneak out to the road—you should be ready to go, too."

"Oh, shit! Did she call for a ride yet?"

"I totally saw you dummies hiding in the bushes. I already called you one."

"Gimme your keys," Bobby said to Tucker. "I'll drive your

car home, so nobody's asking why it's here and you're not."

"Oh my god, thank you both so much." Tucker turned to Nina. "I promise I'll pay you back."

Nina laughed. "That won't be necessary."

# 48

## ERIKA

Tucker escaped from the parking lot as Destiny climbed on top of a trash can and said that she sincerely hoped whoever had done this would confess. Erika found her own way there from behind the bushes, and then the two headed out to the main road, where they huddled off the shoulder, fingers intertwined and kissing, ignoring the people who honked at them.

After they'd been waiting about five minutes, their ride arrived. Tucker climbed into the back. Erika slid into the front.

"Hi, hi, hi," Erika said. "You're a hero. And oh my god, I forgot your car was busted! Thanks for borrowing your dad's."

Marissa turned to her very slowly.

"Oh, this was the least I would have done, to be part of this very sexy heist. Nice hand, by the way."

"Yeah, it's kind of a situation. Can we go now?"

Marissa nodded but kept the car idling. She turned the music up ridiculously loud, then took a slim green can from the cup holder, giving it a little shake.

"Would you like some of my ginger ale?"

"Would I *what*? No. We need to get out of here!"

"Okay, okay. It's just that my ginger ale is very yummy. Sometimes I tell you things are yummy, and you don't listen to me. You should always listen to me."

Erika stared her dead in the eyes, then snatched the can from her hand and put it back in the cup holder. Marissa shifted the car from park to drive, but she still didn't hit the gas.

"You know I heard about this scientific study? It was on NPR or some shit. It said the most satisfying feeling in the world isn't sex or love. It's getting to say *I told you so*."

"Start driving or I will literally kill you."

"*Literally*, Erika? As an English major, you should know how to use that word correctly."

"Oh, I'm using it quite correctly."

Tucker leaned forward from the back seat. "Can you turn the music down a little? What are you guys talking about?"

The girls both turned around, shouting *nothing* in unison. Then Marissa pointed a finger in his face.

"Put on your seat belt, please, so we don't get pulled over. God, it's like this is your first getaway or something. And where am I taking you?"

Erika chewed on her thumbnail. They hadn't exactly gotten that far. All of this work and now what? They had to come up with something good or this would all be a total bust.

"I feel like we need to go to the water or something," she said. "The ocean's obviously too far, but I don't know. Maybe there's somewhere else?"

"Maybe," Tucker said. "Or should we go into DC? There has to be something in DC. We can head that way and figure it out as we go."

"That sounds good," Erika said. "Let's do that."

"Okay, you crazy kids," Marissa said. "I'll drop you at the Metro?"

"Yes, yes," Erika said. "That's perfect."

Marissa took a right, heading in the direction they'd agreed upon, which led them down a busy thoroughfare of a road, big box stores and fast food, laser tag and Starbucks. As they rolled past all those familiar places, the girls started telling stories. Erika almost running into the side of McDonald's right after she got her license. Marissa insisting that they only go to that one dumpy movie theater because the kid who worked the ticket booth kind of looked like Zane. The more they talked, the warmer Erika felt, and the happier she was to look back and remember all of this as home.

"WAIT!" she shouted. "Take a left up here."

"Why would I . . . Oh!" Marissa laughed. "I get it."

Tucker leaned forward from the back seat and poked Erika's shoulder. "You're a total secret romantic, for the record."

"She *so* is," Marissa added.

Erika put down the visor and busied herself with trying to fix her hair.

"Shut up. I'm definitely not. I just want to see what they

turned the place into. I'm sure it's, like, a mattress store or something dumb."

As they approached the parking lot, Erika felt a pang in her chest, because part of her didn't want to see the place gone, turned into something else. But as they made the turn, she felt a rush of confusion, of excitement.

"Wait, I don't understand—is it *not* closed?" Tucker asked.

Erika leaned over, straining to see.

"No, no, it's a bar now, but they kept the name! OH MY GOD, THEY KEPT THE NAME."

Glowing over the entrance was a new sign. The Fun Cave had finally, officially become just the Cave. As Marissa pulled closer, Erika rolled down the window, leaning out to get a better look.

"I'm embarrassed to admit how happy this makes me," she said.

Tucker was leaning forward again, touching her arm.

"Erika. This is it! We have to go in."

She came back into the car, laughing.

"I don't think that's going to happen."

"Why not?"

"Do you have a fake ID? Because I don't."

"So what?"

"*So what?*"

"I can totally talk our way in. You'll see."

Erika looked at Marissa, who threw her hands in the air.

"C'mon, you know what I'm going to say! I'll wait in the

back of the lot, in case you don't get in, but I have a good feeling about this. *A very good feeling.*"

Eyes shining, Erika turned and looked at Tucker.

"Okay. Let's see you work your magic."

# 49

## TUCKER

Tucker strode up to the door as confidently as he could, when really his pulse was hammering and his heart felt like it was stuck somewhere up in his throat. The bouncer was short and squat with an enormous beard and a leather vest, and . . . there were an awful lot of motorcycles parked out front, now that Tucker thought about it. But there was no way this was a biker bar, right? Were there biker bars in the suburbs? Across from the fro-yo place and the Target?

When they arrived at the door, the bouncer ignored them and kept staring at his phone, but that was fine—that gave Tucker a little bit longer to prepare himself.

After they'd gotten out of Marissa's car, as they were trying to psych themselves up, a couple of guys had walked by and said something about how many people were coming tonight, for Dean's party. Now Tucker had a plan.

Finally, the bouncer looked up at them.

"I need both your IDs."

"Cool. Right. Of course. So listen, you probably hear stupid stories like this all the time, so I hate to do this to you, but . . . I'm sorry, what's your name?"

He stared at Tucker, unblinking. "John."

"Cool, cool. Hi, John. So I know this is ridiculous, but we went right from the office to the gym today, and I threw both our wallets in my gym bag, and then left that in *my* car, but we drove *her* car here, so I don't have either of our IDs. I mean, I totally have cash, for our drinks or whatever. Oh! And we're here for Dean's party."

John took a toothpick out of his pocket and started chewing on it, very intensely.

"You're here for Dean's party?"

"Yes."

Leaning forward slowly, John pointed at the line of motor-cycles in the parking lot.

"So which one's yours?"

Tucker frowned. "What?"

"Well, everyone else who came for Dean's party came on one of those, so I just assumed you did, too."

Tucker wanted to argue that the guys he'd overheard in the parking lot had come in a pickup truck, but he wasn't sure that was really going to help his case.

"Uh, I left my bike at home."

"With your gym bag?"

Tucker was officially sweating too much. He licked his lips, tried to think. Erika had been standing right next to him when they first walked up, but now she'd slipped behind him a bit. She must be totally mortified. She probably wished they'd stayed at Dave and Buster's. No, she probably wished she'd never come out with him at all.

"All right, all right," Tucker said. "You got me. We are not here for Dean's party. But I swear we are twenty-one, and we really, really need to come in here tonight."

John nodded, grinning. He was definitely enjoying this, which was probably the only reason he hadn't yet told them to get lost.

"Why do you really, really need to come in *here*, of all places?" He indicated the bar with his thumb.

Tucker fidgeted. Erika had slunk even farther behind him. He was totally failing her right now. He really didn't want to fail her.

*The best lies have a hint of truth. Give him a hint of the truth.*

"We met here, years ago, when it was a crappy arcade. We worked together. And we got engaged *literally* an hour ago. I promised her we'd celebrate here with one drink. Just one drink."

John tilted his head. "That's a very charming story."

"Thank you."

Now John was smiling a little bit too much.

"How'd you do it?"

"How'd I do it?"

"Yeah. You said that you proposed an hour ago, so I figured it was fresh in your mind. I'm just wondering how you did it. I have a girlfriend, you know. It's always good to get ideas."

*Nope, nope, nope.* This was officially over. Tucker had been defeated. He'd thought he had what it took to bullshit his way through anything, but this day—wonderful as it was—had been very long and very exhausting, and he had nothing left, nothing . . .

But then Erika poked him in the ribs.

"Come on, babe. Tell him how you did it. It was so romantic."

Tucker turned around and saw that her lips were pressed desperately together. She wasn't hiding behind him because she was mortified—she was hiding behind him because she was trying not to laugh.

Her cheeks were all pink, and she was loving every second of this.

As Tucker looked at her, he was struck by the force of his memories, filled with the power that came from a year's accumulation of moments as magic as this one. All the times the two of them had clicked perfectly. All the times he'd made her laugh when she'd needed it most. All the times she'd helped him feel happy to just be himself.

*You're close. So close. Keep going.*

Tucker took a breath, dug deep.

"Okay, sure. Yeah. I can tell him. I, uh, got down on one knee, because you have to do that, right? So, I got down on one knee and I said . . . I said . . . Erika, I love every single night that we've spent together. Every night we've spent together is a night that I wished would never end. I want more of them, if you do too."

John stared at Tucker in silence. Erika did not say a word, did not move a millimeter. The only sounds were the cars rushing by on the busy road behind them and the heavy metal coming from the open door.

"That's pretty good," John finally said. "But I still don't believe you."

Tucker groaned in frustration, and Erika squeezed his arm, whispered to him that it was okay. With a sigh, he prepared to turn and walk away, but first he peered inside, trying to see what the place looked like now. There was a row of bikers lined up on the stools, while the bartender was polishing a glass . . .

Tucker's mouth fell open in surprise.

"HIM! Oh my god, ask him. He can vouch for us! He knows us!"

John turned to look at the bartender, then back at Tucker.

"That guy's going to vouch for you?"

"Yes! I swear. Ask him."

His face appearing more skeptical than it had throughout the entire exchange, John turned very slowly on his stool.

This was their last possible shot, and Tucker had no idea if it was going to work. Erika was standing on her tiptoes to look over his shoulder, and he could feel her breath warm against his neck.

"Hey, Mikey," John called. "Do you know these two?"

Mikey leaned over the bar to get a look out the door. His face broke into a huge smile.

"Hell yeah, I know them! I've known them for years. They worked with me at the first version of the Cave."

John looked mildly surprised that even that much of the story was true.

"Are they twenty-one?"

Mikey tipped his head back and laughed, long and hard.

"Are *they* twenty-one?"

Picking up the glass, he inspected it for spots, then placed it neatly back on the shelf.

"*Of course* they're twenty-one! We were all partying together just last week."

With a profoundly bored shrug, John gestured for the two of them to go inside.

# 50

## ERIKA

Erika was in physical pain, she was laughing so hard as she sat next to Tucker at the bar, recounting the last five minutes to Mikey.

"I almost lost it when he said that we'd come from 'the office.' I was actually praying that John would ask *what office*, just so I could hear what Tucker would come up with."

"Oh, I was ready for that. I was going to say we worked in an IT office. That's a thing, right?"

"I'm in school for IT right now!" Mikey said. "I make a ton of money in this place. It's helping me cover my classes."

"That's awesome!" Tucker said.

As Mikey talked more about school, about his future plans, about his girlfriend, Erika peered around the bar. The basic layout hadn't changed—it was still a great cavernous room, still poorly lit, still a little grungy. Now it had pool tables and a lot of people in leather and . . .

Erika grabbed Tucker's arm.

"Holy shit. They kept the ball pit."

Tucker whirled around.

"Oh my god," he said. "Do you think people use it? Do you think they ever clean it?"

"Did *we* ever clean it?"

"Fair point. We should go jump in it with Dean, whoever he is."

There was rustling then, from the man who was sitting next to Tucker. He'd been facing the other way, talking to his friends, but now he turned to stare at them. He was absolutely enormous and covered in tattoos.

"I'm Dean."

"Oh!" Tucker said. "Hey. I, uh, heard you're having a party. Is it your birthday or something?"

Dean started to slowly and systematically crack all of his knuckles.

"I just turned forty. What are you—twelve?"

"No!" Tucker said. "I'm, like, thirteen and a half."

Erika poked Tucker in the arm. "You should buy him a drink! For his birthday."

Tucker turned and gave her an incredulous smile, like he still couldn't believe she was all in on this. Then he looked back at Dean.

"Uh, what can I get you? I am very familiar with grown-up

drinks. Do you like fancy beers? My stepdad's super into micro-brews. He has an app on his phone where he tracks all the new ones he drinks."

Dean continued to stare at Tucker, blank-faced.

"Whiskey," he finally said. "I drink whiskey."

"Cool, cool. Me too. Mikey, can we have two whiskeys? Oh, wait." Tucker turned to Erika. "Do you want a whiskey?"

"Ew, no. I'll have a Miller Lite."

Mikey had their drinks ready in less than a minute, then disappeared down to the other end of the bar. Erika took a long, awkward drink of her beer, holding it with her left hand, since she was busy hiding her bright blue one in her lap. She watched as Tucker picked up his glass and took the smallest sip.

He coughed so hard, people all down the bar turned to stare at him.

"Oh my god. Is it supposed to taste like fire?"

"Definitely," Dean said. "It puts hair on your chest."

Erika leaned forward and gave Tucker's shoulder a protective little pat. "He has hair on his chest! Just, you know, not a lot."

Tucker threw his hands in the air. "What's wrong with that? Who wants *a lot* of hair on their chest?"

"I have a lot of hair on my chest," Dean said.

"Well, sure, sure," Tucker said. "I imagine that's a good look for you. Not that I'm, like, actively imagining it."

Dean watched Tucker for a few long seconds, then got out his phone and started typing.

"Uh, you're not calling the police or something are you?"

Tucker asked. "Because I'm not really thirteen, I swear."

"I'm not calling the police. I'm texting my brother, telling him to hurry up and get over here. This party's finally getting interesting."

Tucker raised his glass to that and tried to take a sip, but as soon as he smelled it, he shook his head and put it back down. Then he swiveled his stool toward Erika.

A giant goofy smile had taken over his entire face.

"So . . . how do you know what my chest looks like?"

Erika took another swig of her beer, pretending to focus on the baseball game that was playing behind Tucker's head.

"I may have gotten a glimpse of it when you were wearing your teeny-tiny Cave shirt."

"Okay, okay. Didn't realize you were looking."

She did her best not to react to that, continuing to stare at the television as though she was deeply invested in what was going to happen in the bottom of the ninth. Meanwhile, she had something that she had to ask him too, but it took her a few tries before she managed to form the words.

"That thing you said outside. The proposal. Did you really come up with that on the spot?"

The noise from the bar was loud—all those people talking and laughing, the music blaring. Tucker started fiddling with his glass.

"No, not exactly. It was something I was going to say to you, that night at St. B's. I'm sorry if it was a little too much, to say it now. I was, you know. Trying to get us inside."

Erika nodded.

"Of course, of course. It's no big deal."

But it was. Erika couldn't stop replaying those words in her head. They felt so real to her. So right. She was thinking of earlier this evening, when Tucker had told that story about the couch at St. B's, how that moment had been given back to her as a beautiful thing.

The memories she had with Tucker—she could hold them in her heart now, take them with her. They were all like Christmas songs.

"Tucker . . . I said that we had to make the most of tonight because it's all we had, but that's not really true. We have a year's worth of parties to remember, you know what I mean?"

He'd been swinging back and forth on his stool, but now he went still. His face lit up.

"Yes, absolutely. You're right. I'm going to think about those nights all summer. All next year. Forever."

He reached out and took her hand.

"Hey, just because this isn't going to work out right now . . . it doesn't mean we'll never hang out again. Right? We'll have more nights like this someday. I'm sure of it."

A smile crept onto her face, and she shifted their hands a little, rubbed his palm with her thumb. "Maybe we could visit Maryland on the same weekend this year? You could stay with Bobby, and I'll stay with Marissa."

"That's perfect. Nina will be there, too. If she and Bobby are both single, that will totally be the weekend they finally make out."

"They'll do something that's completely unlike them. They'll hook up in front of a million people on the campus shuttle or something."

"That's so going to happen. It will be super gross, and we'll make fun of them for years."

Both of them were laughing. Then Erika leaned on his shoulder, and they sat like that without saying anything. Her eyes were brimming with tears, but she managed to hold them back.

"Thank god we escaped," she said. "Because this was very, very worth it."

"One hundred percent worth it."

"This is better than the other Cave party. Better than the Christmas party."

Suddenly, Dean slammed his fist on the bar, hitting it so hard that both Tucker and Erika jumped. He was pointing at Tucker with a big smile on his face.

"I knew you looked familiar. You're the kid who sat on my lap."

Tucker looked at Dean, then at Erika, then back at Dean.

"I . . . don't think so? I feel like I would remember that."

"It didn't click until I heard your girlfriend say 'Christmas party.'"

Tucker covered his face with his hands and mumbled that he needed a second, because his mind was completely blown. He shook his head a few times before he finally looked up, placing both palms flat on the bar.

"Okay, first of all, she's not my girlfriend, she's my fiancée.

Second of all, were you eavesdropping on us? And third of all, oh my god—you're fake Santa!"

Dean squinted at Tucker, like something might be wrong with him.

"Well, I'm sure as hell not *real* Santa."

"Why is everyone so mean about that? But seriously, this is unbelievable. Do you think we're cosmically connected? Also, I can't believe a biker was fake Santa."

Dean leaned closer to Tucker, peering at him. "Do you know a lot of bikers?"

Erika was laughing out of control now, hiding in Tucker's shoulder as she did.

"Actually, I do know *one* biker," Tucker said. "My stepdad's an orthodontist and one of his techs rides a Harley to work every day. Her name's Steph."

Dean's mouth twitched. He twisted his stool so that he could look to the other end of the room, then turned back again and started stroking his chin.

"You mean that Steph over there? The one playing darts?"

Tucker's mouth dropped open. Slowly, he stood and peered out into the gloom, to the farthest corner. Then he cursed and ducked back down.

Panic-stricken, he looked at Erika.

"Oh my god, we have to get out of here. She hates me! She will totally rat us out."

"Why does she hate you?" Erika hissed.

"I told you about this! It was my job to make the retainers, but I always messed them up and she had to fix them."

"That does sound pretty annoying," Dean said.

"Okay, yeah! In retrospect it was super annoying, but I'm way more mature now."

Tucker looked at Erika, crestfallen.

"I'm sorry, but she will seriously get me in trouble. I think we have to go."

Erika shook her head at him and smiled.

"Tucker, I don't care. This was amazing. You got us in, and we got to see the place again. We can go. It's fine."

"Are you sure?"

"Very sure."

"Steph just got in line for the bathroom," Dean announced. "I'd make a run for it now."

Tucker started fumbling for his wallet, but Dean gestured for him to stop.

"Don't worry, I've got it."

Tucker thanked him profusely, then shook his hand. Dean patted him on the shoulder and wished him good luck.

Tucker turned to Erika and asked if she was ready.

"Almost," she said. "One more thing?"

# 51

## TUCKER AND ERIKA

"You have to go first."

"No, you have to go first. This was your idea!"

"All right, all right. How about we go together?"

"That's a good plan, but before we do—I have a serious question. You don't have to answer if you don't want to."

"I'm listening."

"I know it's probably too much to hope for that we might find each other again when the timing is right. But just in case, could you hold on to your candy cane tights? Because . . . OH MY GOD. Did you just snort? While we're surrounded by bikers? You totally snorted. I totally got you."

"Fine, fine. You got me. You always get me. Now can you stop talking for once in your life so we can do this?"

"I will in one second, I swear. But I had to say . . . someday, when I'm older, I bet I'll be sitting around with my friends, talking about the first time I ever went to a bar. I love that this is the story I'll get to tell."

"Yes, yes! Me too. That's why we need to do this! Because it's so perfect."

"Okay. Should we cannonball in? Meet at the bottom?"

"We'll jump on the count of three. One, two . . ."

# ACKNOWLEDGMENTS

Thank you . . .

To my first readers. Elisabeth Dahl, you are always so kind to me and so generous with your time. Nate Gunsch, you have no idea how much I needed your Chris-Traeger-like enthusiasm or your reports of crying man tears. I'm so thankful for your thoughtful critiques. And Maggie Master, without a doubt you have been my Marissa on this whole publishing journey, and that is my highest compliment. You are stuck with me for life.

To my agent, Steven Chudney. I'm so thankful for all the hard work you put in for me, and I would not want to navigate this publishing world without your wisdom and dry wit. I will not forget how remarkably chill you were while I wildly stumbled around trying to write a second book.

To Andrew Eliopulos. I still can't believe you read those

meandering early pages and managed to find some unexpected potential in what—at the time—was just a poorly paced story that lingered too long on a couple of nights. The party book would not be a party book, or a book at all, without you. Thank you for your endless patience, support, and guidance while I found my way. I feel ridiculously lucky to call you my editor.

To all the people who made this story so much better and its packaging so beautiful—Bria Ragin, Alexandra Rakaczki, Jen Strada, and Joel Tippie. Books are such an extraordinary team effort, and I'm so glad to have you all on my team.

To the Sweet 16s. I'm not sure I would have survived my debut year without you all, and I feel so fortunate that I was able to meet such incredible and talented friends through this group.

To everybody who reached out to tell me that my first book meant something to them. Please know that you helped me keep going as I struggled to write something new.

To the Rivers and Hattrup families. I couldn't ask for better supporters or loved ones, truly. Thank you for buying entirely too many copies of *Frannie and Tru*, for giving me reassurance on this one when the nerves kicked in, and for so much more.

To Kevin. Can you believe we started dating when we were Erika's age and we're still not sick of each other? That toga party will always be like a Christmas song to me. Thank you for putting up with me when my head is in the clouds, for being superdad when my nose is to the grindstone, and for coming up with amazing fake-song lyrics, not to mention so many excellent names for a terrible sexting assembly. I'm sorry I didn't use GeniTales.

To Nora and Liam. You are exquisite and magical little people, and I can't wait to watch you grow into exquisite and magical bigger people. Someday we'll have to have an awkward conversation about gum and stuff, so I apologize in advance. In the meantime, always write your own stories—don't let the world tell you who it thinks you should be.